I0691904

i

A Good Death

David E. Lawrence

Pocol Press
Clifton, VA

POCOL PRESS

Published in the United States of America
by Pocol Press
6023 Pocol Drive
Clifton VA 20124
www.pocolpress.com

Publisher's Cataloguing-in-Publication

Lawrence, David E.

  A good death / David E. Lawrence. – 1st ed. –   Clifton, VA : Pocol Press, c2010.

  p. ; cm.

  ISBN: 978-1-929763-45-0

  1. Terminally ill—Fiction 2. Terminally ill—Family relationships—Fiction. 3. Industrial accidents—Fiction 4. Death- Pyschological aspects—Fiction. I. Title.

PS3562.A9118 G66 2010
813.54--dc22   1005

PROLOGUE

I flicked off the radio of my big Chevy Tahoe. It's December 21—the shortest day of the year. It's cold. The sky is lowering. The weatherman just predicted snow. I turned southeast onto Hamburg Road, heading toward my job and thinking, *It's the perfect day for a death.*

1

My name is Paul Stepping. I work at Ft. Detrick, Maryland. Perhaps that rings a bell: chemical warfare; bio-terrorism. Since our signing onto the Chemical Weapons Convention (CWC) we've actually been out of that business—the offensive aspect, that is. But there are still bad actors in this world, so my job is to develop protectants for our soldiers who might encounter chemical or biological agents in the field.

I'm an organic chemist. I received my doctorate from the University of Virginia in Charlottesville twenty-nine years ago. Within a month I married Kay, we moved to Frederick County, and I began my career as a civilian employee of the US Army. I've been at Ft. Detrick ever since.

Roughly 5800 people labor here. Ft. Detrick is home to the United States Army Medical Research and Materiel Command (USAMRMC), the National Cancer Institute (NCI), and thirty-six other tenant organizations. I'm with the Army's Medical Materiel Development Activity (MMDA). We research new medical products, conduct clinical trials, and submit applications for approval to the FDA.

Right now I'm working on a prophylactic for ricin, as no antidote exists. This poison, derived from castor beans, acts inside the cells of the body, preventing them from synthesizing certain critical proteins. These cells die, and if enough of them are affected, organ failure and death may occur. In the 1940s the US military experimented with ricin as a possible warfare agent. It is suspected it was used in the Iran-Iraq war in the 1980s. Apparently we have intel suggesting that terrorist organizations today think it might be a useful weapon. That, combined with the facts that the castor bean plant is widely distributed, can be cultivated, and that extracting ricin is a relatively simple matter, explains my assignment to this

1

project.

Kay and I have three grown kids. She's an elementary teacher—3rd-Grade. We both have less than a year until retirement. We've had good lives, good careers. Excitement had been building for our post-work plans—until this.

2

I had been working on the preventive for some time. My research was guided by the architecture of the ricin molecule (it is a protein composed of two hemaglutinins and two cell toxins), and by what is known of its biochemistry. My approach was to synthesize a compound I thought might confer protection, then test it on laboratory mice. I had gone through seventy-one such compounds. I was now involved with Ricin Protective Agent-72 (RPA-72). The particulars of my work are of course classified. I can say, however, that RPA-72 was effective on the test animals. It rendered them immune to an inhaled ricin mist, while an unprotected control group died within hours. But a week later, the surviving group also died. There was no apparent suffering. One minute they were running around their cages, exhibiting normal behavior; the next they just keeled over. Necropsies revealed an accumulation of RPA-72 in the heart muscles. There were no other abnormalities. I treated another group of mice with the protectant, but did not expose them to ricin. They likewise died within a week. So it wasn't the combination of the two.

I had been thinking about this problem, and had come up with some ideas. One morning three months ago (September 19, to be exact), I entered my state-of-the-art lab at Ft. Detrick, greeted the technicians who work with me, then proceeded to my alcove and the locked cool box where my supply of RPA-72 was stored. I retrieved a sample. I walked to the fume hood where I would be working and placed the sample inside. I secured the door. I flipped the switch on the exhaust fan that would suck out any vapors, passing them through neutralizing chemical baths and beds of activated charcoal. I placed my hands into the rubber sleeves that protruded into the hood, working my fingers into the tight latex ends. *Like ten little condoms*, I remember thinking, just before it happened.

3

Kay works in Washington County, our neighbor to the west. Though Maryland consistently votes blue in statewide elections, as you move into the more sparsely-populated panhandle toward the mountains, things turn conservative. The Washington County School Board recently adopted a sex ed policy that has 5th-Graders receiving basic information about (among other things) condoms. It has caused a firestorm of protest. Though Kay's students are not directly involved, the 5th-Grade parents at her school have been among the most vocal objectors in the county. She has kept me apprised of the situation, thus my *ten little condoms* thought. It wasn't just prurience.

4

Giving details about the accident is forbidden. Suffice it to say glass broke, rubber was sliced, and I was exposed to RPA-72. It was freakish, highly improbable—but it happened. The safety systems operated as designed. I had closed the door to my alcove, so no one else knew or was involved.

Joy Smalls, one of two MDs assigned to MMDA, was just down the corridor. I like Joy. She's friendly, competent, and asks about my work. I considered going to her, then thought better of it. I needed time to think. There was a first aid kit nearby. I treated myself. Once I was satisfied the hood had cleared, I opened the door and dealt with the mess. We had several sleeves in reserve. I replaced the damaged one. I got a fresh sample of RPA-72, and worked the rest of the day as planned—as if this were some minor, run-of-the-mill laboratory mishap.

I drove the five miles northwest on Hamburg Road to our place outside the little community of Yellow Springs. Our five acres backs up to Gambrill State Park and the Catoctin Trail. Kay and I arrive from work about the same time. Today her year-old Civic was already at the end of

3

our long gravel driveway, parked near the front door.

When I walked into the living room she was relaxing in her La-Z-Boy, sipping a Caffeine-Free Diet Pepsi, and watching the tail-end of *Oprah*. She had changed into some pink shorts and a tank-top with sea turtles printed all over it.

"Looks like someone's ready for a little exercise," I said. "You want to walk The Trail?"

The Catoctin Trail winds for twenty-seven miles through Gambrill State Park, the City of Frederick Municipal Forest, Cunningham Falls State Park, and Catoctin Mountain Park. Camp David, the presidential retreat, is in Catoctin Mountain Park. Established by FDR in 1942 as Shangri-La, it was re-named by President Eisenhower in 1953 for his grandson. We walk practically every day (not always The Trail). We aim for an hour, which translates into three-to-four miles.

"Sure," she said. "Hot though."

We were finishing up the third week in September. There had been hints of fall. We'd even had a light frost one morning. But Kay was right: today it felt like summer again.

"Hey," I said, "there are no scientific studies showing a causal link between sweat and poor health."

When I met Kay Bishop she was a junior elementary ed major at UVa. She's a city girl, hailing from the Hampton Roads region of southeast Virginia—Newport News, to be specific. My roots, by contrast, are just up the road from Charlottesville, in rural Madison County. She had me from "hello," as they say.

I let my eyes play over her, appreciating how good she looked at fifty-one: fit, nice breasts, thick honey-colored hair that never needs L'Oréal. She worries about a few wrinkles, but I don't see them. I'm fifty-four. I've managed to keep the weight down, but there's snow on the mountaintop. People think I robbed the cradle with Kay. I've been salt-and-pepper sliding toward white since I was forty—a genetic thing with the Stepping men. But we don't go bald.

Kay frowned. "Paul, what happened?" She had noticed my bandaged hand.

4

"Clumsy me. I broke something in the lab and cut myself."

"Is it okay? That gauze is pretty thick."

"I think so. It was deep; it bled."

"Any stitches?"

"Oh, no—it's maybe a quarter inch long."

Kay had long ago stopped asking about my work. Everything was classified, and the kind of secrecy I was sworn to, forbade my discussing it even with her. When someone hired on, the Army made it crystal clear that any breach of the rules would result in dismissal, no retirement benefits for the employee *or* his/her beneficiaries, and a widespread blackballing that would make it difficult to find other employment. That was for minor violations. Anything more serious could result in prison time.

She brightened. "Then let's go for a walk."

"Good. Let me get out of these clothes."

I moved toward our bedroom. No one had seen the accident. I had hidden the dressing from my co-workers with lab gloves. Maybe I should keep this whole thing to myself.

5

"Dr. Stepping, would you come to my office please?" That was Major Leonard Essex, head of MMDA, speaking into the intercom.

It was the next day. I had just gotten to the lab. "I'll be right there." I communicated regularly with Essex of course, generally via planned meetings involving my entire research team. This was unusual. Two minutes later I was sitting in a chrome chair before his desk, whose large surface area was all but devoid of items. "How can I help you Major?"

My estimate put Essex in his early forties. He was lean, with blue eyes and a strawberry blond crew cut. Despite some grad school problems (not academic) of which I later became aware, he had earned a PhD in biophysics from Rensselaer Polytechnic. He once informed me that Rensselaer, founded in Troy, New York in 1824, was the oldest school of science and engineering in the US. His education had been funded by the Army, so he had an obligation to the military. Apparently he liked the life,

5

and had decided to stay. He had been the main man at MMDA for five years. I still didn't know him very well. He's a good boss—just all business, which actually I don't mind. It's the glad-handing, I'm-just-one-of-you-guys types that make *me* nervous. One minute they're slapping you on the back; the next, that hand has a knife in it.

Essex was looking over a document. "This is MMDA-Form 210. Are you familiar with it?"

"No, I'm not."

"It's a notification of laboratory accident."

I had decided not to report the problem. There had been quite a bit of bleeding. That was outflow, which would have made it unlikely that RPA-72 could have gotten into my bloodstream. But maybe this was not about my accident. Maybe one of the techs had knocked over something. I waited for him to continue.

"Yesterday morning there was an abnormal spike in the effluent from the fume hood in your alcove. I did not receive a report from you within the time specified in the handbook, and I was wondering why? Are you unaware of that regulation? That seems unlikely, as your records show you've worked here a very long time."

Hood effluent is monitored? When did *that* happen? Was staff notified, or was it a stealth initiative to check behind people—make sure they were following the rules? "I am aware of the accident report regulation."

"Then where's the report?"

"To tell you the truth, I didn't consider it significant enough to report."

"What happened?"

I related the incident.

He frowned. "After the deaths of the test animals, you didn't consider this significant? You might be at risk."

"I doubt it sir." I explained my reasoning.

He studied me for a few seconds. "Dr. Stepping, two things: have that report on my desk by noon today; and I'm arranging for you to see Dr. Smalls at 1300 hours. You need to be checked out."

6

Joy Smalls has very white skin (freckle-free), and very red hair. It looks like she has never been in the sun for more than five minutes at a stretch. Maybe she has a family history of melanoma. She's a good ten years younger than me. Her office opens into an examination room. When I arrived she was standing in its doorway wearing a bright smile. Her teeth are as flawless and white as her skin. I have never seen her drinking coffee or tea. She's unmarried. I've heard nothing of a former husband or present boyfriend. I don't think she's lesbian.

"Hey, Paul—it's been a while. Come on in and let's take a look at that hand." We went inside and she closed the door. "Just sit there and rest your forearm on the table." She retrieved some items from a drawer behind her, then sat in a swivel chair and rolled herself up beside me. "I'll just take off this dressing." She began snipping with scissors. "Essex says this happened yesterday morning; you were working with one of your anti-ricin compounds. Can you provide some details?"

I gave her the blow-by-blow, complete with all the specifics I could remember.

"Essex says the agent you were exposed to has killed some mice."

"That's true, but the cut bled a lot, so I figured—"

"This is deep," she said, palpating the wound. "We'll give you a tetanus booster." She pressed harder. "Does that hurt?"

"A little."

"I'll prescribe an antibiotic. It's not really inflamed, but there could be some infection. You're not allergic to penicillin or any of its derivatives, are you?"

"I don't think so."

She watched me for a moment, then said, "Cuts are funny. Even with bleeding, stuff can get in. How much of your anti-ricin was given to the mice?" When I told her she blinked and said, "That's not much."

"No, it's not—and it's possible an even lower dose might have been effective. When they died, I cancelled the planned dosage trials, and turned my thoughts to a new compound."

"They were dosed orally?"

"Yes."

"But you were not."

"I hope I wasn't dosed at all."

Joy pursed her lips. "All right, what we'll do is take some blood. I assume your techs have a test for this . . . ."

"RPA-72—yes, we've developed one."

"Okay. We'll take some of your blood and test it for RPA-72. If we're negative, then no problem except for a nasty cut. If it's positive, we'll look at the concentration and see if it's something we need to deal with."

I told her about the accumulation of the substance in the heart muscles of the mice, and of our presumption that this is what killed them.

She raised her eyebrows. "So you dosed them orally, it was absorbed into their bloodstreams, but it ended up in their hearts."

"That's right."

"And this took time."

"About a week."

"Then if we get a positive on this first sample, we need to take subsequent ones—maybe every twenty-four hours—and see what's happening." She had a rubber cord around my biceps, and was swabbing the crook of my arm. "Make a fist for me. A little sting." She drew the blood. I watched her concentrating on the task. She was good. I felt nothing. "Take this back to your lab, get your people to run it, and forward the results to me pronto. Will it take long?"

"Maybe an hour."

"Good. Then you can bring me the verdict yourself. I'll have the booster ready then, and your antibiotic prescription. My guess is we have nothing to worry about." She gave my hand a squeeze. When I winced she laughed and said, "Sorry Paul—my fault. You better get out of here before I do any more damage."

7

Forty-five minutes later I handed her the results.

"I see you did five trials—good; some variation—that's to be expected. Now, this mean concentration—how does it compare to the initial mean concentration in the mice who died?"

"It's lower by about a third. I just can't believe this got into my blood."

Joy gave me a level stare. "Do you have confidence in the analysis?"

"I have no reason to doubt it."

"Should we re-do the test?"

I shook my head. "No, no—it's accurate."

"Then RPA-72 *is* in your blood, though not via absorption from your small intestine, as was the case with your test animals."

"Correct," I breathed. Then, as if she had accused me, I added, "I'm not in denial here; I would just like to know . . . ." I dropped the thought. Why repeat myself?

"I understand. It raises the whole question of why things happen? Are there *really* coincidences? Chance, fate, destiny—all that."

That was not what I had meant. Actually I hadn't considered these issues for some time; when I had, the result evidence-wise had pretty much been a dead end. Seeing little value in correcting Joy, I said, "Right, but how do we proceed?"

She watched me for some seconds before saying, "You realize Essex has to be kept informed about everything."

"Yes, I do."

"I predict he'll decree any treatment you receive will have to be on-base, administered by medical personnel who have a high security clearance. He considers your project top priority. So regardless of this accident, he'll insist everything be kept under wraps." We were in her office, sitting in a couple of those military-issue chrome chairs like the Major had in his. Joy adjusted her lab coat and crossed her legs. "That's my guess at least."

"I'm sure you're right. So for now we just monitor things through periodic blood samples."

"Exactly. We'll do that—see if there are changes. Plus, you'll tell me

9

if you experience any unusual symptoms."

"Absolutely."

"You mentioned that prior to their deaths the mice behaved normally; there seemed to be no distress, no discomfort."

"None that I could see, and I've worked with a lot of test animals in my day. If there had been significant aberrations, physical or mental, I think we would have noticed. One of my technicians—you know Boyd Markham—is exceptionally good with the mice. He would have caught anything I missed."

Joy nodded. "Yes, Boyd. It's all over MMDA that he's a master with the mice." She looked away and chuckled, as if musing about my tech. Returning to me she said, "Yes, samples every twenty-four hours for at least the next few days. We'll determine the trend, then make some decisions based on that data. Sound good?"

I didn't know about good, but it sounded reasonable. We stood. "Thanks Joy," I said, trying to sound lighthearted, unconcerned. "See you tomorrow for some additional bloodletting."

8

The trend was down. This meant one of two things: either my liver was dismantling the RPA-72, destroying it, like this magic organ did with so many contaminants; or, the compound was accumulating in my heart, as it had with the mice. There *were* other possibilities. Despite many similarities, human and mouse biochemistry are not identical. So maybe something else was going on. Regardless, this news was disturbing.

Joy informed Leonard Essex. His response was to call a meeting.

Four of us gathered in his office, our shiny chairs lined up before his desk, pupils summoned by the headmaster. There was Malcolm Mellwood (the other medical doctor assigned to MMDA), Ward Emmerton (a biochemist from another MMDA lab), Joy, and myself.

Major Essex got right down to business. "Several days ago Dr. Stepping had an accident. He was exposed to RPA-72, a ricin protectant that has proven fatal to laboratory mice. Tests have shown the

10

concentration of RPA-72 to be dropping in Dr. Stepping's blood. That would seem to be good. However, post-mortems on the mice revealed that the compound had accumulated in their hearts. It is assumed that this is what killed them, though the precise mechanism is unknown. As the compound built up in their heart muscles, it was being depleted in their bloodstreams. So the drop in Dr. Stepping's level, if indicative of same, would be a bad thing. Our purpose today is to decide on a course of action. The one stricture that I must impose is that everything connected with Dr. Stepping's case—all discussions, tests, diagnoses, and treatments—will be conducted within the confines of Ft. Detrick. His ricin research is very important and highly classified. Off-base involvement would inevitably raise questions, and that would not be in the security interests of the United States." Joy and I exchanged a look. Her prediction had been correct. "Now, any initial observations or comments before we move on?"

"When do I get to examine Dr. Stepping?" That was Mellwood. While Joy's specialty was internal medicine, Mellwood was a cardiologist. He was rail thin, coffee-and-cigarette thin. He had a mug of black coffee with him now, and everyone knew he smoked. The fact that a heart doctor used tobacco was unsettling. Either he was addicted (and was making no attempt to get the monkey off his back), or he was arrogant (thinking that somehow *he* would escape the dire statistics that continued to mount). Neither of these possibilities inspired confidence.

"Today," Essex replied. "And I want it thorough; I want his heart put through every test you have."

Mellwood took a sip of coffee. His lips tensed and quivered, I guessed from the bitterness. "No problem, Major. I don't work any other way."

"Good." His blue eyes slid a few degrees to his left. "Dr. Emmerton, I suppose you're wondering why you're here?"

"Correct sir." Emmerton was short, pudgy, affable.

"We're thinking worst case scenario here. We have to." Essex didn't even give me a glance. He had a problem; it had to be handled; sympathy, sentimentality, mawkishness of any kind, was an impediment. "If Dr. Stepping goes the way of his mice, the ricin project must continue. You're going to be his back-up. Posthaste, he will bring you up to speed on all

11

aspects of his research, including the next moves he has planned." Now he looked at me. "Is that clear Dr. Stepping?"

I let the moment drag out before responding, "Yes." His eyes narrowed. Maybe he saw this as a small challenge to his authority. Maybe it was. Whatever, I felt a need to hi-lite the off chance that he was crossing the line from efficient professional to cold chump.

Silence hung as the Major and I watched each other.

Then Joy spoke up. "What is my part in this going forward?"

"You will remain Dr. Stepping's prime medical contact. He will report to you daily. You will report to me daily. If treatment decisions are to be made, you will first consult with Dr. Mellwood and myself."

"What about Dr. Stepping?"

"Regarding what?"

"Regarding treatment decisions."

"He's not a Doctor of Medicine."

"With all due respect Major, neither are you."

Essex flushed, but recovered quickly. "That is correct Dr. Smalls, but I *am* head of MMDA, and thus must be involved in all decisions affecting its operation and mission."

"It's Paul whose life is at stake. I'd say his participation is absolutely crucial, not to mention morally requisite. If *he* does not wish to proceed with a given line of treatment, that settles it, regardless of what I, Dr. Mellwood, or you, think. Paul Stepping is not a test animal."

I saw Emmerton cast an admiring glance at Joy.

Leonard Essex successfully intimidated most people by his position, intelligence, and demeanor. Joy Smalls was unfazed, unimpressed. To her, these were style components. She was only interested in the substance of the Major's position, and in this case, she objected to that substance.

Essex blinked. "Of course we would not compel Dr. Stepping in that way." He said this as if it were absurd for Joy to have supposed it. Then he asked, "What are our options here?"

After another slug of coffee Mellwood said, "If Stepping's heart is being infiltrated with this agent, I see two possibilities. One would be to inject the heart muscle with something that would modify the agent, that

12

would change it chemically so it could no longer have adverse effects. That presupposes we can find something to disable the bad molecule that's not harmful itself. We would also need info concerning how the agent is distributed. Is it evenly dispersed, or has it collected in certain areas—around the valves for instance? Then there's the whole issue of actually sticking needles into the heart. That's risky. Even if we didn't open up the chest, we'd have to stop the heart for what would likely be multiple injections." He stopped for more coffee. He patted the pocket of his lab coat. Mellwood was beginning to itch for a cigarette. No one spoke. "The other thing would be a transplant: cut out the compromised organ and stitch in a new one. Some people wait years for a new heart. I don't know how much time we have here."

"I've done some calculations," I said, "trying to extrapolate from mouse to man—more precisely, from the average mouse used in our tests to *this* man. They're based on certain assumptions of course, any one of which might be invalid, or partially invalid. But given all that, I've come up with three months—ninety days—plus or minus four days—from the date of the accident."

"Then forget the transplant," Mellwood said, "unless the military gets some kind of priority."

Essex didn't respond. He was up for promotion to colonel. Maybe he didn't want to jeopardize that by making such an eyebrow-raising request. Just what kind of operation was he running over at MMDA?

"There's complete blood replacement," Joy said. "But we're likely too late for that to do much good. And it's a delicate procedure. I doubt we have the equipment here to do it."

"So three months," Essex said to me. "You're beginning to work on a successor compound to RPA-72. Let's say you synthesize it, and it protects test animals from ricin without killing them. What if you treated yourself with this new compound? Would that help?"

"I'm no pharmacologist, but I doubt it. And again, there's the time issue. It took four months to produce 72 from 71, then six more weeks for the animal trials. But, who knows? Maybe this will go faster. The modifications I have in mind *are* less extensive than the previous make

13

over. I'll keep working. If somehow I beat the deadline and the mice survive, then sure, I'll take some of the stuff."

Looking down at what I presumed was his meeting agenda, Essex said, "Good," and made a check mark with his Cross ballpoint. Kay gave me a Cross once for my birthday. It was a nice pen, but I found it too thin, too smooth (unless I put a vice grip on it, the barrel slipped in my fingers when I tried to write), and too heavy to be useful. He glanced up to Emmerton, but I spoke first.

"Sir, I have a question for Dr. Smalls."

"All right."

I turned to her. "Could my liver be dealing with the RPA-72? Maybe it's not even making it to my heart."

"It's possible, but even if that's true, it couldn't destroy *all* the protectant before *some* of it lodged in your heart. The chemical seems to have an affinity for heart tissue, like iodine has for the thyroid. And don't forget, some substances, some medicines even, can damage the liver, even as the liver is destroying the substance. One thing we know for sure: the mice livers didn't keep the RPA-72 from reaching *their* hearts." She gave me a sympathetic look. "I'll do some checking—see what's known about the differences between mouse and human hepatic physiology. I have a vet friend."

"Off-base?" Essex yelped, as if he'd been jabbed with a cattle prod, or was afflicted with Tourette's Syndrome.

"No sir—she's over at MRIID."

That was the Army's Medical Research Institute of Infectious Diseases.

"All right. But don't provide any context. She has no need to know the reason for your inquiry." Joy made no reply. The Major scanned his underlings, making eye contact with each of us. Then he consulted his agenda once more. "And Dr. Emmerton, here's what I want you to do."

The biochemist looked startled. He had been watching Joy with uncommon intensity while Essex spoke to her. Now he turned to the Major. "In addition to consulting with Dr. Stepping about his research?" he said with a smile.

14

Essex looked up. "Yes, in addition to that. We have no clue as to just how RPA-72 impregnating the hearts of those mice resulted in their deaths. At some point in time, at some critical quantity, at some site or sites within the heart muscle, and for some biochemical reason or set of reasons, this agent caused those hearts to stop beating. I want you to find out why."

The smile faded. "But sir, three months. That's a tall order."

"Yes it is. But if you can uncover even one fact about how RPA-72 is metabolized by the heart tissue, it might give Dr. Mellwood guidance concerning the injection possibility he mentioned."

"I'll do my best sir."

"Anything you need, let me know."

Emmerton was smiling again. "Yes sir."

Essex was thorough. He was covering all the bases. I had to give him credit for that.

"I have nothing else. Any closing comments?" There were none. "Dr. Stepping, you will report to Dr. Mellwood at 1500 hours for your heart exam. Dr. Mellwood, you will forward the results to me first thing Monday morning. Dismissed."

I later learned that even prior to this meeting, Major Essex had put out feelers concerning a replacement organic chemist for MMDA.

9

According to Mellwood, my heart was fine. At one point during the tests he turned things over to an assistant so he could go outside for a smoke. His clothes, his hair, his entire office suite, stank of tobacco. As I said before, this did not engender confidence. Yet Joy had told me the man was competent, and that he enjoyed an excellent reputation among his specialty peers. Fine.

It was quitting time. It was Friday. Though the school year was just cranking up, Kay had taken the day off to drive down to Newport News. Neither of her parents were doing that well. She tried to get down every couple of months to spend a little time with them. Her sister, Joan, lived thirty minutes from the home place. She kept an eye on the old folks, took

15

them to their doctor appointments and such. But soon decisions would have to be made concerning the care of Ruth and Wade Bishop. Kay would likely discuss this with Joan while she was there.

She would take the scenic route to Hampton Roads, crossing The Bay at Annapolis, driving south through the Eastern Shores of Maryland and Virginia, reaching Norfolk via the Chesapeake Bay Bridge-Tunnel (an engineering marvel that had been built without a cent of taxpayer money). Kay despised the traffic nightmare of the Southern Maryland-DC-Northern Virginia metropolitan area, and would gladly drive an extra hour or two to avoid it.

The weekend was mine—but to what purpose? I knew I needed to think. Maybe I needed to talk to someone. But to whom? And what would be my objective? I had just had a meeting with four fully-informed scientists. The considered judgment coming out of that powwow was that Mellwood and Joy would continue to monitor me for abnormalities, Emmerton would try to figure out how RPA-72 had killed the mice, I would move ahead with my work on RPA-73, and Essex *might* check into the transplant deal. He hadn't committed. I needed to press him on that. He prided himself on being a straight-shooter. Let him give me a yes or no. The bottom line, the professional consensus, was wait and see—or "watchful waiting," as it is sometimes called when referring to older men with prostate cancer. Keep tabs, but no treatment. So if I talked to someone, it wouldn't be about the medical contingencies of the situation. It would probably center on my emotional reaction to this unforeseen turn of events, and what my plans would be for the next three months.

10

Soon after moving to Maryland, Kay and I joined First Baptist of Frederick. Tim Rouzerville, a young man fresh out of seminary, was the pastor. Now, twenty-nine years later, Tim Rouzerville is still the pastor. I'm sure that's unusual. It's been good for me though. It's allowed me to get to know him gradually over many years. I've seen him in the pulpit, in committee meetings, in social situations. He officiated when Kay and I

16

renewed our vows at Year 20. He baptized our three children. We've had Tim and Grace, his wife, over for dinner many times. I classify Tim Rouzerville as a friend—a label I don't paste on very many. I like him, and I trust him.

Saturday morning I picked up the phone. "Tim—Paul Stepping. I was wondering if we could talk?"

"You bet. My office? Around nine?"

That was one of the great things about Tim. First Baptist is no small church. The minister is busy, pulled in many directions day in and day out. Somehow Tim is always available, and he never seems rushed. I find that remarkable. This man has obviously found his calling.

He met me on the front steps of the church, his hand poked out in greeting. "Hey, Paul—good to see you. Listen, does this *have* to be in my office?"

"Not really," I said with a shrug. "It is private however."

"Oh, sure—naturally." He looked up into a bright blue sky. "It's just that it's such a gorgeous day. Back behind, between the sanctuary and the education building, there's a small area—shady, fountain with goldfish, couple of benches. I go there quite often for some quiet time."

"I didn't know it was there."

"I don't advertise it. Selfish I guess. There are thick boxwoods on either side, shielding it from the walkways. You won't tell, will you?"

"Your secret's safe with me."

He broke into a big smile, as if I'd just revealed that the Second Coming would be tomorrow during the service. "That's great Paul! Thanks!" He clapped me on the back.

I've never been much for the glad-handing religious types. I met a few in college. They were fine until you wanted to have an open and fair discussion about something. Then the conviviality stopped, and the superciliousness began. Some were downright surly. I have a cousin who runs in this vein. I'm not saying Blake's a bad guy. It's just the fake over-friendliness, combined with his dogmatism (yet super-sensitivity) about his religious beliefs that . . . I don't know—I can't handle it. I make it my business to steer clear of Fake Blake. Tim has shown me that it's possible

17

to be religious, even glad-handing, and *not* fake. But he's the exception. Most of the solid, genuine church people I know are cordial enough, but not uber-jolly.

We walked up the front steps, through the sanctuary, down a narrow stairway behind the baptistry, and out into the little garden Tim had described. It was indeed nice. The maple trees that provided shade were just beginning to show touches of color.

"I really like this spot," he said as we sat on one of the wooden benches. It appeared to have been recently painted—no nicks or peels in the smooth green coat.

"You don't suppose anyone would be lurking beyond the shrubbery?"

"I doubt it—not at this time on a Saturday morning. I can check if you like."

I was being overly cautious. I certainly wasn't going to lay out any technical details before Tim Rouzerville. In the first place, there was no need; in the second, he likely wouldn't follow. So I said, "No, no—that's all right. We'll just keep our voices low. But this *is* confidential."

"Of course, of course. Just like *you* said: your secret's safe with me."

I knew I could rely on that. You don't remain pastor of the same church for almost three decades if you go around violating confidences. "Thanks Tim. I certainly need someone outside of work to talk to."

Tim knew I was employed at Ft. Detrick, and he knew my work was classified. "Some kind of personnel problem?" he said.

"Not really—well, sort of." I went on to relate the bare bones of my predicament, including the Major's seeming reluctance to pursue the heart transplant option.

"That's quite a situation," Tim said, watching me closely. "You say three months, give or take. Are you sure this is going to happen?"

"I'd say it's at least 50-50—at least. I *really* think the odds are more like 70-30 that I'll be dead 86-to-94 days from the accident."

"And no suffering."

"Not if things go as it did with the mice."

Tim ran fingers across his mouth and chin. "So, foreknowledge of death, no suffering (other than mental perhaps), plus time to say good-byes

18

and make all necessary arrangements. I can think of less appealing scenarios."

"Well, sure—but I'm still going to die."

"And you were thinking that unlike the rest of mankind, you would somehow escape this?"

Smiling at his little jest I said, "I was hoping to avoid it for another twenty years or so." Tim often made jokes at serious times. But he was by no means flip. The humor took the edge off the gravity, yet those involved never seemed to doubt the depth of their pastor's concern. It was really quite amazing.

"And maybe you will—you say it's not a sure thing. But I've known you for a long time. You're not a wishful thinker. I'm guessing you want to deal with that worst case."

"Correct."

"And I'm guessing you're not interested in a lot of sympathy."

I thought about that for a few seconds. Truth be told, I *had* spent some time feeling sorry for myself. I had asked "Why me?" quite a few times. But as I'd learned earlier in my life, that line of questioning often proves fruitless. It stirs you up emotionally, which in addition to being itself unpleasant, distracts you from grappling with the problem at hand. So I said, "If I die this young, it will be unfortunate. But no, sympathy would not be helpful. I think what I'm looking for is guidance on how to proceed, assuming the three month termination date to be accurate."

"All right!" Tim cheered, his head jerking up and down like a bobble-head doll that had just been flicked hard. "That's good. That gives me direction. Now, if it were me, Job One would be getting your superior to give you an up or down on the transplant. From what you've told me, the other aspects of the situation are pretty well firmed up. I think you'd rest easier knowing yes or no on this. Certainly the man owes you that."

"Yes he does. And Monday morning I'll be marching straight to his office before going to the lab."

"Good, good. I think that would be an excellent first move." Something dropped onto his lap. He looked up. "Ah, manna from heaven." Ten feet above us, on a sturdy branch of one of the maples, sat a gray squirrel. He was sitting on his haunches, holding a fat acorn in his front paws, enjoying a snack. I assumed it came from a towering oak on the church property, some thirty yards outside our cloister. Yellow crumbles were raining down on Tim. "Now check out that little fellow. He's just doing his thing. He takes life as it comes, no complaints, just a straight-ahead kind of guy. My guess is he can sense ahead of time when he's about to die—assuming it's not in some abrupt accident of course. I've had three dogs die of natural causes, and that was definitely the case with them. Now he won't change his program; he'll just keep looking for food, eating, drinking, doing his social things and whatnot, for as long as he can. Then he'll die. I'm thinking that's an option for you."

I looked at the squirrel. He was bright-eyed, bushy-tailed, and well fed. He certainly seemed to be enjoying his life. "So you're saying just keep on, regular routine, as if the accident hadn't happened."

"Pretty much. I mean, if you make big changes, it's tantamount to saying you haven't been living right. Now if you've left some important things, practical things, undone—a will, for instance—then by all means go ahead and take care of that. Otherwise, just cruise on as normal until it's time to cross that River Jordan."

I frowned. "I don't know about that, Tim. Take Kay: I can't provide her any details; but I've got to give her *some* clue, some *inkling*, that this might happen. To know it, say nothing, then drop dead a few days before Christmas—that would be pretty damn cold."

"But it's tricky, given the classified nature of your work."

"Well, yes it is. Unless I give specifics, it's like we're talking hypotheticals—which we've done many times over the years, on a variety of issues. And since I *can't* give specifics, she won't see the urgency."

"Like I said—tricky."

The gray squirrel had finished his acorn. He hopped along the branch back to the trunk and scurried down. He darted in front of us and dove into the boxwood hedge. He was headed for the big oak. I wondered how much of his behavior was programmed—how much freedom he really had. I looked over at Tim. "Any other ideas?"

"Sure," he said with a wide grin and expansive arm gestures. "You could go big time—you know, dramatic. Bring Kay flowers every day; take her out to expensive restaurants in Baltimore and DC; go see the pyramids; make a big contribution to your church." He closed his eyes while arching his eyebrows: another bit of drollery.

"You just said that option would admit I haven't been living right."

"Well—"

"*And* would bring all kinds of questions from Kay that I really couldn't answer."

"Hey, don't sell yourself short. You're a creative guy. You could come up with something. I'm just saying I've known a few people in your general circumstance who've taken this route: going for the gusto—grabbing for it." He reached out and snatched a handful of air. Then he shrugged. "It's another possibility."

I looked away. I saw movement in the top of the big oak. It was the squirrel. He was savoring nature's bounty today, but I knew he was also stockpiling food for the winter. He believed he had a future, and was planning for it. My future was in doubt, but I still needed a plan—at least a decision about the thrust my remaining days would have. "Look Tim," I said, you know me. I'm not the dramatic type. I'm low-key. I'm deliberate. That would be way out of character."

"True: that's your temperament—your day-to-day posture. But I think you'll agree these next three months won't exactly be routine. You might choose to *act* in a routine manner. But knowing what you know, they can't *be* routine."

I took a breath. "Maybe there's some middle ground—some golden mean of moderation, or compromise, between carrying on as usual, and the big blow-out. I don't like extremes—they get you into trouble."

"Maybe they just make you uncomfortable."

That earned him a sharp look. "Yeah, because they've just gotten me in trouble."

"Maybe. But a more radical approach can shake things up, get the ball rolling, get things done—while your middle ground business is just weak sauce, refusing to challenge the status quo."

"Maybe the status quo is fine."

21

"May be. But what if it isn't? What if it's comfortable, but not fine? Comfort, absence of conflict, can be very seductive. We tend to see it as evidence that all is well. A good dose of heroin would have the same effect."

Now you're being ridiculous, I thought. But I said, "Maybe it *is* fine. Why is it, when things *seem* fine, we must always worry that they're not *really* fine? That's one of the things I don't appreciate about the church experience."

Tim gave me a long, contemplative look. I was fairly sure he wouldn't take that comment personally. I had no desire to offend him. He said, "It's all something to think about. You've got to take *some* tack— *some* approach. We're just chewing the fat of options." He continued watching me, a light in his eyes. I knew this man cared for me, my family—and that felt good. Then he asked, "You're not afraid of dying, are you Paul?"

"I have a fear of suffering," I replied, "but not of dying."

"No fear of punishment or judgment in the afterlife?"

"There could be something along those lines—some after-death insights that might not be one hundred percent pleasant. But if you're asking about eternal damnation, I don't think so. As I understand it, the Gospel is about *good* news; eternal damnation is very bad news. Plus, I don't see how the Almighty, in His beneficence, could countenance such a deal. Like me going big time, that's a country mile out of character. I feel the sacrifice Jesus made was for everyone—even people who don't know about it, don't care, even outright reject it. On this issue, I guess I'm a universalist."

Tim Rouzerville looked shocked. Then, waving his arms, he yelled, "Hey—me too!"

11

So, a Baptist preacher who doesn't believe in hell—the traditional concept of it at least. Interesting. I wondered if that were unusual, and figured it probably was. As I drove home from our meeting, I scanned back over the years. I recalled sermons dealing with poor choices and their consequences; I remembered sermons dealing with various life priorities and the fruits they might bear. I could pull up nothing on hell. In his long tenure at First Baptist of Frederick, I don't think Tim Rouzerville ever preached a sermon on the topic. Again, interesting. How did the congregation let him get away with that? Surely some hardcore deacon or Sunday School superintendent had noticed, and had called his hand on it. Yet he survived. Tim had probably been a closet universalist for a long time. What would happen if he came out?

Our conversation had been good, but inconclusive. I've heard that good counselors don't give advice. Instead, they help the counselee explore his or her feelings, and they delineate possible courses of action. That's exactly what Tim had done. He had clarified that my choices were three: do nothing; do everything; or steer somewhere between.

Kay would be back tomorrow evening. Hopefully I would have settled on something by then. I would take a long hike on The Trail this afternoon. I would think, and I would pray.

12

"Dr. Stepping, what can I do for you?"

Monday morning, first thing, I had asked to see Major Essex. I stood before his desk and got right to the point. "Major, I need to know if you intend to recommend me for a heart transplant, if there is a mechanism to bump me up the list, and if you intend to activate that mechanism?"

His blue eyes watched me. They seemed cold. Maybe it was just my imagination. "I just got Mellwood's report. He says your heart is fine."

"Yes, he told me that Friday after the exam. Based on our evidence from the test animals, it's what I expected. We saw no incremental debilitation. They were normal—behaved normally—until the day they died. Now, about the transplant."

"Would you like to sit down, Dr. Stepping?"

I figured Essex didn't like me standing there, looking down on him. It threw some ambiguity into his sense of peck order. "No thank you sir. I

23

need to get to my lab. I have a lot to do."

So he stood, but remained behind his desk. "I've given this some thought. Emmerton could replace you on the ricin research, but I doubt he could become your equal—not in the time we have. So yes, I'm recommending you for a transplant; yes, there is a bump-up mechanism for personnel considered essential to national security; and yes, I'm activating that mechanism."

I was stunned. A ray of hope. Maybe my distress over the accident had caused me to judge Essex too harshly. Close to stammering, I said, "Why, thank you sir. I appreciate that—very much."

His face did not change expression. "Less than three months," he said. "There are no guarantees."

13

The week was fairly routine. I continued working to produce RPA-73. I made only small progress, finding that one of the structural changes I had envisioned for the RPA-72 precursor molecule was more difficult to effect than I had anticipated. I consulted twice with Emmerton, filling him in on my research in the event he had to step in. He told me he was initiating experiments to gain info on how 72 stopped the heart so abruptly. He thanked me for allowing Boyd Markham, my main tech and animal expert, to assist him. Joy Smalls got back to me after touching base with her veterinarian friend at MRIID. That news was not encouraging. Mouse and human hepatic functions are very similar. After all, why would we use them to test medical products destined for human use, if they were significantly *dis*similar? True, this vet didn't know everything about mouse livers, and Joy didn't know everything about human ones. And no one knew *my* complete genome, the detailed sequence of base pairs in *my* DNA that impacted the structure and physiology of *my* liver. Maybe I had some small variation that would make a crucial difference. But this chance was small. To place undue focus on it would be grasping at straws. And I don't grasp at straws. I go with the odds.

Kay's visit with her parents had not gone well. While she was there

24

her mother had taken a fall. There were no broken bones, but she was bruised up and sore. Ruth had been complaining of weakness, of feeling tired, for some time. Somehow she had gotten off balance just walking down the hall from her bedroom to the bathroom. Had she been at or near normal strength, she would have compensated and righted herself. Kay returned home worried. She and her sister Joan had thought about hiring someone to stay in the home at night, perhaps sleeping in the room with their mother. (Wade slept in another room, was hard of hearing, and was somewhat feeble himself.) They had also wondered if Ruth's problem stemmed from something specific, as opposed to the fact that she was just getting older. Perhaps they should get some tests done. All this was up in the air, and so was Kay.

I was prompted to think of my own mother. Anna is seventy-seven and doing very well. She continues to live in the Criglersville area of Madison County, in the house my sisters and I grew up in. Cliff Stepping, my father, died the year I got my Bachelor's at UVa—ironically from a heart attack that struck without warning. Mother never re-married. She lives alone, and seems to enjoy it.

Her neighbor (a quarter mile away) is Clemmie Finks. Miss Clemmie is almost ninety, and beginning to falter. Mother looks in on her every day—sits with her and drinks coffee. Clemmie was my chemistry teacher at Madison County High School. She wasn't that well-qualified; I had a fair number of questions she couldn't answer. But she worked hard, gave a good course within the limits of her abilities, and was fair. I liked her. I began to see the possibilities of chemistry in her classroom. She retired a few years after I graduated.

I call Mother once a week or so, but hadn't seen her in a while—since Easter, actually. Kay's going to visit her folks made me think I needed to make that journey. While there, maybe I would drop in on Miss Clemmie.

Kay was all for the idea. I said I wouldn't stay any nights. If I left early Saturday morning, I could spend the bulk of the day with Mother, eat supper with her, and be back home before bedtime. Kay suggested I drive her Civic instead of my gas-hog Chevy Tahoe. Fine with me. I called Anna and told her I was coming.

I took US 340 from Frederick until it hit US 17 below Winchester, Virginia. I drove south on 17, picking up US 29 in Warrenton. This four-lane artery took me through Culpeper, and on into Madison County. I pulled into Mother's driveway around 9:00 AM. The trip had taken a little over two hours.

"Well aren't you a sight for sore eyes?" she said, meeting me on the porch all smiles and with a big hug. "Have you had breakfast?" She was wearing a checkered apron. I could see a flour hand print on it.

"I got an Egg McMuffin and some coffee in Warrenton; I ate that on the road."

"Now look Paul—I've got a pan of biscuits in the oven. Biscuits, butter, and syrup—your favorite. I tried to time them for your arrival, and I hit it right on the button. Come on in."

Daddy had built the frame house just after he started working for Sperry Marine in Charlottesville. It was tiny—all he and Mother could afford at the time. I was born two years later, and they added a room. There were other additions when my sisters came along. It was a great comfort to be here this early fall morning.

Anna led me into the kitchen where I was greeted by the aroma of those fresh biscuits baking. "I can fry up some bacon, scramble some eggs; that coffee was brewed not ten minutes ago." She indicated a little four-cup maker on the counter, the carafe of which was half full. I tried to remember a time before this ancient Hamilton Beach appliance, but could not. To my recollection it had always been in the kitchen—in that very spot.

"No Mother, the biscuits will be fine. Don't go to any more trouble. I will have some of that coffee."

I poured myself a cup. Mother still had the thick porcelain mugs she had bought when Beulah's Restaurant in the town of Madison went out of business thirty years ago upon the proprietor's death. The mugs were part of the consolation of this place: symbols of endurance, of continuity, of stability—commodities in short supply with me just now.

I tore open the biscuits, releasing steam, and from the action of the yeast, probably a few trapped molecules of carbon dioxide and ethyl

26

alcohol. The butter melted at once; the syrup permeated the maze of smoking channels, soaked up as by a sponge. It was wonderful, perfect: another of those grand memories of days gone by. I loved my mother. My eyes blurred, so I looked away.

Anna sat there watching me eat—she always had. At length she stated, "Joanna says she can retire next summer."

Joanna is one of my sisters—four years my younger. She lives in neighboring Orange County. Joanna went to Virginia Tech, never took a summer off, and finished in three years. She's been teaching Health & PE at Orange County High School since she was twenty-one. The General Assembly recently passed a "30-and-out" provision for state employees, dropping the age requirement, which used to be fifty-five. That meant Joanna could retire at age fifty-one with full benefits, come the end of the school year.

"You think she'll do it?"

"It's a toss-up. I'd say she grew weary of teaching some time ago. But you know how she loves that softball."

Fresh out of Tech, once Joanna's three-year probationary period had expired, she had been asked to take over the struggling girls softball program at OCHS. Within two years the Lady Hornets won district; within five they won the first of four state championships under Joanna's leadership—the most recent just two years ago. It wasn't like things were slacking off.

We talked a while about Joanna's situation, then I asked, "What's the latest on Lucy? I haven't heard from her in months."

Lucy is my other sister, three years younger than Joanna. She was a 9th-Grader when Daddy died. It hit her hard. I was out of the house; Joanna would be headed to Blacksburg in a month, so it was just Anna and Lucy. Mother had relied on Daddy's firm hand in dealing with us as teenagers. Lucy began acting out, and Mother was at a loss. Looking back, I should have intervened. But I was just starting graduate school and was self-absorbed almost to the point of autism. Lucy made a series of choices that put her on a difficult road. She resents me—at least that's the vibe I've gotten for a very long time. I imagine her thinking is something like,

27

"Daddy died; I was crushed; Mother was in shock; you're the oldest—you're a man; why the hell didn't you *do* something?"

"She's still in Colorado," Anna said, "working in a bar in one of those ski resort towns. She called about a week ago. Didn't stay on the line long. I could hear somebody in the background yelling for her."

"Maybe it was her boss."

"Or her latest boyfriend," she said, her face clouding.

"Lucy's forty-seven years old, Mother. She's a grown woman. She makes her own decisions—lives her own life. Don't worry."

Telling mothers not to worry, even about their thoroughly adult children, is like telling a dog not to wag his tail when he's happy. It's not a matter of reason; it's an affair of the maternal heart.

I told Mother I'd try to get in touch with Lucy soon. I complimented her on the biscuits. Then I said, "You know, I'd like to go see Miss Clemmie. You suppose she's up to it?"

"I think so. I check on her about this time each morning. I'll give her a ring—tell her you're going to take my place today."

"Actually, I'd like to surprise her."

"All right. Just be prepared to drink coffee. She'll have a fresh pot ready."

14

More coffee? I love the drink, but if I exceed moderation, my bladder lets me know, and I get jittery to boot. Three cups in two hours would be pushing it.

Clemmie Finks came to the door with the help of a walker. She squinted through the screen and said, "Anna?"

"It's Paul, Miss Clemmie. I'm filling in for Mother this morning. You're getting the second string."

"So you're down from Maryland. Nothing wrong with Anna, is there?"

"No, no—she's fine. I just wanted to drop by—see how you're doing. It's been a while."

28

"Well come in Paul."

It was dark in the hallway that led to Miss Clemmie's living room. *That's not safe*, I thought. I heard her slippers scrape over the hardwood. The walker thumped as she raised, advanced, then dropped it. I smelled the coffee as I entered the house.

Madison County rests in the foothills of the Blue Ridge. The large windows of the living room faced west. I could see Old Rag Mountain ascending, its higher reaches lost in the slowly rising morning mist. I had climbed it many times as a boy.

A silver service occupied one end of a solid oak coffee table, with cups and saucers on the other. Clemmie and I sat on the sofa, upholstered in maroon damask. I have known Clemmie Finks all my life, and have been in her home dozens of times. Both sofa and coffee table have always been there beneath the big windows.

She poured the coffee, her hands steadier than I would have guessed. "Your mother takes hers black. How about you?"

"No," I said with a chuckle. "I wish I could. Lots more convenient. Mother once told me if I would drink my next five cups black, I'd be converted. I got to Cup Three, and that was it. Too bitter."

"I'm with you Paul," she said, stirring in a teaspoon of sugar and a few drops of Half & Half. "You could have the most expensive brand in the world, and without these small additions, the bitterness would overwhelm all those essential oils that provide the delicate flavor. You might as well be drinking something that had been sitting on a hot plate in a convenience store for six hours. I buy the beans, you know—grind a fresh batch every day."

"Well, it's certainly good," I said, taking my first sip. "I wish I could drink coffee all day. I knew a guy once—he was in our church for a while—he told me he drank fifteen to twenty cups a day. Does that seem possible? I thought he was pulling my leg, but he said no."

Clemmie looked thoughtful. "I'd say he was addicted."

She raised her cup and blew over the steaming surface of the coffee with pursed lips. She used her left hand, which was missing the ring finger. Clemmie Finks was your stereotypical old maid schoolteacher, so it wasn't

29

as if she would have had a wedding band on that digit. She had shown us this anomaly the first day of chemistry class. "I was careless," she had said, holding the hand out and rotating it so every wide-eyed student could see, "and this was the result. I broke a thermometer, got mercury in the cut. I thought everything was fine, but it didn't heal properly. By the time I got it checked out, gangrene had set it. They had to amputate. Follow the safety rules. Don't let this happen to you."

Thanks in part to this high school teacher, I'm generally quite careful in the lab. I've tried to think back, but I still don't know what happened the day of my accident. I guess I never will. I wish the only price I had to pay was the loss of a finger.

"Guess I last saw you around Easter," she said, settling back against the sofa cushions. "Everything going well?"

"Not too bad."

"Your wife still teaching?"

"Yes she is—3rd-Grade." We had been over this back in April.

"And your kids?"

"They're fine—well, except for Amy. I mean, she's okay; she's in Louisiana. She dropped out of school and went down there to find herself, she said."

The old woman offered me a grave look. "As I recall, your sister Lucy did something like that—after Cliff died."

"Yes, she did."

Amy had done so-so through high school, with things beginning to erode during her senior year. She had shown little interest in further education, saying she could learn more by going to work. But Kay and I were adamant. She was going to college, and given some of her recent antics, she would be staying close to home. Hood College was right in Frederick. If she couldn't get into Hood, it would be the nearby community college for two years. We wanted Amy to continue living with us. She desperately wanted to be out of the house. Here was the compromise: you get into Hood, you can live on campus; if it's community college, since they have no dorms, you live with us. No, you can't get an apartment.

30

Amy's grades picked up the last two marking periods before she graduated. She re-took the SAT and tacked 300 points onto her combined score. I had a conference with the chief admissions officer at Hood, who was also Dean of Students. Science majors at the college could apply for a limited number of summer internships at Ft. Detrick. In fact, the previous summer I'd had a very bright young fellow working in my lab. It was then I had met the Dean. These students were not given the big picture of course, but they got valuable real-world research experience; Ft. Detrick got good PR, plus a pool of possible future employees.

Amy got into Hood. After four semesters of piddling around, and after a series of embarrassing meetings with professors, counselors, and finally the Dean again, Amy quit and hopped a Greyhound south. That was back in early May. Amy's our youngest, our only daughter. We've heard from her once since then—a letter, and no contact information. Kay and I are worried sick.

Clemmie said, "I guess Lucy had good reasons. What about Amy? Finding herself sounds a little vague."

"I couldn't agree more. I'm puzzled. She's turned away from us, and I don't know why." Not wanting to pursue this, I said, "But what about you, Miss Clemmie? Mother says you've been struggling a little lately."

"Well," she said, shifting on the damask, "I'm just weak. I do the least little thing and I give out. I think it's the diuretic they have me on. I've got congestive heart problems. That leads to a build-up of fluid." I had noticed her ankles were swollen. "So I take this diuretic, and as it flushes out the excess fluid, it takes along some of my electrolytes, making me weak. Figure in a hip replacement a year ago, plus Type-2 diabetes, and I guess that does add up to struggling a little."

"I see you put sugar in your coffee."

She laughed. "You remember Rhonda Shifflett? She graduated with you." When I frowned, she went on, "Rhonda is Type-1—juvenile onset. She was eight or nine when her folks found out she had it. Rhonda balanced her diet, exercise, and insulin perfectly. She still lives in the county, and after these almost fifty years, shows no signs of the problems diabetes can cause. She's very disciplined, and that comes from her early training. The trouble with your average Type-2 is that we have our patterns well set before we're struck down. That's not to say I haven't made changes in my eating habits. I have. And I take my medicine regularly, and test my blood regularly. That dab of sugar in my coffee—I tried the artificial sweeteners, but they were just awful. I love coffee. It's my one indulgence. Why ruin it? I'm ten years older than your mother for God's sake—more, truth be told. I'm not that long for this world, Paul. It's not like I'm hoping to get married before Christmas!" Clemmie Finks threw back her head and laughed again.

I smiled. It was all I could manage.

15

The drive back to Maryland was good: perfect weather; traffic not an issue; Kay's Civic purring along, sipping gas, getting great mileage. I listened to the radio for a while—first some braying news talk individual who would take a call, then never let the caller finish a sentence, much less a point; second an oldies soft rock station, which I generally liked, but when they hit four songs in a row that I *didn't* like, I cut it off. I motored on in silence, thinking about my day with Mother and Miss Clemmie, wondering what RPA-72 was doing to *my* heart.

Mother is a rock. She had struggled after Daddy died, but she had certainly never given up. To this day though, she considers Lucy her fault. But Lucy would likely have taken the path she did, regardless of Anna's actions. Her youth had been the critical factor. Losing your father at fourteen is a crippling blow—more so than if you're seventeen like Joanna, or twenty-one like me. That's my take at least. Mother's always been there. My tendency (and I doubt it's unique) is to think she always will be. That's not a rational assessment of course. What *is* likely, is that she will outlive me. If that's the way things play out, then she *will* have been in my life from Day One to Day Last.

Clemmie Finks is inspirational. The world needs inspirational people. As I drove along I tried to identify what features put her in that select group.

For one thing, Miss Clemmie is straightforward. She doesn't pussyfoot. Which is not to say she's mean, rude, or bullying. High school teachers have the opportunity to be all three. I had a few that strayed into one or more of those territories. But not Clemmie. She was simply clear, transparent, concerning what she wanted from you. She delivered those expectations with little affect, and no value judgment. That's the way I liked it—the way I still like it. As Sergeant Friday on the old *Dragnet* TV series would put it, "Just the facts ma'am." I don't need a cheerleader or a taskmaster. I certainly don't need a constant barrage of editorial comment. Maybe some do, or did, back in high school. If so, they didn't get these things from their chemistry teacher.

Another factor is optimism, which I don't equate with smiling a lot, or even with looking on the bright side of the proverbial penny. Miss Clemmie doesn't whine, she doesn't complain, she never makes excuses. She takes things as they are, as they come, and deals with them. I call that optimism because it implies that situations *can* be dealt with, and the outcomes *can* be successful. To me, that's huge.

I'm sure there are more. But these characteristics are enough to engender encouragement, confidence, hope—in a word, inspiration. The world needs inspirational people. I know I do. Clemmie Finks is one, and though almost through her ninth decade, like Mother, she will likely outlive me.

When I walked in Kay was in the La-Z-Boy, watching a DVD of *Napoleon Dynamite*, her "favorite movie of all time." When earlier I had questioned that proclamation with, "I thought it was *Doctor Zhivago*—I thought you said Omar Sharif was the man," she had cocked her head, squinted a few seconds, then had replied, "No, Napoleon is what high school kids are *really* like; it's hilarious, and beside, I can actually follow the plot."

She hit the PAUSE button on the remote, freezing a close-up of Napoleon's mouth as he participated in an FFA milk-tasting competition. She walked over and gave me a big kiss. "How's your mom?" she asked, then added, "There's no problem, is there?" I figured she was projecting her concerns about her own parents.

33

"Oh, no—she's fine. Listen, let me run to the bathroom, then we can talk." When I returned she was back in the recliner, staring at the inert image on the TV screen. I dropped into the pine rocker. "Mother's fine," I repeated. "No changes that I could see. Still makes a mean pan of biscuits."

"So what did you do—did you go anywhere with her?"

"No, not really; just sat around and talked. She caught me up on Joanna and Lucy." I gave Kay a recap of all that.

"And what about Clemmie Finks? I'll bet you went over to see her."

Soon after we married, I had introduced Kay to Miss Clemmie. Since then, whenever she traveled with me to see Mother, we called on my former teacher. "I did. She's not doing so well—not that you would know it, but Mother's kept me informed. Actually, I was surprised when Clemmie discussed some of her ailments. It was straight information though—no whining—and I think she did it to lay the groundwork for stating, and I quote, 'I'm not that long for this world, Paul. It's not like I'm hoping to get married before Christmas.'"

"She's a mess," Kay said. "You're worried about her, aren't you?"

"I guess I am. If Miss Clemmie goes, Mother might not be far behind." Normally I would have reported something like the "married before Christmas" comment with a chuckle. This time I was deadpan, if not glum; Kay, of course, picked up.

"Oh, I doubt that. She's in good health. My folks are much farther down the road than Anna." She looked away. "I suppose Joan and I will have to make some decisions in the near future."

Any mention of the future brought my own foreshortened one into focus. But Kay's worries over her parents was another reason not to burden her with my situation.

"You know what?" she said, brightening and switching gears. "We're out of eggs."

Kay and I both love eggs. Trying however to eat "right," we limit our involvement to Sunday mornings. (I say "right," because eggs, like milk and red meat, have experienced a yo-yo reputation in the world of nutrition and health.) Before heading out to First Baptist, I scramble up half a dozen

34

large, and we split them. Kay's an okay cook, but her big problem is patience. And patience is the key to perfect scrambled eggs. You can't just dial your burner up to seven or eight and walk away. You cover the bottom of your skillet with Pam, then crack your eggs, dropping them one by one into the cold pan. *Do not* put them into a bowl first and beat them. Then you set your burner on *four (4)*, and you stand there. You break your yolks with a large metal spoon—not a Teflon spatula—and begin to mix things up in the gradually warming skillet. You stand there, and mix, and watch carefully until that delicate balance of solidified yolk/white and moisture is realized. Then without delay you transfer your achievement to a waiting bowl and cover it with a dish cloth. Seriously, is there anything worse than dry scrambled eggs? And there's never a legitimate excuse for that abomination.

Now we had no eggs for tomorrow morning. "Why didn't you pick some up on your way home yesterday?" I asked.

"I didn't know we were out."

"When did you discover it?"

"A couple of hours ago. I went in the fridge for something—I can't remember what—and I noticed, no eggs."

"Why didn't you run into town and get some?"

"I thought about it. Then I got busy doing a little cleaning and straightening in the garage. Then I ate a bite of supper. Then I started watching *Napoleon Dynamite*, and . . . ." She gave me an apologetic smile and a shrug. "I forgot. I'm sorry. Maybe I was waiting for the Civic to get back so we wouldn't waste gas with the Tahoe."

I watched her a moment. "Yeah, maybe that was it." Kay's impatience caused problems. So did her forgetfulness and her disorganized approach to things. The impact was infrequent at work. I figured the structured school environment kept her pretty well in check. But here at home there was a never-ending succession of these screw-ups. "Well, the Civic's back," I remarked.

She frowned. "Now you're being mean."

"I am?"

"Yes—you said that with a mean tone in your voice." I waited a few seconds. She was staring at me with hurt eyes. Then she asked, "Do you want me to go get the eggs?"

Of course I did. I'd been gone all day visiting my elderly mother. She had been home all day doing what she pleased. I just learned we were out. She had known earlier in the evening. Of course she should go get them. But I said, "I'll go. Finish watching your movie."

I left, calling "Sorry" over my shoulder, but not meaning it. I got back in the Civic and drove to Wal-Mart just inside the Frederick city limits. I retrieved the eggs, then walked up to one of the 20-items-or-less check-outs. It was 9:30. Even at this hour I was the fourth customer back. I stood behind a three hundred pound woman who had at least thirty high-calorie items in her cart.

"I notice you drink Coke Classic," I said.

She turned around to see who had spoken. I doubt she was twenty-five. She had a pretty face, once you got past the triple chin. "I'm used to it," she said. "And I tell you what—all those diet drinks leave one nasty aftertaste." She looked wise, as if she had just revealed some deep truth. Then she smiled.

"Diet Coke's pretty good," I said. "You might try getting use to *it*, considering . . . ." I gave her an arch expression while letting my eyes play over her bulk.

Her pleased look evaporated. "You know what? Mind your own business."

I thought about that suggestion, but decided otherwise. This was something I had wanted to do for some time. "People don't get fat overnight," I stated. "What do you do? Eat five, six thousand calories a day, every day, and never exercise?"

"It's none of your damn business," she said in a louder voice, her face flushing.

"It is if I and other Americans have to pay more for health insurance because of irresponsible individuals such as yourself."

"You go to hell!" she shouted.

"You go on a starvation diet," I replied.

I thought she was going to take a swing. Instead she whirled to face

36

the cashier and shrieked, "Miss! Miss! Get security! This man is harassing me!"

Everyone within a fifty foot radius was looking our way, including a tough-looking bald guy lounging near the automatic doors. The cashier motioned to him. He began to move.

I placed my carton on the conveyor belt and walked away. From a distance I looked back to see the fat lady conferring with the plain-clothes security guard. She was being comforted by a fellow behemoth who, drawn by the commotion, had abandoned her laden cart and waddled to the rescue.

I left by the other set of doors at the far end of the store. On my way home I stopped at a 7-Eleven and bought a dozen eggs for twice the Wal-Mart price.

16

The next morning Tim Rouzerville's sermon was on the Golden Rule. It was an intelligent exposition, exploring not only why this approach to relationships is generally practical (as opposed to being merely "good" or "right"), but also admitting that it assumes the one doing unto others actually *knows* what is best for himself/herself, as well as what is best for the others. He noted that such assumptions are not always warranted. He pointed out that praiseworthy intentions do not inevitably produce praiseworthy results.

As I sat in the pew and listened, I reviewed my encounter with the obese woman. I tried to think about it in the light of what Tim was saying—wondering if it was in any sense defensible. It was clearly out of character for me. I don't get involved in other people's issues unless specifically invited, and I'm reluctant even then. I tried to fathom why I had precipitated this interaction with a complete stranger. *Someone has to confront these mastodons*, I found myself justifying. *Someone has to get their attention—tell them the truth*. Then I debated what the "truth" might be in this situation. The woman was grossly overweight—*that* was true. Her caloric intake, degree of exercise, and health risks, were matters of conjecture on my part. I had been straightforward, like Clemmie Finks, but not loving, or even neutral. When being direct, Miss Clemmie is neutral. At best, I had been insensitive—at worst, malicious.

During the altar call I breathed a prayer of repentance. I had been judgmental and ill-intentioned. These were not virtues. After the service I apologized to Kay about last night. This time I meant it.

17

The next three weeks at work were part soothing routine, part unsettling surprise. I made some progress on RPA-73—nothing to write home about. It was becoming clear that this new variant would not be ready in time to help me, if help me it indeed could. One option would be to treat myself with it a week or so before DP-1, regardless of its stage of development. That would be a risk, especially if no animal tests had been done at that point. A breakthrough was always possible of course, with things moving along faster than anticipated.

A word about DP. At the meeting Major Essex had called, I shared that I had done some calculations. They showed that if I were to die as a result of this mishap, it would happen within a nine-day window I have dubbed the Death Period, or DP. DP-1 is the first day of this window.

Mellwood checked my heart each Monday, Wednesday, and Friday: no changes. I told him I might die from the smell of tobacco before the RPA-72 killed me. He did not find this particularly funny.

Emmerton held out a ray of hope. Boyd Markham, my tech who's expert with the mice, treated a small group of them with 72. When after a week they died, he rushed the little corpses to Emmerton, who removed the hearts and did some tests. He discovered that the RPA-72 molecule was binding to a protein that is specific to cardiac tissue. My team knew the protectant was accumulating in the heart muscle, but had no knowledge of the actual receptor. If Emmerton could determine the nature of the bond, perhaps he could find a way to break it. Once released, whatever damage the 72 was doing would be stopped. Emmerton said he had put one of his technicians on the job of determining the distribution of RPA-72 in the

38

mouse hearts: Was it everywhere, or did it collect in particular areas—around the valves, for instance, or within the two nodes that control the electrical impulses essential to a rhythmic beat? Mellwood had raised this question in the meeting with Essex. That would be nice to know, but time being of the essence, I urged Emmerton to concentrate on a possible antidote.

Before my dates with Mellwood on the appointed days, I went to Joy Smalls. Essex had originally directed me to check in with her daily, but later agreed to the MWF routine as being more time efficient, and likely as effective. Joy did a quick physical each time, and drew some blood. Her main objective was to monitor my liver function via these thrice-a-week blood profiles. Significant changes in the levels of certain enzymes or hepatic metabolites would signal that the organ was experiencing something new—perhaps that it was destroying the RPA-72. To this point there had been no such changes.

On October 17, a Wednesday, I entered her examination room and sat down. She closed the door and prepared to draw blood.

"Monday's numbers were normal," she said, tightening the rubber hose around the muscles of my humerus, "and the protectant level continues to drop." She swabbed the crook of my arm with alcohol. "Make a fist for me." She took the sample, pain-free as usual. I stood and stepped over to the examination table. I sat on the end of it and unbuttoned my shirt. I knew the drill. She used a mini-flashlight to examine my eyes, looking for signs of jaundice, she had told me the first time she did it. "Now lie back." Her hands explored my abdomen—pressing, pushing, palpating—seeing if there were any gross abnormalities, such as a general enlargement of the liver, or a tumor. She smiled down at me. "Okay. All good."

I sat up. "Joy," I said, pushing a button through its eye, "I really appreciate you. You're professional, but you also have a bedside manner that's encouraging. I leave here every time feeling cheered."

"That's good to know. You're dealing with a unique situation, but there's no need to be disheartened, is there?" She gave my arm a squeeze.

"There might be, but my patient confidence index still goes up every time I see you."

She watched me with her green eyes. Her face was still. After several seconds she said, "Well, I'm glad." Then her white cheeks went pink and she turned away. With her red hair, a red, white, and green image of the flag of Italy unfurled in my head. This morphed into the orange, white, and green of Ireland's banner. Joy was more likely Irish than Italian. And people don't really have red hair—it's more like orange. I blinked, thinking, *How weird is the mind anyway?* She kept her back to me, fiddling with something on the counter while I closed my shirt.

I walked to the door, and with my hand on the knob said, "Thanks Joy. I'll see you Friday."

She half-glanced over her shoulder. "Okay Paul. We'll hope things keep going well."

I waited for more, or for her to turn and face me. But nothing happened, so I left. As I walked away down the brightly-lit corridor toward my lab, I felt my heart tick up a notch or two.

Two days later I was in Leonard Essex's office, standing before his desk and saying, "Major, today is my daughter's birthday." It was Friday, October 19, a month since my accident.

He looked up from the single page on his otherwise clear desk. His expression conveyed, *And why do I need this piece of information?* But he said, "Very good, Dr. Stepping. How old is she?"

"She's twenty, sir."

I hesitated after saying that, waiting for some affirming word I guess. The silence was awkward. He repeated, "Very good," cleared his throat while sliding his eyes over to his watch, then asked, "How can I help you?"

"Amy's down in Louisiana, sir. I'd like to go see her. I'd fly down tomorrow, stay Sunday and Monday, return Tuesday, and be back to work Wednesday."

"That's two days you won't be working on RPA-73," he observed. "But that's your business. Employees get two personal leave days per year. I don't think you've used yours."

"I haven't."

"Then fill out the paperwork. I see nothing standing in your way."

"Thank you, sir."

Personal leave could be vetoed by the head of MMDA if the situation demanded. Essex was big on the ricin project, but apparently a couple of days missed by his lead researcher was neither here nor there.

"I'm assuming you can arrange things so your team will be productive while you're gone. I don't want them twiddling their thumbs."

"No problem Major."

"Tell them I'll be checking."

"Will do."

"And I want you to inform Emmerton, Mellwood, and Smalls today. Emmerton might have questions he planned to ask, assuming you would be here Monday and Tuesday. I don't want your absence to hold up his work. You'll miss your Monday check-ins with Mellwood and Smalls. They need to be aware of that."

"I'll take care of it sir."

Returning his attention to the document before him, he said, "Then see you on Wednesday."

This transaction was over. I thanked him again and turned to go.

He called after me, "Nothing yet on your transplant, Dr. Stepping."

18

That one letter we had received from Amy back in May bore no return address, but it did have a postmark: Alexandria, LA. I have a cousin who lives in Pineville, just across the Red River from Alexandria. Eileen is the daughter of Aunt Harriet, my father's half-sister. Eileen and her husband, Jerome, are both professors at Louisiana College, a Baptist liberal arts school located in Pineville. Amy's letter had said she was waitressing. It didn't say where. Once I got down, my plan was to get the Alexandria phone book and start calling restaurants—see if I could track her down. Then it occurred to me to give Cousin Eileen a buzz.

Driving home from work I flipped open my cell and punched her up. Pineville is an hour earlier than Frederick; I hoped she'd be available. She answered on the second ring.

41

"Eileen—Paul Stepping up in Maryland. Glad I caught you."

"Well Paul! I'll be damned! How many months of Sundays has it been?"

"Too many—too many."

"Yeah, my last class on Fridays ends at noon. Woo-hoo! So I cruise on home, take me a solid nap, then grade papers until Jerome drags in. Once he decompresses for an hour or so, we go eat out."

"Sounds like a sweet program."

"It's not bad. You still doing the cloak-and-dagger thing at Ft. Detrick?"

"Yes I am—but not for much longer. Retirement beckons."

"Well hey! Congratulations! I'm afraid I'll be at the old grindstone here a fair while longer." The next thing she said was garbled, then I heard, "Paul, you still with me? Paul?"

"I'm here."

The transmission cleared. "Listen, Paul—I'll bet you're calling about Amy."

My breath caught. "Well, yes. How did you—?"

"Surprised the deuce out of me!" Eileen yelled. "One Saturday morning—must have been back in June—Amy shows up at the front door. We have a nice cup of coffee together. She says she's down here working for the summer. Just wanted to let me know she was around. Then, end of August I think, I get a call. She says she's going to take a semester off from school and keep working. I told her to drop by sometime, but I haven't heard from her since."

"I'm really glad she got in touch with you. She can get unreasonable about being on her own—not wanting Kay and me to hover over her, you know."

"Hey, I deal with that syndrome every day."

"I'll bet you do." I paused, wondering how to proceed without giving the impression that our daughter had basically run away from home. "Listen, Eileen—today is Amy's twentieth birthday. Did she happen to leave you a phone number? I'd like to give her a call."

She laughed. "So your youngest is twenty? You must be getting old,

42

Cousin." She laughed again. "No, I don't have her number, but I know where she works."

"You do?"

"Sure—the Paradise Catfish Kitchen. It's just a few miles up 165 toward Ball. Jerome and I were thinking about going there tonight. I'll wish her a happy birthday—tell her you called."

"No, ah—listen, Eileen—actually I was thinking about flying down— you know, surprise her. So if you wouldn't mind, don't say anything. I mean, you could wish her happy birthday, but . . . ."

"Oh, sure—no problem. Of course she might not even be working tonight. But if she is, we'll request her, then slap down a big healthy tip for a birthday present. But we'll keep it quiet about Daddy making a special trip to see his baby."

"Well listen—thanks, Eileen. So Paradise Catfish Kitchen, 165 . . .?"

"North—toward Monroe."

"Between Pineville and Ball."

"That's it. And hey, Paul—stop by. We need to do some catching up."

Fifteen minutes later I was on orbitz.com booking my flight to Louisiana.

19

Kay arrived just as I was printing out my itinerary. I asked if she wanted to go. She inquired about the airfare. When I told her she breathed, "My God!" then said, "No—you're more understanding. I'd lose my cool with Amy, especially after paying that kind of money, and considering if she were being responsible, *neither* of us would have to go broke checking on her." Kay is nothing if not frugal.

We discussed the car situation. We figured I'd drive a hundred miles getting to and from BWI, while Kay would total more like sixty in her round trips to Washington County Monday and Tuesday. There was the cost of long-term parking, of course. But when you factored in Kay taking me to the airport tomorrow, then missing half a day of school Tuesday to come pick me up: I'd take the Civic; she'd use the Tahoe.

I mentioned earlier that Kay and I were adamant about Amy going to college. That's true, but there's more to the story, and it also centers around money. Kay had let it be known that she deemed ultra-cheap community college a fitting reward for Amy's lackluster high school performance. Why should we waste our hard-earned resources on someone who obviously didn't care? When Amy changed her ways and got into Hood, Kay had not been happy. When Amy reverted to type and began making noises about dropping out, Kay had said, "Let her go." But I, the "more understanding" one, urged, wheedled, encouraged, coaxed, and reasoned. As a result, Amy stuck at Hood for two non-productive years, then quit anyway. At the outset Kay had declared I was making a big mistake, that it damaged Amy's character to be repeatedly begged to do what she clearly ought to do, and that we were throwing good money after bad.

Now here I was again, spending yet more cash trying to rescue our youngest child, who seemed to want nothing more than for her parents to leave her the hell alone. But do twenty-year-olds really know what's best for them? What kind of father doesn't make every effort to protect his children—to save them from themselves if necessary? We hadn't heard from Amy in months. I needed first-hand information. It might be the last time I would see her. If I'd set this up two months ago, sure, I'd have saved some serious coin. But two months ago was the Stone Age. Beside, I didn't give a damn about the money.

Delta had a one-stop deal to Alexandria via their hub in Atlanta. The flights were on time, I had nothing but carry-on, and I touched down at AEX around 6:00 PM in a light rain. Alexandria International uses the extensive runways of the closed England Air Force Base. It's really just a low-volume regional airport, but it has a new terminal and convenient parking. I picked up a Chevy Cobalt from Avis. It was equipped with a nice little GPS unit—a Garmin. I had thought about getting one for use in our vehicles. When I mentioned it to Kay, after hearing the price she had asked, "So what's wrong with maps?" I punched in some data, then headed for I-49 South with my wipers set on intermittent.

44

20

I had reserved three nights at the Hotel Bentley in downtown Alexandria. A placard displayed on an easel in the lobby gave a little of the Bentley's long history, focusing on its use as a convention center. Things were not exactly bustling as I checked in this wet Saturday around dusk. Maybe the next-to-last weekend in October wasn't prime convention time in central Louisiana.

I took the marble stairs to the third floor. The carpet in the hallway was faded and worn. It was printed with foot-wide magnolia blossoms, no doubt striking when new. I inserted the key into the lock: metal into metal; no plastic cards with magnetic strips for the Bentley. The room was clean, but I found myself wondering about the last time anyone had slept here. I also wondered if I was the only person on this floor. Stephen King's *The Shining* crossed my mind. I placed my duffel on the bed and left.

I rolled over Red River via the Jackson Street Bridge. I drove through Pineville on Main Street. Everything was closed down except Huey P. Long Charity Hospital; it watched from a low hill a hundred yards off to my left. At the entrance to Louisiana College, Main split into Military Highway and Donahue Ferry Road. I took Military. It was 165 Business, and it went right by Eileen and Jerome's. They lived at 1709, not a mile from the college. It looked like they were at home. As I drove by, lights showed through the lower branches of the huge pine in their front yard. Maybe I would try to see them while I was here—maybe not. Certainly not tonight. It *had* been a month of Sundays, true. But why did it have to be me who made the call and flew 1300 miles? Eileen has a phone—a computer. She has a credit card. And why didn't she notify me when Amy first contacted her in June? That's been almost five months. Didn't she realize that . . . ? The answer was no, she probably *didn't* realize anything was amiss with her second cousin. Who knows what my daughter had told her? Amy's very good at giving the impression that everything's fine— everything's normal. So no, it wasn't Eileen. It was my own thoughts thrashing around. I was anxious.

45

The business route re-joined 165 near the Proctor & Gamble plant just north of Pineville's city limits. The Garmin showed 1.7 miles to the Paradise Catfish Kitchen.

21

Unlike the Bentley, and despite the fact that we were now involved in a cold steady rain, this fish house in the Paradise area of Rapides Parish was hopping. I had trouble finding a space for the Cobalt, finally parking in a far corner of the gravel lot near a dumpster. I had no umbrella. I waited five minutes for a lull. There was none, so I made a run for it, avoiding a soak, but my hair and shoulders got good and wet.

I pushed through the plank doors to be greeted by warmth, bright light, chatter, and the smell of fried fish. I blinked at a fiftyish woman behind the hostess lectern who gave me a big grin. "Lil wet out there tanaht," she drawled. "Come on in the house."

"Thanks," I said, intercepting with a forefinger some droplets creeping from my scalp toward my eyebrows. "Guess I should have been more prepared."

"Well, you're here now honey—that's the main thang. Let's see if we can find you a spot." She began scanning the large dining area crammed with circular tables and ringed with booths.

"I'd like Amy to be my server, it that's possible."

"Oh, Amy!" the woman yelled. "Lots of people request her. She's a good one, and usually jam packed." She squinted across the crowded room. "But look—that couple's leaving one of her tables now. Let's go get it!" She bustled from behind her counter and led the way, speaking to half the people we brushed by. "And here we are. Now you take a look at this menu, and Amy'll be with you in a few minutes."

The menu was a single laminated sheet, printed front and back. There was a small section devoted to seafood, and an even smaller one for steaks. These were on the back. The entire front was taken up with eight catfish entrées, ranging from baked, through blackened, to fried. I checked out the diners within my purview; deep-fat fried was the people's choice, and no

46

doubt the specialty of the house. Instead of napkins, each table had a roll of brown, unperforated paper towels. As I surveyed the menu offerings, I tore off a yard or so and began blotting my hair and flannel shirt.

When Amy walked up, my head was down. "I'm Amy—I'll be your server. Can I get you something to drink?"

I could barely hear her over the crowd noise, but the sound of her voice caused an ache behind my eyes. "I'll have coffee."

She stepped closer. "I'm sorry sir—did you say—?" I looked up. She dropped her order pad. "Daddy?" Her face lost color. "Oh, my God—Daddy, what are you doing here?"

"This is a restaurant. I'm here to eat. The Paradise Catfish Kitchen has quite a reputation. And oh—happy birthday."

Amy is a beautiful girl: fluffy blonde hair, big blue eyes, slender, olive skin; this is not fatherly bias—I'm a scientist, don't forget. The one flaw that surfaced as she moved into adolescence was her mouth. There were some issues with bad language, but that's not my reference here. She has good teeth and well-formed lips that can add up to a pretty smile—unless you cross her. Then those same attributes can twist into a sneer that is quite unattractive.

After staring for a moment, she said, "Well, thanks." She stooped, picked up her pad, then stood there looking uncomfortable.

"Your mother and I were worried."

"You talked to Eileen." Ah, connecting the dots. My daughter's no fool; well, she's sharp—there's a difference.

"Yes, I did. I called her from back home. Did you ask her not to contact me?"

"Not really."

"I'm glad you got in touch with her," I said. "That was prudent. What did you tell her?"

"I said you and Mom knew I was in Louisiana, and that I had written you."

"But you didn't share the circumstances under which you left, or that you had provided us no contact information."

I saw her lip tug upward. "No, I didn't. Was there an obligation?"

47

She glanced around. "Look, Daddy—I'm really busy. Do you want to order?"

"Yes I do: fried catfish."

"And your sides? You get two."

"Fried okra and a bowl of gumbo."

"The gumbo's pretty spicy."

"That's all right."

Amy was jotting with authoritative strokes of her pen. She seemed at ease in this job—confident. That was good to see.

"And to drink?"

"Coffee—and water, in case that gumbo sets off a three-alarm blaze."

She looked up from her pad and gave me a little smile. My heart melted. I thought I was going to cry. I carry a photo of Amy in my wallet. It's from her fifth birthday. She's sitting at the kitchen table behind a three-tiered German chocolate cake with five candles. Her hair is a halo of cotton. She's smiling into the camera—a little smile, just like now. "It's not *that* bad, Daddy. And four hushpuppies come with the fish. It'll probably be fifteen minutes. The cooks are working like crazy, but we're slammed."

She walked off toward the kitchen. Soon she was back on the floor, moving about, checking on her other guests. She was attentive, but not fawning; she appeared friendly—friendly enough—yet never obsequious. Amy was no bootlicker, grubbing for tips. I've seen a few of those: they're like Fake Blake, my beyond-religious cousin. She was a competent server—as the hostess had said, "a good one." No doubt the owners of this establishment were glad to have her.

It took twenty minutes to get the food, but it was worth it. The menu had proclaimed, "Our catfish are fresh, farm-raised, and never frozen." Apparently all that made a difference. Amy dropped by my table twice as I ate, replenishing my coffee and water, asking if things were okay.

When she brought the check I said, "I'd like to sit down with you—chat a while."

"We don't close until 10:00."

I looked at my watch. "It's 9:30 now—I'll wait."

"Daddy, you're still on Eastern Time. It's only 8:30. Beside, I have to help shut things down after the doors close. And it takes the late customers a while to filter out. I wouldn't be available until at least 11:00—maybe later."

I was tired. I wanted to be fresh when we talked. "Okay, how about tomorrow morning? You got a place here—an apartment?"

That dumb question elicited a look and, "No Daddy, I sleep on the street."

"Yeah, well—sorry. Of course you have a place. Maybe I could meet you there—take you out for breakfast or something."

"Okay, but could we make it not too early? I need to sleep in."

"Sure. How about 10:00?"

"Fine, but fix your watch."

She provided directions. I told her I was staying at the Bentley and gave her my room number. I left the Paradise Catfish Kitchen feeling pretty good about things.

22

According to the dashboard clock, I eased the Cobalt into Amy's driveway at 9:33 AM Sunday. I stopped beside a rusted-out Plymouth. A cold front had moved through. The weather had cleared, and the single-wide loafed in the morning sunshine like a bum. I walked through tall brown weeds to get to her front door. There was no bell, so I knocked. I waited ten seconds or so, then knocked again and called out, "Amy—it's me." I heard sounds from inside; soon the door opened.

"Daddy? What time is it? I thought we said 10:00." Her hair was mussed, her eyes puffy.

"Should I come back? I didn't think half an hour would be a problem?"

I've always been an early riser. I'd been up since 6:00. I had watched the local news, the national news, The Weather Channel (a hurricane was brewing in the Caribbean), and one of the TV preachers. I had stayed in the room as long as I could. I should have gone for a walk around the

49

hotel.

"No, Daddy—come in. It won't take me long to get ready."

I stepped inside. It smelled musty. "Little cool in here," I observed. "When you said across Cemetery Road from Tioga High School, I didn't realize you meant a trailer."

"I got a good deal on it. And it's month-to-month. I can leave any time." She was wearing something flimsy and hugging her arms.

I was standing in the kitchen. The linoleum under my feet was split. The plastic veneer of the counter had peeled up in several places along the edges. One of the sink faucets had no handle. I saw a pair of pliers beside it.

"So what's goin' on Amy? I'm tryin' to get some sleep here." I looked past my daughter, through the den, to where a skinny individual with no shirt stood in the doorway of what I presumed was the bedroom. His skin was the color of school paste. He had a sunken chest, a sparse beard, and was lighting a cigarette. "Damn—when you gunna turn the heat on in this place?" Then he saw me. "Hey, who's this? Is there some kinda problem?"

Amy flushed, then turned toward him. "There's no problem. This is my father."

He took a draw on his cigarette, his cheeks collapsing from the suction. He blew smoke out the side of his mouth. "Good to meet you sir. Amy didn't say nuthin' about her daddy cummin' to visit."

With her back to me Amy barked, "Frank, I need you to leave."

"Leave? Now how'm I gunna do that?"

"Take my car. Could you hurry?"

"All right, all right." He disappeared into the bedroom.

Amy spun around. "I'm sorry Daddy. If you had come when you said—when we agreed—there would have been no Frank." That ugly sneer was beginning to form.

I watched her eyes challenge me for a moment, then I said, "I'll wait for you outside."

23

50

Five minutes later Frank emerged, looking maybe ten percent better than he had five minutes before. At least he had a shirt on. He gave me a wave and a big grin as he dropped behind the wheel of the clunker. The old Plymouth struggled to turn over. It probably hadn't had a tune-up since Amy was in middle school. It started, and Frank raced the engine. He backed up, rolling through a thick cloud of exhaust. That meant bad rings. Oil was getting into the cylinders and burning with the gasoline. The thing needed an overhaul.

I sat in the Cobalt, watching in my rearview mirror as Frank eased out onto Cemetery Road, then roared away. I put him as older than Amy, but not by much—maybe twenty-five. I shook my head. How in God's name did my attractive intelligent daughter get mixed up with this miscreant? What could possibly have been the fascination?

Amy stepped out of the trailer looking fresh, but still scowling. She got into the car without giving me a glance.

"Any place special you'd like to eat?" I asked, slipping the key into the ignition.

"Not really. I'm not that hungry."

"I am. By this time on a regular day, breakfast would be a memory."

"MacArthur Drive has lots of places." I reached out to fiddle with the Garmin, but she added, "Just go back to 165 and head south."

As I began retracing my route to the main highway, keeping my voice friendly, non-threatening, I said, "So tell me something about Frank."

"He's a dishwasher at the Kitchen; I met him there."

"He from around here?"

"Yeah—he lives with his uncle I think it is, up in Ball."

"So not with you?"

"No." Then, as if I'd asked another question, she said, "Daddy, I'm twenty years old. I know that's young, but legally I can leave home, vote, go into the military, get married, and work fifty hours a week if I want. I rent my own place, I have my own car, I don't ask you or Mom for anything. And I have a right to choose who I associate with."

I dropped the friendly. "And Frank is the best you can do?"

51

"You don't know him."

"It doesn't take that long to size people up."

"How would you know?" she flared. "You haven't met anyone new in years. It's just you and Mom and those freaks you work with—and Reverend Rouzerville. What kind of recent experience have you had sizing people up? Frank's someone I can talk to; he's supportive." She looked over at me. I turned south onto US 165, back toward the Red River, and she asked, "Why are you being so critical?"

Our children, all three of them, made this judgment early: Mother is engaged, emotional, impulsive; Daddy is detached, grounded, reasonable. I'm sure the characterizations were more nuanced than this, especially as they got older—but I'm convinced these are the general impressions they developed of their parents. Amy was surprised that her reasonable father would jump to conclusions about her boyfriend when his evidence was so scant. I've tried to be evenhanded along the way—fair-minded. I've listened to Amy's side of every story. Look where it's landed her. Now things have changed for me. Maybe my unflappable voice of reason approach is good for the long haul. But I doubt I have that long.

"All right," I said to my youngest, "you're an adult; maybe you're ready for some adult talk."

"Sure—fine." She looked out the window.

"Good. Then here you go: your place is a dump; your car is a wreck; you don't have an education; you do have a minimum wage job with no future; your boyfriend situation is, to put it mildly, stupid. My question is, with your background and upbringing, how have you come to this point? Why the hell have you made these ridiculous choices? What's your excuse? What are you trying to prove?"

That got her attention. She gave me a brief stunned look, then her mouth transformed into the full-blown sneer. "What am I trying to prove? That your sterile, narrow world is not the only one—that other ways of living are valid."

"And what would you mean by valid? I doubt you even know. Your existence seems to be dominated by that huge chip on your shoulder, which causes you to make one unwise decision after another. Where did it come from? That's what I've wondered about you for a long time. It makes no sense."

We were passing Lake Bulow; I could see the O.K. Allen Bridge up ahead. Amy looked away, out over the glittering surface of the lake. "And that's it Daddy: you're clueless—you've always been. As long as I can remember, your head's been in your spooky little scientific world at Ft. Detrick. You've been a good father I guess—in an aloof sort of way. I mean, you haven't been bad. You've just been sort of nothing—nothing I've needed at least. And Mom, my God, just the opposite: in my business day and night, year after year, controlling and directing—but never listening. So you see Daddy, it *does* make sense. The parenting combo of you and Mom just didn't do it for me. I had to get away or go nuts—so I got away. Is that so crazy?"

Now *I* was stunned. Kay and I had been good parents—*were* good parents. We had complemented each other in our approach to the children. We had been firm but fair disciplinarians. We had maintained high expectations for their schooling. We had kept them in church through high school. The boys seemed fine. Amy was being willful and perverse.

"Your assessment is overblown, inaccurate. And then you make decisions based on your skewed assessment. No wonder you're having problems."

"I'm not having problems. That's your delusion. I didn't ask you to come here."

I looked down from the bridge. Red River was greenish-brown. That probably meant it had been dry, so red clay from the north Louisiana hills had not been washed into the tributaries, then dumped into the main waterway. "No, you didn't ask me to come; and no, as you said, you haven't asked your mother and me for anything. But you are being unfair when it comes to us. We love you. We want the best for you. We think you're on the wrong track here. Should we just sit back and do nothing?"

"Look, Daddy," she said, responding to my softer tone, "I know you're doing what you think is best. You say I'm on the wrong path, but when you get down to it, that's just your opinion. You're not a prophet or a psychic. You have no idea how things will turn out. All you know is that

53

my path is atypical—not what you and Mom had envisioned—and that makes you uncomfortable, worried. So you categorize it as 'wrong,' and feel you need to do something about it. But you don't."

We were approaching MacArthur Drive, a four-lane by-pass with service roads just west of Alexandria. "Amy, what I wish you would do is take stock, count your blessings, consider all the advantages you've been given, and see if this is really what you want to do. You come home, get back in school—your mother and I will be behind you one hundred percent. Honey, don't throw everything away."

She didn't answer, looking out the window again. We passed a Denny's, then a Presbyterian church whose entire front consisted of a single stained-glass window dominated by the color blue. The steeple was a tapering tower of stainless steel, topped by a cross of gold. I've noticed that when it comes to architecture, the Presbyterians and Episcopalians win, with the latter being quaint, while the former are more avant-garde.

She turned back to me. "Daddy, I'm young. I have time." She smiled. "I appreciate your concern—I do. But at this point I need to be here, doing the things I'm doing. It's very important that I be my own person—that I be authentic. At Hood, I almost went under; I came this close to losing myself." She held up a thumb and forefinger a centimeter apart. "But Daddy, you know what? I'm seeing a side of you I didn't realize was there. It felt harsh, but it felt real. You've always been great—I mean, I admired you and all—you're so smart and together—but there was something under wraps, something behind that squared-away front that I wanted, but you never offered it up."

My little girl was perceptive. She had hit on something about her father. I felt my defenses rising. "If parents are too revealing, how does that affect their young children? That was my question. The truth, Amy? I'm quite an emotional person; I'm moody. I saw this in my own father, and it scared me as a kid. I never knew which Cliff Stepping I was going to see when he came home from work on a given day. He could be fun, generous, loving; he could also be a hateful bastard. I know he loved us, but he made Mother cry on a regular basis. That was destructive. That was wrong. As I got older, especially after Daddy died, I felt these same

54

tendencies in myself. Maybe it was learned; maybe it's genetic. Whatever, I vowed to keep all this under control. Why should my children, my wife, suffer, because I let every emotion that blew through my mind be unleashed upon them? I had seen the results of that, and I simply wasn't going to let it happen. If that makes me a bad father, then . . . ."

When I glanced over at Amy, tears were standing in her eyes. "You're not a bad father. But maybe you went too far, closing yourself off. I think I *needed* some emotion. I saw the value in being steady and dependable—that definitely provided security. I wasn't afraid. But as time went on, I felt cold. It's not that I didn't feel loved, or valued—I did. It's more like I wasn't understood. That's such a cliché, I know. And it's very possible that no one could have understood and met my emotional needs at that point. Mom thought she did, because she was so involved in all my activities, and because she's *not* one to hold her emotions in. I know she was well-intentioned, but to me that felt like intrusion and bluster. I don't know Daddy—maybe I'm just a hard case. I do know that right now it's important for me to find my own way. Don't give up on me."

Now *my* eyes were blurring. Amy was assuming a time frame for me that likely was in error. She was my baby. Of course I would never give up on her—not as long as I had breath. "Sweetie," I said, "that is not going to happen."

Amy decided she was hungry after all. I turned the Cobalt around and we went back to Denny's. We ordered a couple of Original Grand Slams. We kept the talk light as we enjoyed our breakfast. I did probe a bit more about Frank, my biggest fear being that her entanglement with him might result in complications she was ill-equipped to handle. She consoled me on that score, reiterating her adult status.

I flew back a day early. Delta had regular flights from Alexandria to Atlanta, and on to BWI. They had seats available, so this presented no problem for the airline. Avis was fine with the early return of the car. The desk clerk at the Bentley offered some hassle about my canceling the third night. I asked to see his supervisor, hoping my assumption about them hurting for business was correct. When the suave middle-aged man strode up and joined his subordinate behind the counter, I said to them, "My

55

daughter lives in the area. I visit her often. I like the Bentley, but I have many other choices." The supervisor apologized for the misinterpretation of the hotel's cancellation policy, then turned on the clerk and commanded him to credit my MasterCard.

I felt good about Amy—about what we had shared. If she stayed here, I prayed I *would* be able to visit her often. As we lifted off from AEX, it seemed a metaphor. I was light, free, rising. I knew I must come back to earth. But for now, I was defying gravity.

24

On Monday night, home again, relaxing in front of the TV, I filled Kay in on Amy. She was glad to hear our daughter was okay, but when I described her living conditions, she said, "You didn't give her any money, did you? We don't need to be subsidizing her situation down there. It was her choice. She needs to deal with it."

"I did buy her breakfast," I said. "And Saturday night I ate at her restaurant and left her a twenty-dollar tip." Kay raised her eyebrows. "But, in return I got all her contact information: cell number, e-mail address, snailmail address, work info. She promised to keep in touch."

"She can afford cell and internet service? And a computer?"

"She has the laptop we got her for college. And listen, she told me she makes upwards of a hundred dollars a shift; and she works six days a week—sometimes doubles. I think she does pretty well. I know they like her there. She has a regular clientele—customers who ask for her specifically. Plus, she gets to eat free."

We talked on a while about Amy—about her personality, her character, her prospects. I pulled back from telling Kay what Amy thought of us as parents. I probably needed to do that. I would—soon—but not tonight. After all these years, I knew my wife. If any of her main thrusts, priorities, strategies, or preferences is challenged, she becomes angry, then hurt, then self-abasing. We didn't need such drama this near bedtime.

I was tired. Half-way through *CSI: Miami*, with Lieutenant Horatio Caine delivering yet another solemn, lame one-liner before stalking off the

56

screen, I bade Kay good night.

25

Joy Smalls is not like Kay. Well, I consider them both good-hearted, which is major—but beyond that, they're pretty different. I'm drawn to Joy. I have been since she came to MMDA, and that's been quite a few years—since before Essex. We're friends. I think she would agree with that assessment. So many things are not worth the risk. The cost/benefit ratio is too high. But with time growing short, I began wondering if maybe I should tell her the truth. Three weeks after my return from Louisiana, after weighing the pros and cons until I was losing sleep, I finally worked up the courage to do it. Even in the face of death, old proclivities die hard.

On Friday, November 16, I went for my third check-up of the week. The Wednesday blood work had been unable to detect RPA-72 in my system. Either my liver had taken care of the protectant, or my heart was riddled with it. The odds favored the latter.

Joy welcomed me with her resplendent smile. We went through our regular routine: nothing out of the ordinary. She was about to escort me out when I said, "Listen, Joy—do you have a minute?"

She glanced at her watch. "Shortly Mellwood and I meet with the doctors from JVAPO and MISSA. Don't you go to Mellwood when you leave here?"

JVAPO is the Army's Joint Vaccine Acquisition Program Office; MISSA is their Medical Information Systems and Services Agency.

"Right, but he rescheduled me for later in the day. He didn't say why; I guess it was your meeting."

"Well good. Then we have a while."

I sat again in the seat with the armrest, the one used for drawing blood. She rolled her swivel chair up close and waited for me to speak. Watching those green eyes, I thought of Kay, our children, my straight arrow life— and suddenly this didn't seem the best of ideas. But that was emotion squawking. I'd thought this through *ad nauseam*. It was now or never.

"I've told you how much I admire you—as a doctor, and I hope I've

57

made it clear, as a person as well."

She nodded. She blinked and her mouth gave a small twitch.

"We're friends; I've made an effort over a long period of time to leave it right there—but I've been unsuccessful."

Her cheeks heated up.

"I guess these frequent visits, plus my narrowing window of opportunity, have brought all this to the fore." I took her hand, and she closed her eyes. "Joy, my feelings for you go beyond admiration or friendship. They're strong, and as I said, persistent."

She examined my face. Her hand was limp. She looked stricken. "Paul," she said, "you're married."

"Oh, sure—of course. Oh, no, Joy—I'm not suggesting anything. It just seemed to me, after a lot of soul-searching, that before I—move on—I should be honest with you about this—just sort of get it off my chest so to speak. I didn't mean to upset you."

"I'm not upset," she said, applying pressure to my hand with her fingertips, then withdrawing. "It's that I don't know how to respond."

"I want to know how you feel—if this is in any way reciprocal. From time to time I've thought it was—that I'd picked up things. Perhaps that was nothing more than projection."

She was shaking her head. "Paul, I don't—I mean I do—I *have* had— I do have—feelings for you. I know I shouldn't. You've been happily married for a long time. That's a marvelous achievement that I deeply respect." Her hands were in her lap now. She was looking down at them.

"Of course—I know you do. And I love Kay. I have no intention of jeopardizing that." Joy Smalls saw me as more than a colleague, more than a friend. I was embarrassed at how much that buoyed me. Embarrassed, but emboldened, so I asked, "Do you not have any men in your life? Intelligent, high-achieving, professional woman—compassionate—a whole grab-bag of pluses: I'd think you'd be beating them off with a stick."

"Not really—I'm not exactly the social type."

"Me either. Family and work, church to some extent—that meets my social needs: more than meets, to tell you the truth. I just don't require a lot in that regard. Everyone's different of course. Kay, for instance, is happiest in a group. Me? One-on-one, just like this: no distractions, no intrusions. You can really concentrate on the other person. I think you catch details that are lost in these large gatherings. So often they're loud." I made a face. "I don't like that. I never have. I find the one-on-one more valuable, more gratifying." I was close to gushing, and that was not Paul Stepping. I stopped talking.

She was watching me. Her eyes were bright. She had regained her equanimity. "Men have been problematic for me," she said, drawing the words out as if this were a conclusion she wanted to make sure she phrased properly. "The ones I found interesting turned out to be *not* so interesting."

"What do you mean?"

"They tended to be self-centered—that was my main objection: a stunted capacity to show sustained attention to anyone else. If it wasn't pretty much about them, they lost focus."

"What was the attraction in the first place?"

"Good looks, charm—and attention. They paid attention at the beginning."

"Then it dropped off?"

"Yes—soon after that first kiss. My idea would be sure, let's go out again. Let's talk, do things together, learn about each other. I liked the kiss. It was exciting. Maybe there'll be more. We'll let that develop naturally. That was my idea. But the guys, that was *not* their idea. They wanted to short circuit straight to more physical. I would resist that progression, and the budding relationship would die."

"Did this happen often? Surely not all—or even most—men are like this." Joy was speaking without much affect, providing little clue as to how she felt about these experiences.

"A couple of times in high school, four or five times in college—and really, all about the same. I began to wonder if something was wrong with *me*, if I was giving off signals I didn't intend. To tell you the truth, I was about to give up on the man-woman-romance thing." She paused, shifting her gaze to my right. I was debating what to say when she continued. "But then there was med school—and Bennett: Bennett Weinstein—like Einstein, but with a W. Bennett was different."

59

I nodded and smiled. "So things went well—renewed your faith." Before she could reply I added, "Listen, there's nothing wrong with you—only a moron would think that."

Joy gave me a soft look. I realized my pronouncement had sounded earnest, protective. "Thank you Paul—that's sweet of you to say. And Bennett was no moron. He's now a top neurosurgeon at Johns Hopkins Hospital."

"You went to Johns Hopkins." I had seen the Doctor of Medicine diploma many times on the wall behind her office desk.

"Yes, both for my undergraduate work, and for medical school. Bennett stayed in Baltimore after we graduated, attached himself to the university hospital, and has become quite a star."

"So what happened?" I asked.

She checked her watch again. "It'll have to be the short version."

"That's fine."

She took a breath. "Like I said, Bennett was different. He wasn't shallow. We talked philosophy, religion, politics. There were minor intimacies, but he remained attentive, asking about my life, my upbringing, my opinions—telling me about himself. We got more physical, but it was gradual—what I considered reasonable, normal. I liked the way things were going with Bennett. I began to think we might have a future together." She looked down at her hands again, and when she raised her eyes, tears were standing in them.

When I saw that, I swallowed and said, "Joy, listen—you don't need to go on with this. You know, maybe another time."

She pulled a tissue from the pocket of her lab coat and blotted her eyes. "No, it's good I'm telling you. I thought I'd gotten past this, but obviously not. So it's okay—it'll be therapeutic." She took another breath and attempted a smile. "This went on for over a year. We were very involved, very serious; I thought he would soon propose marriage, and I was going to accept." Her mouth trembled. She shook her head, as if still unable to believe what she was about to tell me. "But he had another woman. In fact, he had two other women—both medical students like me. A friend of mine tipped me off. When I confronted Bennett, he didn't even

60

bother to deny it. I remember exactly what he said: 'Look, Joy, I never promised you anything—so no problem, right? It's been fun. You have a good day.' He patted me on the shoulder, then walked away. And that was it. I was crushed. I never really tried again—never ventured out. Oh, I've had men show some interest along the way, but . . . . It was the blasé factor—the nonchalant, casual way it ended: that's what broke my heart. How trivial *was* I, that I could be tossed aside with that degree of carelessness? If he had been remorseful, or even embarrassed, that would have softened the blow. If he had offered some rationale, some justification for his behavior, I would have listened. But it's-been-fun-have-a-good-day: the lack of importance implied in that—the lack of value—well, I just figured—I concluded that I must be . . . ." She closed her eyes and tears squeezed out.

I shouldn't have done this. Stirring the pot is almost always a bad idea. Predictability is skin deep—a surface phenomenon. Dig below that, and the raw nerves of drama are exposed. Touch them, and you're playing with fire.

At a loss, I began to mumble, "Joy, I'm so sorry; I know that you—"

Then she was sobbing, and kissing me, and declaring, "Oh Paul, I *do* love you! I don't want you to die!"

26

That afternoon, when I went to see Mellwood, he said my blood pressure was up. His sympathetic comment was, "Things are getting close. Guess you're starting to feel the heat."

A month to go. True, that was weighing on my mind. But the issue today was Joy Smalls. My time with her that morning had been unsettling. It had also been euphoric, like a tonic. This BP elevation was likely due to the adrenalin released during that encounter.

The next morning Kay and I decided to walk the Catoctin Trail. It was half a mile from our back door, across our large yard, past the boundary of Gambrill State Park (our property line), down a path we had made through the woods, to the trail proper. There we would turn left (south) and hike

61

the three miles to the picnic area at the lower end of Gambrill. We would eat lunch, then retrace our steps. This would be a seven-mile trek—double our normal distance. With lunch, we'd be gone from the house well over two hours. It would be a good workout. We would have plenty of time to talk. That's what I wanted.

Kay was cheerful as she got together the tuna fish sandwiches, celery sticks, peanut butter, and Triscuits. Exercise was a priority for her. She was looking forward to this.

It was chilly and overcast, though neither rain nor snow had been forecast. Understanding that predicting the weather is anything but a precise science, I slipped a couple of hooded ponchos into our knapsack, along with the food, bottled water, a thermos of coffee, and a few first aid supplies.

We never locked our doors, not that there was much of value to interest thieves. We lived a good distance off Hamburg Road; our nearest neighbor was a quarter mile away. It seemed our situation didn't warrant much in the way of security measures.

We left around 10:30. The wind had picked up. We wore jeans, ski-type jackets, Thinsulate gloves, and hiking boots. We hurried across the back yard toward the woods, hoping the trees would serve as a windbreak.

To some extent they did, but here in the second half of November, most of the leaves had fallen. The oaks and beeches hung onto maybe half their brittle brown foliage. But the maples, poplars, hickories, and walnuts, were bare. A hundred yards into the hardwood forest, the wind, somewhat gentled, still found us. By the time we turned onto the main trail, we needed to turn up the collars of our jackets.

"That thing getting too heavy for you?" Kay was referring to the knapsack.

"No way. The extra weight is good for these less than six-pack abs." I patted my stomach.

Kay laughed. "Hey, those abs look pretty good to me. Feel pretty good too." She gave me a look. Now she was referring to last night. Here in our fifties we still enjoy the bedroom. After three children and almost thirty years, I'm not claiming things are exactly as they once were. But we've made our adjustments, and we have fun. Friday nights are a regular for us, and last night I would definitely put in the ABOVE AVERAGE category.

"Well thanks. I hope you're not just trying to make an almost-retired guy feel good."

"Hey, I wouldn't do that." She laughed again. "And speaking of feeling good, thank *you*. It was marvelous, but a lot of effort on your part."

I looked over at her, glad she had been pleased. "Guess what? I didn't mind. You're worth it."

I meant that. I loved Kay. She deserved satisfactory sex and a whole lot more. Before we met I had read a few books, learning that often women do not achieve climax during intercourse. Suggestions were made for how this situation might be remedied. When Kay and I began our sexual involvement, I vowed that so far as it was within my power, she would have an orgasm every time. I've kept that promise, and Kay has been appreciative. It's been good for our relationship.

"Aw, now isn't that a sweet thing to say? You're worth it too. Did you enjoy?"

"Always."

"You were quite enthusiastic. That brought me right along."

At home I seldom pass Kay without touching her—often in places I never would in public. She remains very attractive to me. But my cheeks warmed as I acknowledged that part of my excitement last night had been due to the meeting with Joy Smalls earlier in the day. Was that something I needed to share—with a month to live? Maybe later. For now I just said, "Good deal."

We walked on, chatting about this and that, crunching on the leaf litter blanketing our walkway. It had been dry. Every so often a puff of wind would stir the brown crisps.

The squirrels were busy. We saw several close up, their cheeks bulging with nuts. I was reminded of my talk with Tim Rouzerville and the furry visitor we'd had. We surprised one little fellow. He was on the ground, ten feet or so off the beaten path. He was digging, preparing to bury provisions against the long cold winter. Leaf mold was flying. It was

63

as if his front paws were mechanized. When he saw us, he froze. His bright eyes watched, unblinking. As we approached, his tail began to flick. Finally he gathered himself and sprang through several yards of gray air to the nearest tree trunk. He stuck like Velcro, then scurried to the far side, hidden from view.

"I wonder if I need more life insurance?" I said this as we neared the picnic area.

"You have some with the government, don't you?"

"I do, but sometimes I think it's not enough—you know, if something happened to me, I wouldn't want you to struggle."

Kay didn't deal with any of the financial stuff. It didn't interest her. Wanting to keep her apprised, from time to time I ticked off the litany of our assets and liabilities, how things would change once we retired, what might happen if we became infirm: it just didn't stick. She was plenty bright about these issues. She asked good questions. But she didn't retain much from one of our sessions to the next.

"What if something happened to me?" she said. "I wouldn't want *you* to struggle. Maybe I need more insurance too." Kay was a bit of a feminist; she didn't appreciate condescension from males.

I said, "Well yeah—sure—it might be a good idea for both of us to lock in some good term rates. We're relatively young, in good health—we could probably get a couple hundred thousand each for twenty years, no problem. That would take us through the bulk of our retirement worry-free, so far as actual death is concerned. After that—I mean, life insurance for people in their seventies is pretty expensive—but hopefully by then our other investments will have grown to the point where it wouldn't be as necessary."

She said, "Can we afford it?" I had droned on a little, but she had been listening.

"I think so. I need to check around a little, get some specific numbers. But what happens, let's say we get it, pay the premiums for a year or two, then decide, yes, this *is* too expensive? Hey, we just cancel. We make no more payments, the company drops us, end of deal. It's not like we're signing a twenty-year contract or anything."

"Then do it," she said.

There was more than a little moral ambiguity here. I would have to hide my situation from the underwriter. They would do a health check of course, but just like my regular tests at work, it would reveal nothing. I would be required to disclose my employer, and while that could affect the cost (my occupation might be considered high-risk), no questions to Essex or anyone else at MMDA would be allowed. Bottom line, I would be lying to the insurance company. On the other hand, I would be providing for my wife, who would be losing her husband and his potential income (maybe I would work after retirement) twenty or thirty years prematurely. Wasn't that the responsible thing to do? These companies were huge. They did the math. They knew some small percentage of their clients would kick off soon after purchasing a big chunk of protection. That was baked into the actuarial cake. But lying was lying. Or was it?

I said to Kay, "I'll look into it."

We saw the picnic pavilions in the distance, just as the first drops of rain began to fall. We picked up the pace, hoping to make it to one of the enclosures without having to stop and unpack the ponchos. We achieved that short-term goal, but enclosure is not the best word. These structures had a roof, plus two walls at right angles. Otherwise they were open. There were three tables at this one. They were heavy one-piece affairs, fashioned entirely of metal, but not bolted down. We muscled one of them into the corner, affording us some sanctuary from the chill blowing rain.

Kay spread out our lunch. "Hey, pour me some of that coffee," she said, nodding at the thermos. "Oh, damn! I forgot the peanut butter!"

"I thought I saw it right there on the counter," I said.

"Yeah, but I must have gotten distracted by something."

"You talk a lot about being distracted. Celery's pretty worthless without peanut butter."

We were sitting on the same side of the table with our backs to the corner. We sat side-by-side in booths when we went out to eat. We enjoyed the closeness. In response to my comment, Kay slid a few inches away. "And what kind of big deal is that?" she said.

"It's not necessarily a big deal; it's just if you know you tend to be

65

distracted more easily than the average person, why don't you do something about it—develop some strategy for dealing with it?"

"I think it's chemical."

"Then go see a doctor; get medication. I mean, why let this go on, messing us up time and again? Remember the eggs?"

"So no peanut butter for celery is messing us up."

"Yes it is. I was looking forward to it. I like celery *with* peanut butter. But the point is, it's symbolic."

"And what does that mean?"

I had poured the coffee. We both took it black. I bit into my tuna sandwich and sipped some brew. "It's symbolic of the way you seem to operate a fair portion of the time. I'm just saying it bothers me, and it inconveniences us—both of us. It's a problem. Let's deal with it."

The animation had abandoned Kay's face. She was looking straight ahead, out into the light rain. "Oh, I've got problems—" she said in a flat voice, "—lots of them. You made a big mistake when you picked me. Sorry. Sorry I can't be perfect like you."

We had played this scene, or something similar, many times before. Yet it never ceased to amaze me how one minute everything could be great (our recounting of last night's sex, for instance), and the next we could be simmering in an emotional crock pot, heading toward a messy boil-over.

But this was typical Kay. It was as if there was this tape in her head. And if the right code was punched, the right words said, a switch was flipped, the tape began playing, and all this spilled out. Of course I was the one who generally punched the code. I felt like doing it quite often, but usually refrained, having learned that the results were counterproductive. But my time was growing short. I had been forthright with Amy, and it had worked out pretty well. I wanted to clear the air with Kay. As I said, I had broken the crust on this and other issues with her before. I generally pulled up short because her response was so dramatic. But maybe I'd never pushed things far enough. Maybe I'd backed off too soon, for the sake of peace and a return to normalcy. I certainly didn't want to hurt her, but I did want to be honest before saying good-bye. I had always worried that rocking the boat would jeopardize the future of our relationship. Now that

66

future had been squeezed down to a month.

So I said, "I'm not perfect, Kay, and I don't pretend to be. Saying that is some kind of self-pitying diversion. Why don't we stick to the issue of your distractibility, and what can be done about it?"

"Now I'm self-pitying," she said, flicking a look my way. "You see—another defect."

"Kay, please—stop being defensive. It's just something to solve."

"Why don't you stop being critical?" Now she looked at me with hurt eyes. "Don't you love me at all?"

Here I usually called a halt. The specter of Kay melting down was too intimidating. I would apologize, affirm my love, extol her virtues, and we would make up.

This time though, I would not back down. "I love you with all my heart, but that's not the question. You've got a problem, and you're not facing it—*that's* the question. You're in denial. You make excuses. And I enable you. I take responsibility for that. But I want us to *deal* with this—find a solution. Why is that so threatening to you?"

"It's not threatening to me. The problem is, *you're* threatened."

"By what?"

"Because sometimes I forget things. Because I'm not predictable like all your science stuff. My spontaneity terrifies you. I won't go into a test tube to be manipulated and exploited. You can't control me, so you're scared stiff." She tore into her sandwich, then stared back out into the rain.

"Unbelievable," I said, chuckling and shaking my head. "You forget the peanut butter, and that's considered spontaneous? You forget the peanut butter, and I'm terrified? Get real, Kay. You're diverting again—denying."

"So this is funny?" she said, turning on me with wide eyes. "I'm not denying. I'm just pointing out one of *your* on-going deficiencies, which is that you're a control freak. That's why your days are spent in a laboratory with beakers and chemicals, instead of with people. Why don't we talk about dealing with that? Don't you think that's a little more important than whether or not I forget a damn jar of peanut butter?" She paused. I was getting angry. She added, "Or do you find that too threatening to discuss?"

67

I do value control. Control brings order to individual lives, families, communities, society in general. And I definitely value order—and predictability. So does Kay and every other person on the face of this planet. Spontaneity! That's nothing more than a smokescreen for lack of planning and inattention. Her life would be a shambles without me. Maybe I should tell her that.

"What kind of dream world do you live in? I'm disciplined, tend to details, keep tabs on things. And this is bad? This means I'm a control freak? A *freak*? Most people—normal people—think this is good: they call it competence, Kay."

I was trying to keep a lid on my escalating outrage. I've only blown that lid a few times in my life, and it was scary. I never got violent, but the dripping sarcasm, the corrosive full-blown vitriol that came out of my mouth, left me wondering if I truly have respect for other human beings, or if that's just something I fool myself into believing. Things were percolating. I didn't want to lose it.

Kay was stung. "I *am* normal!" she almost shouted. "Most people are like me—not like you—some cold, anal, Nazi!" Tears were standing in her eyes. Her face had gone white.

Cold, anal, Nazi. Well by God, that was it. "Let me tell you something Kay! In a few short weeks you won't have me to worry about—nobody to bring up your ADHD or whatever the hell it is; nobody to clean up after you when you leave clothes and dishes and God knows what else all over the damn house—you'll have it like a pig sty; nobody to deal with the trail of blunders left by your impatience and disorganization and laziness; and best of all, you'll be able to live happily in your delusion, with no one to disturb that thin scab on your pitifully fragile self-esteem!" My voice was low. I was snarling.

"You're threatening to leave me!" she yelled. "You want a divorce? Fine—you got it!"

We had used the D-word a few times before during combat. That wasn't my reference here, but it was natural that she thought so.

"I want you to grow up, Kay! You're fifty-one years old, for God's sake: act like it!"

She slapped me. It sounded like a rifle shot.

In reflex, I struck back. I almost knocked her off the bench. I stared at my open hand and moaned, "Oh no!"

Kay jerked herself upright. The side of her face was red. "You bastard!" she screamed. "I hate you!"

"Kay, I'm sorry. I—"

But she was gone. She bolted from the table, tripping and sprawling on the cement floor of the shelter. She scrambled to her feet, then plunged out into the weather. The rain was changing to snow.

I was paralyzed. I couldn't call after her. I couldn't move. Within seconds she was lost in a swirl of white.

I sat there for several minutes, shut down, feeling more dead than alive. At length I gathered everything up, slipped on one of the hooded ponchos, and headed for home.

When I walked in an hour later, numb with cold and remorse, Kay was sitting at the kitchen table with our younger son. Joel looked at me with wary eyes. He said, "You hit Mom. What's going on, Dad?"

27

Joel is our middle child. He's twenty-five, unmarried, lives in DC (a little apartment near Capitol Hill), and works as an aide for a newly-elected Maryland congresswoman. There had been rumors he was involved with her. But with Representative Versa Brooks being first-term, and therefore low on the name-recognition totem pole, these rumors, even if true, had been stillborn so far as the thrill-seeking press was concerned. They had bigger fish to fry, thank God.

I shrugged out of the knapsack, then slipped off my gloves and jacket. I had removed the poncho on our screened-in back porch, draping it over one of the plastic chairs to dry. "Did she tell you the whole story?" I said to Joel.

"She said you guys had a fight while walking The Trail, and you ended up hitting her."

I placed my items on the counter and sat down at the table. I

69

responded to Joel while staring at Kay. "That is true. But like many truths, it's out of context, incomplete, and therefore as misleading as a lie." Kay did not take that bait. She refused to look at me.

"Well what happened? Set the record straight."

Of course I regretted striking my wife. That had never happened in our long marriage. Walking back through the snow I had tried to formulate just how I would apologize. Now, with her sitting there like a statue, and with Joel having shown up unannounced with an accusatory tone in his voice, my frame of mind changed. "The main fact your mother apparently omitted, is that she slapped me first." I started to offer more, but decided to let that statement hang unadorned for the moment.

Joel turned to Kay. "Mom?"

She pressed her lips together. She folded her arms across her chest.

"Mom, is that true?"

Kay got up. She walked out of the kitchen, down the hall, and into our bedroom. I heard the door lock.

"It's true, Joel. That doesn't excuse me of course—but it's true."

My son's face was a portrait of confusion.

"One time when you and Bill were little—this was before Amy was born—your mother and I had a disagreement. You probably don't recall it. I doubt Bill does. But Kay didn't talk to me for three days. I think something like that is brewing." I gave a little laugh at that memory.

"Dad, this is serious." Joel seemed to think I was down-playing the present situation. "Did you and Mom come to blows back then?"

"Oh, no. Listen, Joel—this is an aberration. Don't worry."

He continued to frown. "When Mother wouldn't talk—what was the problem?"

"You know, I can hardly remember: something to do with correcting you two boys I believe."

"The silent treatment is pretty extreme."

"Kay can *be* pretty extreme."

"So you think her reaction was unjustified—that your disagreement didn't warrant that kind of response."

"It didn't. All we had to do was lay out our concerns in an emotion-

70

free manner, sketch out some possible solutions, then agree on one of them. But she chose to go nuclear."

"How did that get resolved?" Joel asked.

"I blinked. I caved. I basically did what she wanted. Then everything was fine."

"Why did you do it?"

"For the sake of peace in the family. You and Bill didn't need to feel those vibes. It was cost-benefit. I didn't like the idea of Kay injecting power into our relationship. A marriage based on power is certainly not a healthy one. And it wasn't good for Kay herself to get away with it. But that kind of thing happened infrequently, and worrying about the effect it would have on you and your brother if things dragged out, I gave in. When she gets her feelings hurt, Kay becomes stubborn. I had no doubt she would have gone on for weeks. So, cost-benefit."

Joel propped his elbows on the table. He laced his fingers. We were sitting across from each other. "What about this time?" he said.

"I don't think so."

"No giving in?"

"No. I'll apologize for hitting—that was indefensible. I hope she'll do the same. But the issue in dispute—namely Kay's careless approach to things, and the trouble that makes for others—no, I'm not backing down on that. If she wants to clam up until hell freezes over, and refuse to face this problem out of pride, or out of spite against me for daring to bring it up, or whatever—then fine. I'm tired of pussyfooting. I'm tired of pretending this doesn't bother me. It does. And I'm tired of fixing her mistakes— checking behind her to make sure we don't break our necks tripping on something she dropped on the floor, but never got around to picking up; that the well doesn't run dry because she was watering the roses and forgot to turn the sprinkler off; that the house doesn't burn down because she put some potatoes on to boil—on high—then just walked away. I'm sick of this. I'm done."

Joel ran a thumb over his lips. "I have to tell you Dad, this doesn't sound like you. Mom's sort of scattered. That's no secret. I thought you accepted that about her. And she does a lot of very good things. You

71

acknowledge that, don't you?"

"I acknowledge it—but so what? You do a good thing, does that mean you can then do a bad thing? Something that could have easily been avoided with the least bit of mindfulness? Is it some kind of balancing the books deal?"

"Mom's not bad," he said with an edge in his voice.

"So you're defending her."

"She's not here to defend herself."

"Well that's her choice, now isn't it?" I didn't like the way this was going. I didn't like the feel of it. Joel was trying to make *me* the bad guy—in my own house. That was not going to fly. So I changed direction. "How are things going with your job? You've made a career out of trying to impress people. Now you've got your chance."

His brow knitted. "What do you mean by that?"

"I was just thinking back to when you were in high school, then college—you seemed to always be talking about how great you were, and about how great *other people* thought you were; I'm just saying Congresswoman Brooks must be impressed, and that as one of her aides, you must have ample opportunity to impress numerous others—some of them quite important."

Truth be told, Amy was an accident. There are five years between Joel and her, but only two between the boys. So while Joel is the middle child, his birth order was not as significant as if Amy had been male, and had been born sooner. Still, Joel exhibited certain middle child behaviors; I found them irritating, but had, when he was younger, made conscious efforts to suppress that irritation. Now he was grown.

"I see a lot of people in my job," he replied. "Some of them *are* important. Are you suggesting I should *not* try to impress them?"

"I'm suggesting you not be so arrogant and self-aggrandizing—that you not try so hard—that you lighten up on the BS."

He watched me from across the table, his face tense. I figured he was sizing me up, wondering whether or not to take on his father. He said, "You mean be more like you."

"You could do worse—but no, I'm not saying be more like me. Just

72

be more authentic; stop trying to put people on."

Joel lowered his eyes for a moment, then raised them and gave a little laugh. "Believe it or not Dad, I learned this from you."

"Now that's an absurd statement."

"Not really. You're sort of quiet, retiring, don't say much—and you equate that with not putting people on. In fact, it's an *egregious* case of putting people on; that's the irony of it."

"I can't wait to hear *this* twisted logic."

"It's not twisted at all. You, as do we all, have feelings, emotions, opinions. Expressing those would be authentic, as you put it. But you don't do that—or seldom do that. So in effect, you're putting people on. You get respect—or think you do—by playing it cool, by operating above the fray. You mind your own business, don't get involved. I'm sure that's comfortable for you, but it's *not* authentic. It's sophisticated BS. It forces others to form opinions about you based on erroneous data, or more precisely, on an *absence* of data. Your calculation is that most of those opinions will be good. People know you're a PhD chemist, a solid family man, a church guy, and you seem nice. And that's all fine—it's not false. But you let it go at that. And it's worked. I've really never heard anyone say a bad word about you. So growing up, I watched you and I said, 'Cool—this BS is powerful stuff!' Trouble was, your brand of BS didn't jibe with my personality. So I tweaked things a bit, and began putting people on in a more direct and pro-active way. I tried to mold their opinions of me, rather than just hope they'd be good. So Dad, I'm just a chip off the old block. We're the same, though a surface evaluation wouldn't suggest that."

Joel had chosen Georgetown. Those Jesuits had done a good job, as they damn well should have, given the cost. He was smart—arguably the smartest of our three, if you limit your definition to raw analytical ability. Of course there's more to intellect than that: judgment and ethics, for starters (think Richard Nixon and Bill Clinton). But Joel was perceptive. He had actually nailed me pretty well, and it made me mad.

But I tamped that down. "So you're saying neither of us is authentic. We just hide things in different ways."

73

"Exactly—and I don't necessarily have a problem with that. I mean, does everybody I meet have some kind of God-given right to know my innermost thoughts? I don't think so. But I do have a problem if you say that I BS people, and you don't."

"You would see that as being inconsistent—hypocritical."

"Yes, I would."

"Listen, something I've wanted to know: Is the Catholic thing part of your snow job, or is it real?"

Joel smiled at that. "I'd say fifty-fifty."

"Did the priests at Georgetown brainwash you?"

"Come on Dad. If eighteen years of Reverend Rouzerville and First Baptist of Frederick didn't brainwash me, I don't think four years at Georgetown would. The Jesuits were impressive, but they weren't into indoctrination. It was an academic experience."

"But it *is* a Catholic school."

"Oh, definitely. And I'm not saying it didn't have an influence. Just realizing that my professors—highly educated, intelligent, thoughtful, scholarly people—were also by and large doctrinaire Catholics: that scored some points with me."

"And then you went to work for Congresswoman Brooks, who is Catholic. How did that figure in?"

Joel ran fingers through his thick hair, which was very much like his mother's in texture and color. "It was a consideration, as was the fact that Versa's district is a good sixty percent Catholic."

"So you converted for political reasons."

"You know what they say: You have to go along to get along. And there's nothing wrong with getting along. You seem to think it's pandering. You could as easily have characterized it as cooperating, or working together, or compromising—all for the greater good."

"But these are your religious beliefs."

"I said fifty-fifty. I'm fine with quite a bit of Catholic theology—enough to justify my conversion. I doubt you're whole-hog Baptist."

He watched me with his blue, long-lashed eyes. Joel was taller than me, with broad shoulders and a trim waistline. He had wrestled in high school. He was a good-looking boy who had never lacked for female attention.

I asked, "Were you hired on *condition* of your conversion? As I recall, both these events happened around the same time."

"I doubt it. When I interviewed for the job, the subject came up. I told Versa I had graduated from Georgetown, political science major, history minor, and that I was thinking of making the switch. She seemed happy with that news. I was hired. Soon after, I converted."

"And you were then seen with her at Mass."

Joel laughed. "That's old news Dad; *no* news, really."

"She single?"

"Divorced. Listen, Dad—"

"Does your romantic involvement interfere with your work relationship?"

"Who says there's a romantic involvement? That's gossip. I thought as a science guy you were all about hard evidence."

"Just trying to be more open," I said with raised eyebrows. "Just trying to cut some of that BS—be more transparent. Let me re-phrase: *Are* you sleeping with the representative?"

Joel stared for a moment, his face devoid of cheer. Then he said, "Frankly Dad, that's none of your damn business. I'm a grown man with a responsible job. Who I see or don't see, what my religious stance is, and why it is, are no concerns of yours. I'm under no obligation to share information on these topics with you. We *were* discussing the fact that a couple of hours ago you hit my mother. Somehow you've turned this into a referendum on me. Very slick, but I've had enough of that. I'm doing fine. You're the one who's having issues. My only question now is whether or not to call the Frederick County Sheriff's Office."

"Unbelievable," I breathed. "That would be a big mistake."

"What? To protect Mom?"

"Kay is in no danger. Don't be ridiculous."

Joel pushed his chair back from the table and stood. He shook his head. "For all I know Dad, that's just a big piece of BS on your part. I'm going to check on her."

75

I glared at him and said, "Yeah—you do that."

28

Joel did not call the sheriff. Kay dissuaded him from that, thank God. I apologized for striking her. She apologized for striking me. Then she went silent. She remained so until we reached her parents' house on Thanksgiving Day. Then for another week she barely spoke. It was miserable, but (initially at least) I didn't budge. Time was short. If I was going to be authentic—if that was my path—then forget the excuses.

And that *was* the path I had chosen. In our talk, Tim Rouzerville had sketched out three alternatives: I could do nothing as I approached my likely death—business as usual; I could do everything—grab for the gusto; or I could find some middle ground. Unclear at first, over the last month I've realized that I am going with the middle ground, and that for me, this means being authentic, or genuine, or open with people. Like Clemmie Finks. Just be honest, straightforward—what you see is what you get. It's definitely new territory though. My inclination, as Joel pointed out, is to lie low. But, he noted, there's an element of falsity in that. Others can be led astray by the detached, unruffled façade. He also raised the issue of whether everyone has *a right* to know what a given person thinks about things. Good point. In addition, I've long questioned if it's *prudent* to be so candid with people. Won't there be unintended consequences, some of them perhaps dire? Until the accident, I had been afraid to test that hypothesis. Now I am conducting experiments. Thus far the results are inconclusive.

Kay and I did not go to church the day after Joel's visit. Tim had missed us, and he called that afternoon. I said we were a little under the weather, having been out in the snow the day before. That was not exactly above board. Already I was violating my own protocol. I guess the Titanic doesn't turn on a dime.

Prior to the Thanksgiving break it was three days of work. Kay drove away these mornings without a word. I knew she was being her friendly, vivacious self with her colleagues, her students, strangers she might

76

encounter—with everyone but me. After she left on Wednesday, I sat down in her La-Z-Boy and cried. That had not happened since Amy's senior year in high school, when at one point we thought we had lost her to drugs. I felt better afterwards: less tense, less troubled, but more fragile—like I might break down again at some small provocation.

My Monday appointment with Joy had been awkward, stiff. Neither of us knew how to follow up on Friday's dramatic episode, so we kept things extra-professional. It was almost like I was a brand new patient.

On Tuesday I sat down with Emmerton. He had invited me over to his lab for a briefing on his search for an antidote. He told me he had succeeded in isolating the RPA-72/cardiac protein complex from the tiny mouse hearts. His problem was sample size. Per my request, he had dropped the idea of determining the distribution of the protectant, and had instead utilized the hearts he would have employed for that, to beef up his quantity of the complex. It still was not enough. Boyd Markham had more mice in the pipeline, but it would be after Thanksgiving before they could be processed. Emmerton said he needed at least half a gram—and three-quarters would be better—for the tests he had in mind. He had patted my arm with a pudgy hand and said, "We're pulling out all the stops on this, Paul." But his normally happy face had been solemn. We both knew the time crunch was our most formidable foe.

Now it was Wednesday—time to see Joy again. I was nervous, and as I said, feeling fragile. The blow-up with Kay, the confrontation with Joel, the now stilted relationship with Joy—these were the kinds of fallout I had feared from being too open.

She welcomed me with an attempt at a smile. She drew blood, then I moved to the examination table and she performed her routine checks.

"All good," she said. "Guess I'll see you on—oh, there's Thanksgiving—guess it won't be until Monday."

She was still standoffish. Understandable, but no, I wasn't going to maintain this course: pretending that nothing of importance had happened last Friday; just ignoring it, letting its oscillations gradually damp out over time, allowing me to continue to live my life in still waters. I said, "Kay and I had a fight."

Joy's white face went chalky, then blinked crimson. She brought fingertips to her cheeks, then jerked them away as if they had been burned. "Oh God!" she breathed. "It wasn't because of . . . ?"

I took her arm and guided her back to our blood-sampling chairs. As we sat I said, "No—believe it or not, it was over peanut butter." It took several minutes to relate the details. I ended with, "She hasn't said a word to me since Saturday—the old silent treatment." I tried to sound lighthearted.

Joy had clearly been relieved to learn that she was not the cause of this quarrel. She now gave me a concerned look and said, "How is this affecting you?"

"It's terrible. You become a non-entity to the other person. And the absence of communication leads to other problems, which can exacerbate the original source of the conflict. It's very aggressive. It's the equivalent of pointing a gun to someone's head, and ordering them to do what you want."

Joy frowned at that analogy. I couldn't tell if it was out of sympathy for me, or if she thought my comparison was over the top. She asked, "What does Kay want?"

"That's a good question. I've asked her several times myself. Since she won't answer, I'm left to guess." And that was another cruel aspect of this approach to problem-solving. The revolver is at your temple, you ask the assailant what her demands are, and all you hear is the click of the hammer being thumbed—the gun being cocked. It's a mind game: an unfair one. I felt myself getting angry. "I suppose she wants me to say that her forgetfulness and disorganization are fine—that they're not a problem. But they are, and I'm sick and tired of sweeping that under the rug. I don't have a lot of time, and I'm not going to spend it telling lies." There was agitation in my voice, despite my efforts to keep it even.

"You're under extraordinary pressure. I can't imagine you slapping anyone. That's evidence of the stress you're feeling. And now to have—"

It seemed our entire Friday conversation flooded my brain at once. Every word, every look, every feeling was replayed. It was remarkable, and it took no more than two seconds. My response was to pull Joy Smalls

78

to her feet, crush her against me, and kiss her with the same fervor and abandon reserved for my wife.

29

Kay and I now slept in separate bedrooms. Early on Thanksgiving morning I heard noises from the kitchen. I roused up to see what was going on. She was sitting at the table, fully dressed, a traveling bag on the floor beside her, eating a bowl of Cheerios.

"I didn't realize we were going this early. Did we agree on that?" She ignored me and took another spoonful of cereal. The wall clock showed 7:00 AM. "Give me ten minutes," I said. Of course there was no response, but I figured she would wait. We had set up these visits before our current problem, and I doubted Kay wanted either to cancel, or to explain why I wasn't along.

We had received calls from each of our children last night. As I shaved and brushed my teeth, I reviewed these communications.

Amy would not be coming home for Thanksgiving. She would remain in Louisiana, and would celebrate with Eileen and Jerome. She assured me things were still going well, and she did in fact sound good on the phone. Amy was expert at glossing over bad situations, but in the context of my visit with her last month, I tended to believe her status report. She hadn't spent much time on the phone with Kay.

Just the opposite was the case when Joel called. I answered to a cool, "Oh, hello Dad. Is Mom okay?" Things remained frosty for the minute it took him to tell me that Congresswoman Brooks had an event in Rockville Thursday, and another in Bowie on Friday. He then asked for his mother. They had a gay old conversation for half an hour. Apparently he had told Kay on Saturday that he couldn't come today, as she didn't seem surprised or upset about it. She just said, "I'll miss you," before hanging up.

If either or both of our single children had made it, we would have taken them with us on our two-day trip.

We had checked with Bill, our oldest son, several weeks ago, before we had made arrangements to go to Virginia. If he and his family had been

79

able to drive up from Florida, we would have had Thanksgiving dinner at our house. But Bill had said Pauline felt she needed to be with her people in south Georgia. When I noted they had done Thanksgiving in Georgia last year, Bill had hesitated on the line, then had said, "Well, Eva's been a little sick. We don't want to take her too far north—winter, you know." So when he called last night, there had been no expectation of their coming. Kay and I both had nice talks with Bill, whom I would characterize as our mildest, our least turbulent, child.

I finished my abbreviated toilette (no shower), stuffed some clothes in my duffel bag, and with no breakfast hustled out to the driveway. Kay was behind the wheel of the Civic, motor running. I pitched by bag into the back, then dropped into the passenger side front seat. Before I could close the door and fasten my seatbelt, she was moving.

We drove the Eastern Shore route toward Hampton Roads in stony silence. Road trips were usually times for good discussions, for catching up. But not this one. The plan was to have Thanksgiving dinner with Kay's folks, spend the night there, go to Mother's in Madison the next day, spend Friday night there, then get home mid-afternoon on Saturday. Thank God I had the presence of mind to bring along something to read.

There was this guy I'd run across a few times on the radio: Neal Boortz. Boortz calls himself a libertarian, and his latest book was *Somebody's Gotta Say It*. I had seen it while browsing at Barnes & Noble two weeks ago. On the back cover he proclaims, "I've come to the conclusion that roughly 50 percent of the adults in this country are simply too ignorant and functionally incompetent to be living in a free society." That had reminded me of the fat lady at Wal-Mart. I bought the book. As I began plowing through, I encountered chapters such as "Homosexuals and Their (Gasp!) Agenda," "The Rainbow Fraud" (where he rails against Marcus Pfister's book, *The Rainbow Fish*, characterizing it as an "anti-individual, anti-property rights tome"), and "What Kind of Mindless Horsesqueeze Is This?" (in which he skewers a 10-question citizenship quiz offered up in the *Asheville* (NC) *Citizen-Times* newspaper, and suggests a more rigorous 66-question replacement of his own). I found Boortz's take-no-prisoners style refreshing. And he was funny. I realized at one point that I began smiling every time I cracked the book, expecting another hilarious line to come up soon. Here was a man who had obviously found his voice. Like Miss Clemmie, he was authentic—what I aspired to be. But as he blasted government, and I cheered him own, it hit me just how disingenuous I, a career federal employee, was. In my heart I was all for capitalism, free markets, risk-taking, competition, and individual initiative. I understood how these concepts constituted the driving force behind the vibrant and prosperous society I enjoyed. Yet my whole working life had been spent in the protective cocoon of big government: a huge instance, an overarching symbol, of my essential inauthenticity. Joel would doubtless label me a hypocrite. Perhaps I am. I'd like to think it's a personality-specific deal, where straightforwardness works for a Clemmie Finks or a Neal Boortz, but not for a Paul Stepping. That would be comforting.

We had just passed through Pocomoke City, and were about to enter the Eastern Shore of Virginia. My eyes were tired. I closed the Boortz book. I was a slow reader. It occurred to me that I might be dead before I finished it. I asked Kay if she would mind if I turned on the radio. She gave a shrug—the first sign in five days she had acknowledged my existence.

My eyes blurred at that simple gesture. What the hell was I doing? What kind of ill-conceived ego-trip was I on? I loved Kay—deeply. She was my heartbeat, my treasure, my Pearl of Great Price. She had been for a very long time. And here, in the final weeks of my life, I was throwing that away in the name of being authentic? What an idiot! I needed to forget this bogus initiative. I needed to go to my grave as I had lived: low-key, reserved, and in the loving bosom of my wife.

30

Kay began to thaw on this Thanksgiving trip. The silent treatment can also be hard on the one dishing it out. Plus, in the context of visiting our parents, never speaking a single word to her husband would have required some tall explaining.

We were forced to spend the nights in the same room, in the same bed.

81

Kay reverted to semi-silence during these times. The first night at the Bishops, I tried to make peace. I recounted some of the harsh things I had said, owning that I had been extreme, that I had been unjustified in painting with such a broad brush. "I was wrong," I said. "I'm sorry, Kay."

That olive branch was rejected. She looked at me for a moment. Then she scowled, blew a derisive snort, and turned her back on me to sleep.

I was floored. In our long history, we had been at odds any number of times. Invariably, upon my apology, Kay had softened, and we had reconciled. This time it seemed I had struck some new nerve. This time the hurt was deeper.

The next night at Mother's, I felt my heart harden. Why should *I* always be the one to give in? Why did *she* have to be treated with kid gloves every time we had a problem? She needed to meet me half way. "I want this to be over," I said before we turned out the lights. "Don't you?"

She said nothing. She reached out and pulled the chain on the bedside lamp.

I lay there in the dark, seething at her recalcitrance. My brain railed at the injustice of this situation. I found myself thinking of revenge. Then I found myself thinking of Joy Smalls. How different things would be if it were Joy there beside me.

31

On the drive from Madison back to Frederick, Kay began speaking to me: just monosyllables for the most part; some short sentences. I attempted to engage her in an evaluation of our visits, which we often did after spending time with family members. But she would not volunteer any observations or opinions. She would respond only to direct questions, and then in the truncated manner described above. She was like a hostile witness at a trial. Still, I chalked it up as progress of a sort. I avoided reference to our dispute, the issue that had precipitated all this: Number One, I didn't want to sidetrack the small amount of headway we had made; Number Two, I had already offered my apologies, they had been repudiated, the ball was in her court.

We did go to church the next day. Our Sunday School class was uninspiring. Kay and I were in Adult III, but she had signed up to help in the nursery. I sat there listening to Clay Winslow drone on, all but reading the lesson from the denominational quarterly. These booklets were dull, written on a middle school level, and the "questions" at the end of each lesson were infantile. A good teacher could liven things up, solicit meaningful inquiry, raise the intellectual level. Clay was a good man, but not a good teacher. Over the years at First Baptist I had sat in a few decent Sunday School classes—too few. Five or six years ago I had been cajoled into taking Adult II, the 35-45 age group. Certainly no master teacher myself, I made an effort to implement the upgrades I just mentioned. I came away from that year-long experience with two major impressions: the average person in the class wasn't much interested in these upgrades; and the Sunday School Superintendent felt threatened by them. He had gone so far as to take me aside at one point, and warn me not to "deviate from the literature." I was upset, but had smiled and assured him, "No problem Joe." It had occurred to me to take this to the pastor (Weren't Baptists all about freedom? Wasn't there a First Amendment to the US Constitution?), but I didn't. Despite my capitulation, I was not asked to teach again. Well, this was a new day; this was a new Paul Stepping. I cleared my throat and raised my hand.

Clay looked startled. I thought for a moment he was going to just ignore me and resume his monologue. But he said, "Yes Paul?" Then glancing at his watch, he added, "We only have a few minutes."

The lesson was from the Old Testament book of Malachi. It was on giving. "Bring ye all the tithes into the storehouse," began the key verse.

I said, "I see the lesson-writer interprets the storehouse to mean the local church. I wonder how he made that jump, and I also wonder if other charities—other helping causes—might be included in the tithe?"

This was not some major doctrinal question. It was not about salvation, or the nature of Christ, or the attributes of God. I considered it more a practical matter, and I figured there might be opinions to be expressed. But no—no response. Had Kay been talking to these people?

After some seconds Clay said, "Paul, the *tithe* is the *Lord's*; offerings

83

for other things—these helping causes you mention—are over and above the tithe. I think that's clear."

"But you know, the Apostle Paul was hardly rigid on the idea of the tithe. I'm not sure I remember him even discussing it as such. He did write to the early churches about giving, thanking them for their hospitality toward him, praising them for meeting the needs of their members, and urging them to support the believers in Jerusalem—but it was always along the lines of do what you can: give as God has prospered you, and as you feel led. I don't recall the ten percent coming up."

There were maybe fifteen of us in an oval, with the teacher's table at one end. I sat directly opposite. Though I was focused on Clay, my peripheral vision caught several people shifting in their seats.

Clay replied, "Well maybe you *do* recall Jesus Himself saying that He didn't come to destroy the law or the prophets, but to fulfil them. Malachi is one of the prophets."

I thought of all the Old Testament dietary and health regulations, the detailed rules regarding various types of offerings and sacrifices, the commandment about the Sabbath Day (Saturday) being holy, and I said, "Yes, I've read that. Jesus also warned against putting old wine in new bottles. I guess my question is, the law and the prophets are full of dictates and decrees about everything under the sun: Why do we pick and choose some—like the tithing deal—say we are obligated to abide by them as interpreted in a debatable way, and ignore the rest? Is that consistent?"

Clay Winslow tapped on the open quarterly before him. "We've got theological experts, seminary people, who write these lessons for us. I'm sure they've considered everything before putting it in print. We should be grateful for the knowledge they have shared, and take it to heart."

And that was it. Clay shut his Bible and his Sunday School book. He asked that everyone bow for the closing prayer. I walked out as he was saying, "Heavenly Father, we thank You so much for . . . ."

32

Essex called me into his office first thing Monday morning. He was seated behind the clean expanse of his desk. "Have a seat, Dr. Stepping." I pulled up one of the chrome chairs. "I have transplant information for you." He looked down at a sheet of paper.

I felt my heart give several hard thumps. Perhaps it was damaged, and hopeful of being replaced. I took a calming breath and said, "That's great, sir."

"That remains to be seen," he replied without raising his eyes. "This is from Sentara Careplex Hospital in Hampton, Virginia. They have a patient, a twenty-three year old male, on life support. He received a brain injury in a motorcycle accident some weeks ago. He matches you on enough tissue markers that anti-rejection drugs would likely be effective."

Once the idea of a transplant had come up, Mellwood had taken a blood sample and had sent it over to the National Cancer Institute. NCI is a non-Department of Defense tenant organization at Ft. Detrick. They have the ability to do tissue typing. As he drew the sample, I had complained again about the stale cigarette smell. Mellwood had laughed (rare for him) and said, "That's incense to the cardiology gods. Aren't you a religious man?" I had expected him to employ a flexible catheter similar to those used in angioplasties, going in through one of my femoral arteries, up the aorta, and into my left ventricle. I figured a small group of cells would be snipped or aspirated from the ventricle wall, and subjected to typing. But Mellwood had explained that NCI used DNA analysis to fingerprint the MHC (major histocompatibility complex). This group of genes controls the antigens that evoke the strongest immunological response. Zero mismatches between donor and recipient would portend the greatest chance of success; six (six genes in the MHC are checked) would forecast vigorous rejection and would require use of the most potent immunosuppressant drugs. These drugs brought their own dangers, primarily vulnerability to infection brought on by disabling the recipient's immune system.

I watched Essex scanning his document. I wondered why the Major had used the term "tissue markers," while Mellwood had spoken of the MHC. No matter—this was good news. "Sounds encouraging," I said. Then I noticed Essex was frowning. "Is there a problem?"

He looked up. "You might say that. The boy's family is not sure they want to pull the plug."

"Is he brain-dead?"

"Yes."

"Then what's the concern?"

He ran a palm over his crew cut. "The concern is time. These people want to wait a while longer. I've talked to the neurosurgeon. He says he's told the family the facts, gone over the EEG readout with them. They wanted a second opinion. He helped them get it. He's actually gone so far as to tell the parents about you—in generic terms of course—but they're holding out hope for their son. Doctors make mistakes, they say. Miracles sometimes happen."

I stared. "In somewhere between eighteen and twenty-six days I'll be dead. Do they realize that?"

"I did not communicate our time frame to the surgeon. That would have provoked questions we are not prepared to answer."

I paused to process those two sentences. Then I blurted, "That's ridiculous!"

"Excuse me?"

"What questions? What are you talking about?" This man's obsession with secrecy could cost me my life.

"If I reveal the nine-day window, he'll ask how we can be so specific."

"You're not obligated to provide an explanation."

"If no rationale is given, the assumption will be that we're trying to strong-arm the family."

"Give me a break," I muttered, looking away. Essex waited. "Listen," I said, returning my gaze to him, "can't you just say this is all a classified Army matter, there are compelling reasons to believe the recipient won't last beyond three weeks, and leave it at that?"

Essex remained cool; he watched me heating up. "I could. And do you know what those parents would say?"

"What's that?"

"They would say in three weeks their boy might rise up and walk."

"But that's absurd!"

"To you, to me—yes. But it's not our son lying there, is it?" Before I

86

could reply he added, "I can't say I blame them."

Well aren't you the compassionate bastard? I thought, my lips tensing, pressing together hard. I took two deep breaths before asking, "Major, will you communicate the time information to the surgeon? It might not change any minds, but will you please do that for me?"

The cold SOB allowed me to sweat and squirm in my metal chair a full ten seconds before replying with a shrug, "Sure, Dr. Stepping, I'll honor that request—if you're prepared to be disappointed."

33

It was thirty minutes until my regular appointment with Joy Smalls. I went to the lab to touch base with my techs, to set up for the experiments I had planned for later in the day, and to settle down from my session with Essex. I had no idea what to expect from her following our unsettling pre-holiday episode.

She was nervous. That was clear right off. There was no smile. Her voice caught, and she had to clear her throat when she said, "Hello Paul. How was your Thanksgiving?"

We chatted a little as she drew blood and did the other routine checks. Over the break she had visited her parents in Parkville, a northeast suburb of Baltimore. Her younger brother had made it home from his Bohemian, hippie-type commune in Fair Haven, a little settlement on the Chesapeake Bay, some fifteen miles south of Annapolis. Joy referred to him as a slacker.

We avoided any mention of the situation between us. I should have pursued it. That's what authenticity demanded, did it not? Keeping true feelings, honest opinions, inflammatory issues, under wraps—that was the way of the coward. But I told myself in *this* case, respect for Joy's emotional state was paramount. Maybe Wednesday we would feel more comfortable being straightforward. Beside, I was due in Mellwood's office right after this. I didn't want it to be difficult to break away. We said our good-byes with neutral faces, without touching.

Mellwood did weekly EKGs. One was scheduled for today. He

87

ushered me into the alcove off his examination room reserved for the purpose. I stretched out on the recliner. He attached electrodes to my chest, wrists, and ankles. He fiddled with the controls on his machine. Then he said, "You lie still; see you in five."

I knew he was stepping outside for a smoke. While he was gone my mind made an attempt to think clearly about Joy Smalls and Kay Stepping. I was emotionally involved with both these women; I had much more invested in Kay of course. And my obligation, my commitment, my duty, was plainly to her.

Joy had feelings for me. She had shown that. I was flattered and excited. But she had been embarrassed by her loss of control that day. She had no intention of becoming problematic—especially given the crisis I was facing. She had not implied that I owed her anything.

Kay cared little for me—at the moment. We've had our issues along the way. I'm not sure it's possible to live with someone almost thirty years trouble-free. But this time of apathy/antipathy was stretching well beyond any precedent we had set in our marriage. We were talking now. But it was perfunctory, lifeless, about trivialities. I had never stood my ground with Kay because I had feared such a reaction. She was infuriated by my courage. She was outraged at my show of backbone. That her husband would fail to blink, would fail this time to fold, was outside her realm of experience, and therefore wrong. Her response had been to assume the mantle of the injured party, and to retreat into an inner sanctum of righteous indignation.

She didn't care for me at the moment? Well guess what? I didn't care for her. Kay's reaction to criticism was juvenile. It didn't lead to improvements or solutions. I had no respect for that approach. Frankly, I despised it.

I had wanted this to be an exercise in objective thinking. Emotion was creeping in. Back to reason.

The likelihood was that at some point Kay and I would resume normal relations—we would climb out of this adversarial pit we had dug, and be grown-up Paul and Kay Stepping again. But I didn't have much time—or did I? What if the Death Period came and went, and somehow I survived?

What if the transplant came through? What if Emmerton found an antidote in time? The real test for our relationship might be if I *didn't* die within a month. If I cleared that hurdle, how long would I wait for my wife to come around? At what point would I choose the warm possibilities of Joy, over the wintry detachment of Kay?

That was not a question I wanted to face—nor would I have to just now, since Mellwood swept into the alcove, invigorated by nicotine, attended by his distinctive aroma. He tore off the EKG readout. Leaving me tethered to the electrodes, he sat beside the recliner and said, "Let's see what we have this time." He scrolled out the long thin graph, holding it up to the light. The spikes and dips were visible.

"At least I haven't flatlined," I cracked.

Mellwood was frowning. "No, but I'm seeing something."

I felt my forehead prickle. "What's that?"

"It's the nodes." He pulled the paper closer, running the entire length of it slowly past his eyes.

In wondering just how the RPA-72 had killed the mice, Emmerton had talked to me briefly about two areas in the heart that control the electrical impulses necessary to coordinate the contractions of the four chambers. Hadn't he called them nodes? Trying to gauge Mellwood's expression I asked, "So what's happening?"

"There are irregularities in the firings of both the sinoatrial and the atrioventricular nodes."

"How irregular?"

"Minor," he said, folding the graph and positioning it so I could see part of the printout. "Check this peak—" he pointed out a tall spike, then ran his finger a few inches to the right, "—and this one."

"Okay."

"In a normally beating heart the peaks have sharp but perfectly smooth crests. If you look closely, you'll see that these crests are jagged—there are a number of slight indentations in the curve."

I raised my head off the recliner pillow to see what he was indicating. Sure enough, the peaks were serrated. I lay back. "So what's going on?"

"The nodes are like electrical capacitors. Voltage builds within them

89

to a certain point, then there is a discharge. Normally both the build-up and the discharge are continuous processes, showing up as smooth crests on the EKG. If there are discontinuities, breaks in the action, that's when you see the indentations. As I say, yours are minor—but they persisted throughout the entire test. They did not come and go."

"What happens if they intensify?"

"Well, that's the concern," Mellwood said, running yellowed fingertips over his chin. "If they remain at this level, then no problem. The worse they get, the greater your chance for arrhythmia, or irregular heartbeat. Now there's a whole spectrum of arrhythmias, ranging from a barely detectable flutter, to a situation where the chambers are working against each other and no blood is being pumped. That, of course, if not corrected within minutes, will result in death."

I knew I had to be stretched out for the EKG, but I didn't like being supine before Mellwood for this discussion. So I said, "Listen, could you get these things off me?"

He looked surprised, as if this would not have occurred to him. "Oh, sure." He peeled away the electrodes, taking a few strands of chest hair with two of them.

I sat up and started buttoning my shirt. "So what's the cause of this?"

"It can be congenital—not your problem. Also electrolyte imbalance, heart disease, certain medications, alcohol, tobacco, caffeine, some herbal remedies, heart surgery, old age, stress. In this case I'd think the most likely explanation is the protectant collecting in the nodal areas and beginning to interfere with their functioning. If that's not it, then I'd say stress. You're under the gun. I'd be surprised if your heart didn't reflect that in some way."

It made sense. Emmerton had found that the RPA-72 was binding to a cardiac protein. If that protein was unique to these nodes, then the 72 would be building up in them, perhaps altering the way they operated.

I needed to get to the lab. I stood, stuffing my shirttail in my pants. "So what do we do?"

Mellwood rose too, and began patting around inside his lab coat. I wondered if *he* had arrhythmia, given the amounts of tobacco and coffee he consumed. "I'm going to run an EKG every time we meet. We're getting down to the wire." He stopped his search to check my chart. "We're at the 26th, right? You say December 13th is the first day you could be in jeopardy." He glanced up. "Essex told me about the transplant possibility. I wouldn't hold my breath on that. So I'll track these abnormalities closely. If things get worse, I won't hesitate to slap a pacemaker on you."

34

A pacemaker. Now there was a concept. If the mice had dropped dead because of acute severe arrhythmia, precipitated by RPA-72 infiltrating these electrical nodes and building up to a critical short-circuiting level, then using a pacemaker to regulate the misfirings would be the ticket. I left Mellwood's office feeling hopeful.

This was Monday. I worked productively through the afternoon, and by the end of the day Tuesday I had solved one of the problems hindering the transformation of RPA-72 into its successor, RPA-73. There were several more roadblocks, but I was getting close.

I was sobered Wednesday morning when I went to see Joy Smalls. It had nothing to do with our dubious relationship. That had been relegated to back burner status by my liver.

We sat in our regular blood-sampling chairs, but she didn't cinch the rubber cord around my upper arm. Instead, she showed me a two-page document and said, "This is your lab work from Monday. There's been a change."

"Elevated levels of tryptophan?" I quipped. "I 'gobbled' lots of turkey over Thanksgiving, but I don't feel sleepy."

Every doctor knew that turkey protein was high in this supposedly calming amino acid. Joy had a decent sense of humor, but this witticism got no applause. "No," she said. "Elevated levels of two enzymes that indicate liver damage."

That expunged the smile from my face. "Liver damage," I repeated.

"Hepatic cells are constantly dying, and that's normal. When they disintegrate, certain enzymes are released into the blood. Cell division

91

produces new cells, and the opposing rates are equal. In a given period of time, if a thousand old cells die, a thousand new ones are born, and the organ remains healthy. If a person has liver issues—cirrhosis, hepatitis, bad reactions to medications—death rate exceeds birth rate, which impedes function, *and* the enzyme levels shoot up, since they are being dumped into the bloodstream faster than they can be metabolized. That's what we have in your blood work from two days ago." She gave the papers a little shake. "Mellwood told me about the arrhythmia."

"Minor arrhythmia," I corrected.

"Okay. And these elevations are minor as well. But the concern in both cases is that you've rolled along for over two months since the accident with all indicators nominal—now, on the same day, both your heart *and* your liver are acting up."

"A little."

"Yes Paul—a little. Don't trivialize this." She watched me with serious eyes, then added, "I don't mean to be harsh. I know you're worried."

I shrugged, and being anything but authentic, said, "Just providing context."

"Duly noted."

"But here's a question: If RPA-72 is bonded to a cardiac protein (as Emmerton has demonstrated), how is it killing off *liver* cells? And why didn't it so at the outset of my exposure?"

"Maybe it did. But maybe the heart mopped up the molecules so quickly the damage was minimal, the liver repaired itself, and enzyme levels returned to normal before we started with regular blood tests. Remember, our first few tests were not broad-spectrum: we tested only for RPA-72." She paused for me to nod. "But as to your first question, I would speculate that it's not the 72 per se that's acting on your liver. I'd put my money on some kind of distress hormone from the heart. Mellwood's hypothesis has the protectant binding to Emmerton's protein in the two nodal regions, disrupting the normal electrical goings-on there. Could be in response, your heart is producing something—I called it a distress hormone, but whatever—and it is *this* substance that's having an

92

adverse effect on your liver."

"Well," I replied, "that doesn't seem very adaptive. The heart has a problem, and its answer is to manufacture something that attacks the liver? Sounds like adding insult to injury."

She raised her eyebrows. "Oh, you're talking evolution. I see your point. But RPA-72 is a synthetic molecule. Outside your mice, no mammalian heart but yours has ever been attacked by it. Given a variety of cardiac responses over geologic time, you're right, this particular one would likely not be selected. But we don't have a variety of responses. We have only yours, and it's problematic."

"So what do we do? Is there some kind of medication that would help?"

"The trouble is, we don't know what we're dealing with. I don't advise taking a shot in the dark. The enzyme up-tick is not insignificant, but it's not in the alarming category. I doubt you're going to be done in by liver failure. I say for now we just keep track."

Joy took her blood sample, then completed the other aspects of the exam. During this we chatted about the progress I had made on RPA-73.

As I prepared to leave she said, "I recall in our meeting with Essex you said if this new compound worked out with the test animals, you'd take it yourself, hoping it might constitute a cure. Are you still thinking that way?"

Giving a small shake of my head, I breathed, "To tell you the truth Joy, I'm thinking a lot of things these days."

35

Wednesday's EKG showed a slight intensification of the arrhythmia, "but not yet pacemaker-worthy," Mellwood had remarked with a seldom-heard chuckle. Maybe he was a *Seinfeld* fan. When I saw Joy on Friday, she said the previous blood sample had shown another increase in the enzyme levels: again, minor. She rushed me through, saying she had another appointment fast on the heels of mine. I wondered if that was true, or if she feared time alone with me would once more prove embarrassing.

Whatever. It gave me a while in the lab before seeing Mellwood again.

Thursday had been productive. I had come in early, and had worked straight through until quitting time, sipping coffee and popping reduced fat wheat crackers when I felt hungry. Using metallic lithium as a reducing agent, I had swept aside another barrier to the ultimate synthesis of RPA-73. Today I would mount my final assault. Before heading to the cardiologist's lair, I retrieved the glassware and reagents I would be using. I organized them on one of the lab tables flanking the fume hood, ready for action.

When I walked in, Mellwood was looking jumpy. I figured things had not worked out for him to catch a smoke in the last fifteen minutes. He hooked me up in jig time, then vanished. When he returned he was a changed man. As he scanned the EKG tape, I tried to read his face: pensiveness, perplexity, indecision. I was not encouraged.

"These jags have deepened again," he said, glancing up at me. "But it's so incremental. And that's what I don't get. You said your mice ran around normally until they keeled over dead. Am I remembering that right?"

"Yes, it was abrupt. There were no behavioral changes to tip us off."

"Well that's what I mean. That's inconsistent with arrhythmia that intensifies by increments. Your animals seem to have experienced an explosive electrical malfunction in the nodes: explosive—not gradual like I'm seeing with you. Now the only way this adds up in my mind, is that we're dealing with some kind of threshold phenomenon. This stuff initiates a biochemical reaction in the nodes. Maybe this is the first in a *series* of reactions, the products of one becoming feedstock for the next. Maybe there are, say, ten steps. Maybe the products of steps one through nine are minimally disruptive of the nodes—the small abnormalities we're seeing in your EKGs. But maybe the products of step ten are devastating." As I lay there, the leads still stuck to my skin, Mellwood extended a hand a foot above my face. He fluttered it like a tambourine. "We have chaotic fibrillation, and then *boom*—" he grabbed a fistful of air, "—cardiac arrest!" I watched his discolored nails dig into his palm, picturing a heart—in this case, *my* heart—grinding to a halt.

94

I left soon after this bit of theater, trying to evaluate Mellwood's theory as I walked toward my lab. I was excited about what might transpire today. The possibility existed that I would complete the synthesis of RPA-73 before going home for the weekend. If that happened, on Monday Boyd Markham would begin animal tests. Should the new compound protect the mice from the effects of ricin without then killing them, two things would be true: it would leave me a week before DP-1 to dose myself with 73, hoping it would function not only as a ricin protectant, but also as a cure for 72; and regardless of other outcomes, including my own death, I would have taken a giant step toward the goal of safeguarding our troops against a chemical attack involving this deadly agent.

I pulled up a lab stool and sat down before my chemicals and glassware. I had just poured 100 mL of n-butylamine into an Erlenmeyer flask when the phone rang. "Essex!" I muttered. I corked the flask, then walked over and lifted the receiver from the wall unit. It was not Essex—it was Emmerton.

"Listen Paul—can you step over for a few minutes? Thanks to your tech, I've now got enough of the complex to begin my decoupling trials. I'd like to run my plans by you before I start."

So when was I supposed to do *my* work? Our day was 8:30 to 5:00, with half an hour off for lunch. It was now 10:38. But this was important. For all I knew, my life depended on Emmerton's research. "Be right there." I placed the flask of solvent under the hood, pulled the sliding Plexiglas door down tight, and latched it.

Emmerton met me with an oversize artist's sketch pad, and a medium-tip red Sharpie. "Over here Paul." He led me to a circular table in the middle of his lab. Its circumference bore eight equally-spaced indentations, so when the chairs were pushed in, nothing extended beyond the perimeter. *Sweet design*, I thought. *I need one of these.*

He got right down to business. He flipped to a clean page in his pad, and with plump fingers gripping the marker, he drew a large oval and printed the word "Protein" inside it. A few inches away he wrote "RPA-72," and made a smaller oval around it. He then connected the two with a heavy red line. Tapping the line he said, "Now this is the bond in question; this connects your molecule to the cardiac protein." He looked over and gave me a big smile. "I've been able to isolate the complex—you know that—*and* I've now got some clues as to the nature of this bond." He scrubbed his Sharpie over the line, making it thicker. "Here's what I know . . . ." He turned the page and began fleshing out the collection of atoms he believed constituted the bridge between the ovals. "This being the case, there are at least three classes of compounds that might act to break this connection." He jotted them down. "I predict that each class will attack at a different point." He drew arrows from the words to specific positions on the chain of atoms. "And I suspect that the attacks will occur with varying degrees of ferocity. What we want is the *least* ferocious molecule that will actually break the bond. That would be easiest on the subject, wouldn't you say?"

"Makes sense," I said. If Emmerton actually came up with anything, some mice would be tested. But of course I was the only human subject to whom he was referring.

He looked at me with consolatory eyes. "Does all this seem good to you, Paul? Am I missing anything?"

I Googled my brain-server for files related to the chemistry Emmerton was proposing: electronegativities, bond strengths, reaction mechanisms. He seemed to be on the right track, so I said, "No, this looks fine. The only thing I thought of was concentration. You might be able to temper the harshness of the attack by dilution, as opposed to selecting a less harsh agent. It would simplify things—possibly expedite them as well—if you choose a single vigorous bond-breaker, begin with a high concentration of it, then taper off gradually until you find the dividing line between break and no-break."

Emmerton lit up. "That's a fantastic idea! That's exactly what I'll do!" He made some quick notes on the sketch pad. "I'll get started right away."

"It should work, plus it would give you some guidance regarding dosage." He bobbed his head while printing the word DOSAGE in block letters. "But Ward, here's what Mellwood told me this morning."

96

"Yeah, the arrhythmia."

Essex was doing a good job of making sure each person involved in this race against time was fully apprised of the status of the other three. "Right. Mellwood's theory is that electrical function is not seriously affected by the RPA-72 itself, but by reaction products that only appear at the end of a multi-step sequence." Emmerton sat up straight. "So I'm wondering if the original 72 in my heart is already half way through the sequence? If it is, then it's disappeared, meaning there would be nothing for your bond-breaking molecule to act on."

Emmerton displayed a rare frown. He jutted a thumb over his right shoulder. "I have 0.76 gram of the complex in that refrigerator, waiting to be tested. It exists, and it was extracted from the mice hearts *after* they died. Even if Mellwood's right, the RPA-72 is not *all* consumed. If I can find something to treat you with, we can still dismantle the remaining complex, disrupting the pipeline so these end-of-sequence products never balloon to critical levels."

"The RPA-72 in my blood dropped quickly," I countered. "The assumption is it went to my heart and bound to your protein. Now why would *some* of the 72 participate in the Mellwood sequence, and not the rest?"

Emmerton took a breath. "Well that's a very good question Paul. The truth is, there are big holes in our understanding of this problem. And the truth also is, we don't have time to close them. All I can do is nail down a promising decoupling agent."

He was right. We could argue theory, ferret out the weak spots, formulate hypotheses, design experiments to test them, and discover exactly what was going on here—if we had six months. What we had was two weeks.

I got back to my lab at 11:30. I didn't break for lunch. Laboring through the afternoon I made further progress, but did not complete the synthesis of RPA-73. The final step was to slice off a methyl radical from the now modified RPA-72, and replace it with a more reactive aldehyde group. This replacement was proving a bigger stumbling block than I had supposed. I would mull it over this weekend. If I could wrap things up

97

Monday, it would still leave time for the animal tests, and if they proved successful, a few days for self-medicating with the new protectant prior to DP-1.

The day had been overcast. I drove home in a cold drizzle. The Civic was not in the driveway. When I walked in I saw an envelope on the counter. My name was on the front. I opened it and read:

I'll be staying with a friend for a while.
I've made sure everything's neat and clean.
-Kay

36

Kay normally left for work a few minutes before me. But not this morning. She had hung back in her room, and I actually had not seen her prior to walking out the door. I guess she had wanted to surprise me with this informative note, rather than tell me to my face what she was planning.

"Excellent, Kay," I hissed. "Nice move." I tore the paper to bits, then added, "To hell with you. I'm going to see Bill."

I called Frederick Municipal Airport. Yes, they ran a shuttle to BWI, the next departure at 6:30. It was a prop plane, a private aircraft, a charter, so no, I couldn't arrange transportation on to Daytona. I reserved a seat on the shuttle, then went on the internet to book a direct flight from BWI to Daytona International, leaving at 8:00 PM. I called Bill. Yes, he could pick me up at 9:40.

I threw a few things in my duffel and headed for the Tahoe. I'd be back Sunday night. Let Kay guess where I'd gone—if she came home—if she cared.

All this cost a tidy sum, being arranged at the last minute, and including the shuttle. That kind of excess is a cardinal sin in Kay's book, second only to someone having the audacity to point out one of her shortcomings. But guess what? It's my money too. And if she wants to get technical, talk percentages, I make more than she does, so it's more than half mine.

"I need to see Bill," I muttered, pulling out onto Hamburg Road, "I'm

98

going to see Bill, so shut up."

The hop to BWI was rough but short—about thirty minutes. Up a few thousand feet the cold rain turned to snow and the air developed potholes. There was no locked cockpit door. I could see the pilot, a younger guy than I would have preferred under these conditions. He seemed to be having a good time as his aircraft lurched eastward through the dusk. The expressions of my six fellow-passengers ranged from impassive mask to damp furrowed brow.

Once on the big jet to Florida I relaxed. My angry thoughts about Kay returned, but I tried to push them aside by considering the options I had in finalizing the synthesis of RPA-73. That helped. Focusing on work always helped. There I could be rational, forthright, honest. And when I was, it bore fruit. There was no energy-sapping melodrama, no absurd mind games. The molecules were quiet, respectful, predictable.

Human beings are another matter. I've met a few along the way whom I could count on (Clemmie Finks and Tim Rouzerville, to name a couple); for the rest, there are too many variables, hidden emotion-laced variables, concealed by veneers of banality, waiting like land mines to explode if disturbed. One of Kay's devices had recently detonated. Historically when that happened, I hustled to stuff the genie back in the bottle. This time I had not, and the genie was metastasizing.

Bill is not like that—at least I'm unaware that he is. I've characterized him as our mildest, our least turbulent child. I felt the need to contact a family member with whom I could be straight, and not have things blow up in my face.

The plane touched down on time at DAB. Bill was waiting with a warm smile and a tight hug. "Good to see you Dad," he said. His puppy-brown eyes were benevolent and calm. "I'm glad you're here." He waited for me to elaborate on what little I had told him on the phone.

But I said, "Thanks for agreeing to the short notice. It's been a long day. I'm looking forward to some rest."

Bill had a Toyota Sienna. I figured the minivan purchase signaled that he and Pauline were thinking in terms of a larger family. We headed west on International Speedway Boulevard. The giant racetrack where the

99

Daytona 500 would be run in February was almost joined to the airport on the south side of ISB. As we drove past, Bill commented that 250,000 fans would throng this facility for that event. Most would be in the stands, he informed, but some would populate the center of the 2.5-mile asphalt oval. A quarter million NASCAR fanatics: so much for baseball or football being America's top spectator sport. I was glad to learn these details, but February could not be part of my present focus.

We turned south onto I-95, our destination being Port Orange, a residential suburb of Daytona Beach. Bill and Pauline lived in SunSplash, one of dozens of subdivisions in this bedroom community. They had a three-bedroom, two-bath, single-storey, Mediterranean-style white stucco, that looked much like hundreds of other homes in the area.

The house was situated half-way down Pendrey Drive. Pendrey ended in a spacious cul-de-sac that bordered a tropical-looking retention pond. Soon after they moved in, Bill had told me gators had been spotted in that pond. He had also relayed that Pauline referred to Pendrey Drive as "Nutsville," owing to the fact that several of their neighbors seemed to be afflicted with personality disorders, or were in chronic conflict with the Port Orange police on a variety of small matters, or both.

They had bought the place new, and by all accounts had gotten a decent deal. Two downsides (in addition to the Nutsville problem): tracks of the Florida East Coast Railroad were situated no more than fifty feet from the back door; beyond the tracks was a hundred-acre swamp, known to be the habitat for a colony of wild pigs. I call these downsides, but Bill says you get used to the eight-to-ten trains that rumble by during each twenty-four hour period, and the pigs pretty much keep to themselves. Okay. But isn't the swamp a perfect breeding ground for mosquitos? Bill claims that for their particular stretch of Pendrey Drive this has not been an issue. The big nuisance, he says, is the so-called "no-see-ums," gnat-like insects that attack for several hours near dusk. They are too small to be seen, but around sundown the tiny vampires descend, seeking blood from ankles and forearms, with a special affinity for the scalp. I understand most Florida jurisdictions have mosquito eradication programs. These little monsters must laugh at whatever chemicals they spray.

100

We pulled into the Stepping driveway around 10:30 PM. The house was dark. "Eva's down by 9:00," Bill said, unlocking the front door. "Pauline's often not far behind, especially if Eva's been extra-active—or sick, like she's been lately."

We walked into the large open space that formed the center of the house. I recalled Bill's excuse for not coming home for Thanksgiving. "She's better I hope."

He flipped on a floor lamp. "Oh, yeah—she's on an antibiotic. She'll finish up with that this weekend."

"Good, good." I glanced at my watch. "Listen, Bill—I'm beat. Where would you like me?"

"Master bedroom—right this way." He led me past the thrift store couch and the 13" color TV, through the kitchen-dining alcove combo, to the bedroom door. He reached in and turned on the light.

Kay and I had visited a few times. We had always slept in the other end of the house. "Guess things have changed since Eva's gotten bigger," I said. Bill and Pauline had loved this large bedroom with its spacious adjoining bath and glassed-in shower. When the baby was born, her crib had been set up at the foot of their bed.

"Yeah, we felt Eva needed a space of her own, but we wanted to be close by. So the other two bedrooms seemed the way to go." He gave a little laugh. "And you're the lucky beneficiary."

"It's very nice," I said, scanning around, refreshing my memory of the volume ceiling, the overhead fan, and the double windows that faced toward the train tracks and the swamp. On our first visit after the purchase, the excited couple had of course given us the tour. After that, I don't recall setting foot inside this appealing chamber. "I'll enjoy it."

"Eva's up pretty early," Bill warned. "There could be a little racket."

"No problem. You might remember I'm an early riser myself. Anyway, I'm anxious to see the little rug rat."

"All right—good enough. Sleep well." He half-turned to go, then asked, "Dad, is there any reason Mom didn't come? Well, obviously there's a reason. But I'm assuming everything's okay."

Everything was far from okay, but that was not a subject I could broach now. So I made a dismissive gesture and said, "Oh, sure. Look, I'll fill you in tomorrow." Bill walked away. I shut the door. I placed my duffel bag on the bed, wondering if tomorrow I would find the strength to be honest with my son—debating if that would even be wise.

37

Eva beat my normal wake-up time by fifteen minutes. Scratches and taps at the door summoned me just as I was drifting off from the latest train arousal. I heard Bill coaxing her away with, "Grandpa's trying to sleep," but the damage had been done.

It was December 1. At home we'd had the heat on for six weeks. Here, one often wore short sleeves on Christmas Day. I pulled on some cut-off jeans and a Red Cross T-shirt they gave me the last time I donated at the rescue squad station near our house. Flip-flops completed my beach bum outfit. A little water on the face, a few brush strokes through the ever-whitening hair, and I made my appearance. I would brush my teeth and shave after breakfast.

Bill and Eva were sitting on the sofa, watching a children's program on the tiny TV. When I walked up, Bill said, "Eva, here's Grandpa Stepping. Go give him a hug."

Kay and I had last driven down back in the summer, just after school let out. That had been almost six months ago—roughly a fourth of Eva's lifetime outside the womb. She sat there in her pajamas, giving me a scowl.

"Eva, Grandpa came a long way just to see you."

That bit of guilt-based cajolery proved ineffective, so I walked over and sat on the worn cushion beside her. "Hi Eva—what are you watching?" I nodded toward the TV.

She had been following my movements as I approached. Now she turned toward the screen and said something fairly close to "Sesame Street." Then she looked back at me while shrinking toward her father.

Eva had Bill's big brown eyes and Pauline's auburn hair. She was a beautiful two-year-old, with a not-so-beautiful disposition. Back in June,

102

Kay and I had stayed a week, and Eva had never warmed up to either of us.

I decided not to push this encounter. Instead I asked Bill, "You said she's up early—is this every day?"

"Pretty much."

"And you always get up with her?"

"Well, I leave for work before Pauline, so it makes sense."

"No switching off?"

"Not really."

This was something I wanted to raise with Bill. He knuckled under too much to his wife. From what I could see, Pauline ruled the roost. Of course it was their business, but I felt it might be healthy to air the situation. I was sure Bill would profit—maybe Pauline as well. I figured I'd wait until we had some time alone. "How about some coffee?" I asked.

Bill gave me a troubled look. "Oh, I'm sorry Dad. We don't have any. Pauline prefers tea."

"I thought *you* drank coffee."

"Yeah, well—I used to. But, you know: too much trouble; also health issues and whatnot. Tea's easier. And I wanted to be on the same page with Pauline—present a united front to Eva here." He patted his daughter's head, only to have her duck away.

A united front to Eva about tea? Give me a damn break. This was the kind of nonsense I was talking about. I said, "I saw a 7-Eleven just before we turned into your subdivision last night. Mind if I take your Sienna and get me a cup o' joe?"

"Oh, sure." He started fishing in his pants for the keys.

"I could bring you one."

"Oh, no—that's okay. Thanks Dad."

When I returned fifteen minutes later, Bill was in the kitchen preparing breakfast, while Eva was across the open space, pitching a fit at the closed door of the bathroom there. "What's going on?" I asked, dropping his keys on the counter and taking a pull on my coffee-straw.

"Pauline's taking a shower. She used to let Eva bathe with her, but we're trying to work out of that." Bill was scrambling eggs, preparing oatmeal, and monitoring the progress of four slices of wheat bread in a bulky toaster ravaged with rust.

"Where'd you get this baby?" I asked, indicating the humming appliance.

"Goodwill," he chuckled. "Pauline's big on bargains. I think it cost a buck. Works well though."

From the other end of the house the kicking and screaming stopped, and I heard, "You can come in Mommy's room and we'll get dressed. Then we'll eat breakfast. And *then* we'll go to LLL and have some fun."

Pauline worked part-time at La Leche League, an organization that promoted the practice of breast-feeding; it provided information, education, and support to interested mothers and mothers-to-be. I made an early mistake with Pauline. Soon after she and Bill married, the newlyweds were visiting us in Maryland. Pauline ran the Daytona chapter at that time. At supper one night she was waxing zealous about the benefits of breast-feeding, going so far as to characterize those who opted for other alternatives as "child abusers," and to recommend they be "horsewhipped." Seeking to lighten things up, I had quipped, "You realize LLL is only one letter removed from KKK." Perhaps that's contributed to the fact that thus far our relationship has not been warm.

"Does Pauline work on Saturdays?" I asked. My information had been that she went in weekday mornings for several hours.

"No, but they have a special event today—kind of an open house. Pauline's in charge."

I helped Bill set the table. Pauline and Eva walked up. Pauline gave me a tight little smile and a peck on the cheek.

The eggs were excellent. Bill had started his post-high school education in the Culinary Arts and Hospitality program at Frederick Community College. He loved to cook, and was good at it.

The oatmeal was for Eva. After a couple of bites she began fussing. In a case of excellent timing, a three-engine freight train began rumbling by, drowning out most of her complaints. I was put in mind of the one-hit wonder, Little Eva, singing "The Locomotion" back in 1962. Looking out the alcove windows you could glimpse the gondola cars piled high with phosphate from south Florida, gliding past. They were just beyond a line

104

of palmetto palms whose fronds screened out some of the sights and sounds. The quality of the vibrations transmitted to the table top changed when the low-riding gondolas were followed by a sequence of swaying boxcars.

At that juncture Pauline threw a shawl over her left shoulder, and behind that shield whipped out a breast. She lifted Eva from her high chair. She thrust the toddler's auburn head beneath the shawl, and the fine dining began. Soon the last car lumbered by (not a caboose: Bill had explained last summer that as a cost-cutting measure, Florida East Coast trains no longer had those, nor the employees who rode in them). As the sounds from the tracks drained away, I could hear Eva slurping her milk.

The only thing Pauline said to me during the meal was, "Don't you like tea?" She had noticed the 7-Eleven cup. My answer had been, "No."

Bill excused himself to go squeegee the dew off Pauline's vehicle. She drove a boxy Volvo wagon with the predictable BABY ON BOARD sign plastered on the inside of the back window. In addition there was a La Leche League bumper sticker: MOTHER'S MILK—NECTAR OF THE GODS. I cleared the table while she wrapped up the feeding session with Eva. Bill returned announcing, "I started the motor dear, and flipped on the defroster. I think you'll be fine."

After a swing by Eva's room to retrieve a toy she was demanding, they left. I was alone with my oldest son. Now what?

38

Bill had been a weak student at Frederick High: not like Amy, who goofed off; he worked hard—just without much success. He was also shy, and not athletically inclined. His lackluster career had been bumped into the painful category when his brother Joel, two years his younger, splashed upon the scene. Joel was bright, outgoing, and a damn good wrestler.

As I mentioned, after high school Bill enrolled at FCC, the community college Kay and I had threatened Amy with. He did a year in what I called "the cooking program," then decided he didn't want to be an executive chef. At the end of his second year he had earned the Transfer Studies

105

Certificate. The school catalogue stated that the holder of this document was assured of "maximum academic flexibility to meet transfer course requirements at four-year institutions." Words of comfort from this bastion of higher learning on Opossumtown Pike.

The four-year institution to which Bill transferred was Flagler College in St. Augustine, Florida. Flagler is small, private, co-ed, not religiously-affiliated. It is named after Henry Morrison Flagler, a Gilded Age industrialist, railroad pioneer, and oil magnate. In 1888 Flagler built the luxurious Hotel Ponce de Leon, a masterpiece of Spanish Renaissance architecture. Thomas Edison personally helped make it the first building in Florida wired for electricity. When Flagler College was founded in 1968, the trustees bought the hotel, making it the centerpiece of the new school.

I learned all this as Bill prepared to make his transition to the Sunshine State. He had told me he was thinking about a biology major. That sounded good. I reminded him that present-day biology leaned quite heavily toward the molecular, and that chemistry had proved especially troublesome to him in high school (despite my tutorial efforts). He told me not to worry, and I soon discovered why. He would be working toward as BS in Natural Sciences. Flagler did not offer a degree in any specific science. The Natural Sciences department had two professors; one of them had a PhD. My enthusiasm had been further tempered when I was informed of the small fortune we would be shelling out over the next two years. Perhaps the characterization was too harsh, but it seemed to me at the time that Bill was transferring from one fluff institution to another. I had been reminded of Randy Travis's great country hit, "Better Class of Losers."

On the positive side, Bill had seemed to thrive at Flagler. He met Pauline, a Communicative Arts major, there. He got his Natural Sciences degree cum laude and on time. The October after graduation they had been married on the Wigglesworth farm in south Georgia, near Valdosta. Kay had been highly incensed at this decision, arguing to Bill that if they were set on an outdoor wedding, how in God's name did south Georgia trump the Maryland panhandle for natural fall beauty? "Let me remind you that our property backs right up to Gambrill State Park," she had fumed. But to

106

no avail. Bill had tried to explain this capitulation to his mother. It was the first of many kowtows.

Bill secured employment as a sea turtle specialist with Volusia County Leisure Services, a position I could not see he was qualified for. The couple moved to the Daytona area, renting at first, then buying the house in Port Orange. Bill was headquartered at the Marine Science Center (MSC), located in Lighthouse Point Park, a few miles south of Daytona Beach. The main mission of the center is the rehabilitation of sick and injured sea turtles and shore birds. Soon after their move from St. Augustine, Pauline took the La Leche League job, switching to part-time after Eva was born.

As Bill washed up the breakfast dishes, I sat at the alcove table and said, "Your mother and I are having a little disagreement. That's why she didn't come."

He raised his eyebrows. "Wow—what's up?"

"Back before Thanksgiving we were walking The Trail. She forgot an item we needed for lunch—peanut butter. I was disappointed and made some comment to that effect. She took offense, and things escalated." I didn't deem it necessary to tell Bill about the slapping. That behavior had been so aberrant, so atypical, I couldn't see sharing it as essential to my authenticity effort.

"You apologized, didn't you?"

"Not exactly."

"Why not?"

"Kay forgets a lot—she's easily distracted—and it causes problems. I've been pretty understanding about that over the years—as you say, apologizing when I've been critical—but it hasn't changed the behavior."

Bill lifted some items from the hot rinse water and arranged them steaming in the drying rack. He looked over at me with a frown. "Why now?" he said. "You and Mom have been married a long time. You've obviously discovered how to work out your differences. Why rock the boat?"

"It actually has to do with something at work—something that's coming up shortly before Christmas."

"I didn't think you could talk about your work."

107

"Well, I can't—not in any detailed way. I'm just saying an upcoming event there triggered this change in approach on my part. Sorry to be so cryptic; this is to provide a little context; I know it's hard to envision how something there could be relevant to this particular relational issue between your mother and me."

"No, no problem," he shrugged, pulling the drain plugs from the double stainless steel sink. "Things are what they are." He dried his hands on a dish towel draped through the handle of the nearby refrigerator. "So, what are you doing? You say things escalated. What does that mean?"

I wanted to get out of the house. It was a gorgeous Saturday here, cloudless and warm. The forecast for this first day of December in the Frederick area was a high of 38, with a 70% chance of snow. I told Bill my wishes, and he suggested we go to Causeway Park, located beneath the Dunlawton Bridge on the Port Orange side of the Halifax River. He said we could be there in ten minutes. He pressed a brief Post-It note onto the counter for Pauline.

During the short drive I fleshed out what "escalated" meant. I told Bill of the silent treatment, and of the memorandum I'd found from Kay the previous afternoon. "I don't even know where she is," I said as we pulled into a parking spot in the shade of the high bridge.

"Are you worried?"

I thought about that for a moment. "I don't think so. My guess is she's staying with one of her school friends."

Bill had parked near an unpainted wooden picnic table. We were no more than a half mile from the Atlantic. The table showed the effects of the salt air. We sat on the same side so we could look out over the river. The Halifax was part of the Intracoastal Waterway, and some interesting vessels plied its waters.

"Does she know where you are?" Bill said.

"No."

"You didn't call around, or leave a message in case she comes home?"

"Look, Kay clearly doesn't want me to know where she is. She doesn't care where I am. I'll be back tomorrow night. I doubt she'll have returned by then, so what kind of worry will she experience? If she does

108

come back, and wonders where I've gone, so what? It'll be a little taste of her own medicine."

Causeway Park boasted an extensive fishing pier, two cement boat ramps, and several floating docks for watercraft tie-ups. Maybe a hundred yards out from these docks was Bird Island, a half acre of salt myrtle and red mangrove, perpetually thronged with all manner of egrets, gulls, pelicans, ibises, and herons. A stone's throw to the right was a much larger island with nary a bird on it. Bill had pointed out this oddity on a previous visit.

I had been staring out toward Bird Island as I spoke. My peripheral vision detected Bill turn toward me near the end of my soliloquy. "Dad," he said, "this doesn't sound like you. Are you okay?"

I shifted to look at him. "Actually, no—or maybe yes."

"You're going to have to explain that."

"I will. I'm trying to be more straightforward—with everyone: be more up front about how I feel. This thing with Kay is a for instance. I'm sick of apologizing for pointing out her counterproductive behaviors. I shouldn't have to do that—apologize. She should make some effort to change the behaviors. Instead, she gets her feelings hurt. That's gone on for thirty years. Now it stops."

"And this change of heart has something to do with your secret work at Ft. Detrick?"

"Yes, but that's just the catalyst. I should have made this move long ago. If I had, maybe things would be different with you."

"Different with me?"

"The way you relate to Pauline. I'm afraid you picked that up from how I've dealt with your mother over the years."

Bill's brown eyes were showing confusion. "Well, sure. I've admired your gentle approach with Mom. Your forbearance was a huge example to me. I considered it one of your major strengths. And yes, I wanted to be that way with *my* wife."

I watched him for several seconds, remembering that April morning almost twenty-eight years ago when he had been born. Kay's water had broken at 2:00 AM. Things had progressed so quickly we had barely

109

gotten to the hospital in time. "Listen, Bill—I certainly want you to respect me. Every father wants his son to look up to him. But on this issue, I think I've missed the boat. And you have too. I mean, look at you: you're henpecked; Pauline calls the shots; you're all about 'Yes, dear'; you're basically a doormat. I've been bad, but you're worse. I'm trying to reverse course with your mother. I think you need to do the same with Pauline. You need to take a stand."

Bill stared at me as if I were from another galaxy. "Our marriage works," he said, pausing between words.

"Uncontested dictatorships always work," was my reply.

He looked away, across the Halifax to where employees of Deck Down Under were making preparations for a large lunch crowd. The name had nothing to do with Australia, but referred to the fact that much of its parking was beneath the bridge. This establishment, with its enormous outdoor riverside eating area (its deck), put Daytona Beach Shores on the map. Otherwise, the tiny jurisdiction's primary claim to fame was an attractive sign welcoming motorists from the Dunlawton Bridge with the weak assertion, "Life is better here."

Bill turned back to me. "You were disappointed about Thanksgiving."

"Well, yes—but that was just a case in point. My concern is the nature of the entire relationship."

"And why is this *your* concern?"

"You're my son; I want you to be happy and fulfilled; I don't want to see you taken advantage of."

"And what if I tell you I *am* happy, I *am* fulfilled, I'm *not* being taken advantage of?"

"Then I would say open your eyes. Either you're lying, or you're in denial—or maybe you're delusional."

Bill squinted, and after watching me for several seconds, said, "Let me get this straight, Dad. You see me—what?—twice a year at most. Yet somehow you're the expert on my relationship with Pauline. Furthermore, you feel comfortable flying down here on a moment's notice to tell me what a fool I am. And this from someone who's just admitted that his own wife has basically left him because he's such a nit-picking,

110

uncompromising—because he's *been* so nit-picking and uncompromising about something as inconsequential as peanut butter. That's not only stunning—if you weren't serious, it would be laughable."

I did a quick memory scan to see if I could recall a precedent for this kind of rhetoric from my low-key firstborn. I could not. I was stung, but I was also proud. If he could stand up to his father, maybe he would confront his scold of a wife. Plus, he had made a valid point, one I needed to acknowledge.

"Son, you're right—I'm no expert on your relationship with Pauline. What I'm doing is expressing how that relationship appears to me, and how I feel about what I perceive. I'm troubled by it. I have been for a long time. I'm finally getting around to saying something. Maybe it's none of my business; maybe it is. Take it for what it's worth. I do think you need to hear it."

An expensive-looking vessel with a billowing orange sail was headed for the channel below the bridge. Fifty yards out, the sail was furled, and the boat proceeded under the power of its small motor. I assumed this was to avoid the possibility of an unanticipated gust of wind pushing the sloop against the pilings that lined the narrow strait.

Bill and I had been watching the sailboat. Now he said, "Dad, I'll try to do that. I'll try to take your advice for what it's worth. But don't you think a positive, long-term approach would be more effective? You once told me you were a rational gradualist. I see your strategy here as marginally rational, and not at all gradual. I feel like I've been hit by the blast of a blunderbuss."

Though I could not recall the occasion Bill had referenced, since college I have considered myself an exponent of rational gradualism. I coined the term. I've never seen or heard it anywhere. It basically means that I don't make snap decisions. I gather information, I ponder that data as it relates to the decision I must make, then I act based as much on reason, and as little on emotion, as I can. I'm not a fan of intuition, or of the oft-vaunted gut feeling.

I said to Bill, "My problem now is time. I'm feeling rushed. So the gradualism is by the boards. That being the case, I want to say a few words about Eva."

"Critical, I suppose."

"Somewhat. Should I proceed? If you're not interested, I could shut up; but then," I said with a chuckle, "you might get a nasty letter in the mail."

Bill did not smile. "Go on," he said.

I watched his face. It made me question the wisdom of my get real enterprise. Still, I forged ahead. "Let me say right off the bat that it's clear to me that you and Pauline love your child and have her best interests at heart. So that's not the concern. The concern is, why do you let her get away with being a brat? And she *is* a brat."

"She's two years old Dad. You ever hear of The Terrible Twos?"

"Oh, I've heard of it—and I think it's a crock. You don't let kids get away with murder just because they're going through a stage. Go down that path, and you'll be making excuses for them until they're forty-five."

"What murder is she getting away with?"

"Whining, complaining, fussing, demanding: I don't see you or Pauline sending the message that this is inappropriate—that there's any kind of problem here. If it was now and then, I'd say fine. But this is Eva's non-stop program. And it works. She gets what she wants, so why should she change?"

"Children come into this world with a temperament," Bill asserted. "Some are mellow and laid back. Some are not. Eva's not."

"So you don't buy the blank slate theory."

"No, I don't."

"Neither do I, but that's beside the point, isn't it?"

"I don't think so. If temperament is genetically determined, then I think it's very much the point."

I shrugged and said, "Fine. But the bottom line is behavior. Eva's, by and large, is unacceptable. I think something needs to be done, regardless of origin."

"And you think Pauline and I do nothing."

"I don't see any present correction. And six months ago when I first observed this stuff manifesting, I saw no correction. So I'm assuming

112

there's not much going on in the way of intervention."

"You assume."

"Well sure. I acknowledge it's an assumption. How could it be otherwise? I don't live with you. Why don't you *tell* me what your strategy is with Eva? Maybe it's fine. But from where I sit, it looks ineffective."

"All right Dad—and I'm sure you'll like it. I would refer to our strategy as rational gradualism."

That, of course, was a dig. "You're right—I like it. However, rational gradualism only makes sense in the context of an identifiable goal—a clear cut problem that needs to be solved. I'm not convinced you and Pauline see that you *have* a problem with Eva."

Bill was keeping his cool, but he was not happy with this conversation. "Eva's strong-willed," he said. "That's a challenge. Strong-willed people meet resistance; they can also be effective leaders."

"*If* they learn how to handle the resistance," I interjected. "What she's learning now is that there *is* no resistance. She demands, others acquiesce, end of story."

With a slight arching of the eyebrows Bill said, "But we're very early in the game. You seem to be confusing the faint beginnings of strategy, with no strategy at all. And that's a flaw in logic."

"So there *is* a plan to clamp down on Eva—you just haven't gotten into it yet."

"Eva needs direction, training. I see that. And it's coming. But if it's too abrupt, there could be trauma. I'm not interested in crushing Eva's spirit."

"So spanking is out?"

"Yes."

"Regardless of the offense?"

"I can't think of anything that would justify hitting Eva."

Bill was mouthing the present-day philosophic pablum regarding child-rearing: trauma, crushing the spirit, hitting—all the inflammatory buzzwords that led modern parents down the garden path of guilt, of permissiveness, and ultimately of heartbreak. Kay and I had been on the

113

same page when it came to discipline. We had spanked, but not much. It had not been necessary. Our cardinal principle had been that we were the parents, we had the responsibility for our offspring, therefore we were the bosses. Of course we cut slack for the mistakes, the bumblings, the indiscretions of youth. But open defiance? No. That was not countenanced. Ever.

A squadron of white ibises flew under the bridge, headed for touchdown on Bird Island. I could see their long curved beaks, so perfectly adapted for ferreting out worms and crustaceans in the fine bottom silt of the lakes and ponds where they waded and fed. I could see their red faces: embarrassed, I thought—ashamed of something.

And what of me? Should I be ashamed of the way I was dealing with Bill? Should I be ashamed of my openness with Joy Smalls? Should my face turn red over Kay, over my hard heart when it came to her these days? A minor celebrity I once read of was asked if he had a motto, some basic rule by which he lived his life. His answer had been, "No regrets." At the time I regarded that attitude as irresponsible and flip. Now I embraced it. Walking around with a load of contrition and remorse is a recipe for pessimism, if not depression. But "no regrets" is not a matter of justifying everything. We all make mistakes. If you commit an error, go astray, transgress—don't waste energy on regret. Instead, be quick to repent, apologize, make amends, fix the problem. But if you determine that a particular course of action is *not* shame-worthy, then forge ahead, and never look back.

I would forge ahead with Bill, but I decided not to pursue the corporal punishment issue. I switched the focus a bit and said, "Here's a thought: Pauline sees in Eva a controlling female in the bud—a controlling female such as herself; this is good, this is affirming; so Pauline encourages the controlling behavior in Eva to legitimize her own need to dominate—her own will to power." Bill was shaking his head, so I added, "And you play along."

He regarded me for several seconds. "You know what Dad? You should stick to chemistry, because your pop psychology here stinks. It's so dire, so extreme, it can't help but be off-base. If Pauline is the monster you

114

paint her to be, she couldn't hold a job, she'd likely be in jail for something, and we'd be long divorced. Yet our marriage is fine, and it's you and Mom who seem on the verge of breaking up. So maybe you need to tone things down a little—try to have at least a passing acquaintance with the facts."

"All right, but look—where do you think all this is going to lead in a few years? Eva's two. What's the situation when she's five? Is she still whining and demanding and getting everything she screams for? School is going to be a very unforgiving brick wall."

"We might home school," was the reply. "Pauline's talked about it."

I should have seen that one coming. "Of course," I said. "That would be perfect."

The sarcasm was unhelpful, and perhaps unwarranted. Bill could have confronted me again—called me on it. Instead he suggested, "Why don't you discuss this with Pauline? I'm clear on what you think, but she isn't. I could take Eva someplace—maybe Spruce Creek Children's Park—and leave you two alone."

"Would she do it? You saw the extent of our breakfast conversation."

"I don't know."

"Maybe you could ask for me."

He frowned. "How forthright would that be?" Then his eyes tugged wider. "You're not afraid of Pauline, are you?"

Another dig. "I'm uncomfortable around her; but fine—I'll check it out."

Bill grinned. "Excellent." He rubbed his hands together. "I'd like to be a fly on the wall for *that* interaction."

I asked my son about his work: Did he like it? Were things going well? Could he move up in the Leisure Services hierarchy? The respective answers were yes, yes, and probably no. The Marine Science Center had a director. That was the only higher rung at the Center, and the present guy had expressed no intention of leaving. Bill said that regardless, the position was too political for his taste. And beyond the MSC, nothing in Leisure Services really interested him.

I voiced my concerns about the quality of Bill's education, wondering

115

how his degree in Natural Sciences had prepared him for his present job. He explained that about half of his science course work had employed a seminar format, with the participants being allowed to select areas of individual interest. He had focused heavily on marine biology, in particular on the anatomy, physiology, and behavior of sea turtles. I asked several specific questions about these endangered reptiles. He knew the answers. Perhaps my judgment of Flagler College had been premature, and the small fortune they had demanded had been well-spent.

We talked on for a while. Our dialogue was becoming less contentious, thanks primarily to Bill's imperturbability. When we started thinking about lunch, he pointed across the river and said, "How about Deck Down Under? If we hurry we could be first in line."

We enjoyed oyster sandwiches in the shade of a striped umbrella on the big deck. I began worrying about my potential sit-down with Pauline. Maybe I *was* afraid of her.

39

Pauline was *not* afraid of *me*. When I inquired about the possibility of a chat, she quickly accepted, all but licking her chops: if her father-in-law wanted to rumble, she'd have him for lunch. That was my interpretation at least. She suggested the next morning, Sunday, out on the back patio. She told Bill to take Eva to church, not to the children's park. When I asked Bill what church, he said the Presbyterian. "Why not Baptist?" I asked. He began, "Well, Pauline's family——," at which point I stopped him with a raised hand. I understood.

It took me a while to go to sleep that night. I had gotten past my initial apprehension, and was actually excited at the prospect of being direct with her, of seeing how she would react. What kept me awake was wondering how our meeting would be different if I prefaced it by announcing, "Pauline, I'll be dead before Christmas, and I just wanted to clear the air with you before I go." I suspected that would prejudice things, making it difficult for her to be genuine, while encouraging me to take unfair advantage. If you hit the little kid with leukemia, you'll be called a bully; if the little kid realizes this and kicks your shins, knowing you won't hit back, then he's the bully, but nobody will dare say it. I've felt frustrated at being unable to share the motivation behind my authenticity campaign. But maybe that's okay; maybe it's all to the good. The rich guy has droves of friends—but why? The dying guy is never challenged: after all, he's dying—give the poor fellow a break. Once I sorted all this out I dropped off, and was only slightly disturbed by the two trains that clanked and clamored by in the night.

The next morning we had breakfast, and once Bill and Eva left I followed Pauline out the back door to the cement patio (or, as they call it in this part of Florida, the lanai). We sat in some cheap plastic chairs. Another thrift store purchase, I guessed. Kay and I have similar seating on our screened back porch, but our chairs are better quality: we bought them brand new at Wal-Mart. The back of the house faced east, but it would be a while before the sun topped the tall pines that bordered the swamp. The sky was clear. The temperature was in the mid-seventies. It was a comfortable setting.

"We've discovered that no trains come by until early afternoon on Sundays," Pauline said. "We shouldn't be interrupted. By the way, sorry about the coffee situation." I had gone to 7-Eleven again. "We just don't drink it." I was about to reply, but she asked, "So what do we need to talk about, Paul?"

Pauline seldom used my first name. Did this portend a cordial exchange? Or was it the condescending familiarity of predator with prey prior to the kill? Regardless, she was avoiding small talk, getting down to business. Fine. I could do that. In fact, I preferred it. "Two things:" I said, "the first being your relationship with Bill."

"What about it?"

"It seems lopsided."

"That's an interesting adjective." She watched me with hazel eyes; for a second, for the briefest moment, my mind flicked to Joy Smalls. With the hint of a smile she said, "And by lopsided you would mean . . . ?"

"When it comes to making decisions, it appears Bill has little say. You call the shots. It's not exactly fifty-fifty."

"You're assuming decision-making *should* be fifty-fifty. Perhaps that's debatable." There was a pause, then she said, "Could you give an example?"

"The most recent was this morning. Bill's plan was to take Eva to the playground. You vetoed that, without discussion, and commanded him to take her to church. I'd call that lopsided."

Pauline laughed, balancing nicely between simple amusement and derision. "Did I command? I thought I recommended. Look, Paul—good marriages have divisions of labor. They have to. Efficiency requires it. Rationality demands it. And the job assignments are based on interest and aptitude. Bill takes care of the cars, for instance. He knows more about all that than I do, and he really likes keeping them clean, well-maintained, and in good running order. Our vehicles are important. Bill deals with them. I don't. It's something I don't have to worry about. When it comes to most of the day-to-day decisions, I take the lead. I have a knack for prioritizing, for organization, for time management. Bill is weak in these areas. Ask

118

him—he'll tell you. So it makes sense for this to be one of my jobs. Are you following me? It seems pretty basic. Surely you and Kay divide things up."

This was the longest continuous sequence of words Pauline had spoken to me in the five years since she and Bill had married. She was cogent and on point. She was doing a good job of shoving emotion to the side. I was impressed. Still I remarked, "Car maintenance hardly seems comparable to making family decisions."

"I believe I said day-to-day decisions." She smiled. "On bigger issues, of course Bill has input."

"But who eventually decides on these bigger issues? Input is good, whatever that might actually mean. But let's say you and Bill have twenty thousand dollars to invest. You talk about it, bat it around, and it comes out that Bill thinks it best to use the money to pay down your mortgage, while you want to set up an aggressive stock-based mutual fund. You've both done your homework, performed your calculations, and made your case. My question is, in situations like this, who finally decides? I'm guessing it's you, and I'm wondering why. Why should your judgment trump Bill's?"

"Now you're sounding like a protective father," she said, good humor still in her voice. Then there was a hardening—ever so slight. "Don't forget, Paul: Bill picked me; he knew what he was getting."

"And you feel things are working out well."

"Yes."

"No buyer's remorse?"

"Absolutely not—not on my part. Look, Bill is a dependable man. He's a faithful husband, a reliable father." There was that smile again. "It just so happens that I'm the stronger personality. Opposites do often attract, and that's not necessarily a bad thing. It makes the division of labor more natural. Spouses tend to gravitate toward different responsibilities, lessening competition and potential conflict."

The rising sun found an opening in the pines. Rays tumbled through, and Pauline was in the spotlight. She was lean, tanned by the Florida sun, seemingly fit. She was twenty-seven like Bill, but looked older. I think it

119

had to do with the way she wore her hair: pulled back and rolled into a tight bun. She reminded me of a librarian. Not that she wasn't attractive— she was, tending more toward the handsome end of the spectrum than the cute. Her demeanor was often dour, her manner brusk. She was quick with a frown. These factors imparted a severe aspect to her face, contributing to the older look. In this interview however, she had been relaxed and smiling. Sitting there with her bare legs crossed, bathed in sunshine, Pauline presented a pretty picture.

I noticed she had managed to evade my question about her judgment trumping Bill's when it came to important decisions. I had also caught her use of the words dependable, faithful, and reliable when referring to her husband. Weren't these terms the master might apply to a good slave? Yes, but how about vice versa? What about employer/employee, and vice versa? And how would I characterize my expectations of Kay, and Kay's of me? I had to admit I was reaching in casting Pauline as a Simon Legree. It was time to move on.

"You're right about opposites. I'm sure if the differences are *too* extreme, it might prove difficult for the people to find common ground. Barring that, and assuming both parties are satisfied with the other facets of their relationship, I'd say your analysis is on target."

The sun was inching higher. Her face moved into shadow. "I hope so," she said. "By the way, you're quite articulate. I've known a few math/science types here and there, and some of them, while competent within their disciplines, had trouble stringing two coherent sentences together. For instance, there was this guy in high school. We took the SAT—max of 800 on each part. He scores 770 on the math; 430 on the English. He was the sweetest boy, but God, the disparity! You're not that way."

"Well thanks. My guess is the left brain/right brain distribution is primarily genetic—so it's nothing I can take credit for."

Glancing at her watch she said, "Whatever the reason, it's unusual— and nice. Listen, I'm going to join Bill and Eva at church. You can come if you like. I'll need to leave in ten, fifteen minutes. Was there anything else?"

120

"Actually yes—and I won't hold you up. It's Eva. I have to tell you Pauline, the way she acts is not very appealing."

"She's two years old."

That had been Bill's initial reaction when I broached this subject.

"Right, but the whining, the complaining, the demanding—and worst of all, the blatant disobedience and disrespect—it worries me. I project down the way a few years, and I don't like what I see."

"She's two," Pauline repeated.

"Yes, but if she continues on this trajectory, she's headed for trouble. I don't want to see that."

There was a slight curl of the lip that reminded me of Amy. "Eva's trajectory is fine. She's a strong-willed child; Bill and I are handling it, so you can relax."

Strong-willed. There was *that* excuse again.

"But the problem is, I don't see any evidence of handling. If anything, I see aiding and abetting. Where's the correction, the discipline?"

"What would you suggest? A strait jacket and some duct tape?"

No good humor now.

"Once, in another connection, you mentioned horsewhipping."

She flushed, apparently recalling my reference. "That's absurd!"

"Exactly. So are a strait jacket and some duct tape. So if you will refrain from putting words in my mouth, perhaps we can be reasonable. What's your plan for Eva?"

Pauline consulted her watch again. Cooler, she asked, "You have no faith that Bill and I can rear a child? Is that the concern?"

"No. I'm merely asking about your approach."

She examined me with her hazel eyes. "I don't have to answer your questions, Paul. I'm under no obligation." I didn't respond. "You know, Bill told me about your sad little foray into psychodiagnostics. Pitiful really. Amateurish. I mean, 'need to dominate'; 'will to power.' Please." I watched the contempt spread over her face. "Who are you? Freud? Nietzsche? And speaking of child-rearing, what happened with your son? Seems a bit cowed, don't you think? What did you and Kay do to him?" Her face advanced a few inches. "I'm merely asking about your approach."

121

She stood and looked down on me. "I'm leaving. We'll be back in two hours. By then, I want you gone."

40

Pauline walked away, confirming my opinion of her as a cold, hegemonic shrew. That judgment had begun to erode during our conversation; it was reinstated here at the end. Nutsville: Pauline was in exactly the right place.

I remained on the lanai for a while, thinking. What did she want me to do? Walk to the airport? My plane didn't leave until 6:00 PM. I would actually have time, and I could use the exercise. But there was my duffel bag. Bill had said it was six or seven miles from DAB to their house. That bag would get heavy, plus I wasn't entirely sure I knew how to get there. I thought about asking the neighbors across the street for a lift. They were retired, in their sixties. The man was crippled, could barely walk. He seemed bitter. He spoke in monosyllables, and only in answer to direct questions. His wife made up for that lack. Bill had introduced Kay and me to this couple, and I had been cornered by her several times on previous visits. She caught me once retrieving Bill and Pauline's mail. She ambushed me at the curb; it was forty-five minutes later that I handed Bill his stack of envelopes, advertising circulars, and periodicals. When I explained the delay, he had laughed and affirmed that yes, the spry, swarthy little woman was nosey, and could be "quite chatty." I had considered that a candidate for the Understatement of the Year award. In those forty-five minutes I had uttered maybe three sentences. If I asked for this favor, I had no doubt she would grant it. But the price would be much too high. I decided to call a cab.

I went inside. Scouting around the phone area in the kitchen I found a pad and pen. I wrote three identical notes to Bill, explaining in less than fifty words what had happened. One I placed by the sink, one I put on the thrift store sofa, the third I taped on the outside of the front door just above the knob. I wouldn't put it past Pauline to open, read, and destroy these communiques. My thinking was that with the multiple copies at least one

122

would reach Bill.

I consulted the Yellow Pages to arrange for a taxi. I changed clothes, stuffed my bag, locked the doors to the house, then stepped out onto the front stoop to await my ride. That was a mistake. Chatty Kathy spotted me. She was out her front door and into the street when the cab pulled up. I gave her a wave and a big smile as I made my escape.

Daytona Beach International is a step up from central Louisiana's AEX, but not a big one. I had time to kill. Rather than pay top dollar for some unknown quantity inside, I crossed Speedway Boulevard and had a Big Mac Combo at a two-storey McDonald's. Then I took a stroll to check out the enormous racing facility beside the airport. When the duffel bag became an issue, I headed back to the terminal. Browsing Hudson News, I found another book by my man, Neal Boortz. I cleared security, walked to the departure gate, then settled down among the other travelers to read and wait for the plane. I halfway expected Bill to call my cell, maybe even come to the airport and have me paged. But he did neither, and I knew why.

We lifted off from DAB on time. In the air I continued with Boortz for a while, then turned my thinking to work. I retrieved a notebook from my bag. This item traveled with me whenever I ventured from Ft. Detrick or from home for any length of time. I opened to a fresh page and began sketching out possible methods for replacing that specific methyl group on the modified RPA-72 molecule with an aldehydic one. This would complete the transformation of 72 into RPA-73. If I scored success tomorrow, Boyd Markham would begin animal tests at once. If 73 protected the mice against ricin, without also proving lethal, I would face the decision of dosing myself with it as a possible antidote for my exposure to RPA-72. By the time we touched down at BWI, I had come up with three novel approaches.

Unlike the hop over, the shuttle back to Frederick Municipal was smooth as silk. I paid my parking fee, and pointed the Tahoe toward home.

I pulled into our long driveway at 8:29 PM according to the dashboard clock. My headlights were on dim, so I didn't notice at first. Closer to the house, I saw the Honda Civic parked near the front door.

Kay was home.

41

"And where have you been?" Kay spoke from the La-Z-Boy. She was watching some old black-and-white movie on TCM. I heard the smooth nasal baritone of Vincent Price. *Must be a horror flick*, I thought. *Fitting*.

"I could ask you the same thing," I replied, toning down my reflexive response, which had I spoken it would have been, "And you have the audacity to ask *me* that question?"

"I left a note," she said, not taking her eyes from the TV screen.

"Yeah, well—let me put this stuff up and I'll fill you in."

I walked down the hall to my bedroom. I placed the duffel on the bed. I went to the bathroom, turned on the hot water at the sink, and let it run. It was a good minute before I could feel the heat. I was tired. It had been a long, unusual day. And Maryland was cold. I splashed the warm water into my face and let it bathe my hands. I felt my body relax. I patted my cheeks and forehead with the hand towel, then returned to the living room.

"Not like you to be out and about on a Sunday night," she said.

"Would you mind muting that?" She hit the button, truncating a blood-curdling scream. She turned to face me as I sank into the heavy pine rocking chair to her left. "I've been to Florida."

"Really? To see Bill?"

A sarcastic retort bubbled up. I was not over my anger at Kay—that was clear. But she was talking, and I needed to avoid derailing that positive development. "Yeah—they went to Georgia for Thanksgiving, and who knows about Christmas? We haven't seen them since summer. I can tell you one thing: Eva hasn't improved."

Ignoring that, she said, "Must have been expensive—last minute and all."

"It won't send us to the poorhouse. Listen, I would have asked you to come along, but . . . ."

". . . you didn't know how to reach me," she finished up. "I have to

124

tell you Paul, I wouldn't have gone—so no harm done. It would have doubled the cost, and to tell you the truth, I'm not that interested in seeing Pauline."

A point of commonality. Perhaps it held the promise of halting our divergence, of placing us on the same page again. So I said, "I mainly wanted to see Bill of course. And I wanted to see Eva and Pauline—but you're right, Pauline is not a pleasant person." I went on to describe in detail my interactions with her. Kay listened closely, nodding, frowning, raising her eyebrows. I felt myself yearning toward her. I felt my tension melting away. This was my baby, my sweetheart, my friend of friends; this was my Pearl of Great Price. I ended by expostulating, "And believe it or not, she kicked me out of the house—just for asking about her child-rearing techniques!"

Kay reacted to that news with, "My God! What's wrong with that woman? And what in heaven's name did Bill see in her?"

This opened the door to sharing information about Bill—and more about Eva. We had a marvelous adult conversation. The discord, the animosity, were gone. There was generous eye contact; Kay even reached over a few times and touched my arm.

I had about concluded that our issue had passed, that we were back together. I was smiling, enjoying once more communion with the woman I loved. There was no need to further apologize for my offense, and I required nothing more from her. I'd confronted one of her major shortcomings, made my case, been authentic, it hadn't gone very well. We'd had our sojourn in the wilderness. That was now over.

Around 9:15 I said, "Listen honey, I'm bushed. I think I'll hit the sack. See you in the morning."

Would we sleep in the same bed tonight? I expected Kay to clarify that.

"I just came to get a few things," she informed. "I'll be staying with my friend at least until mid-week. I'll leave a number."

42

125

I was stunned. I went to my room and shut the door. I heard the TV come back on. A few minutes later it clicked off. The front door opened and shut. I heard the Civic crank, then crunch away down the gravel driveway.

Sleep proved impossible. After almost an hour of tossing and turning, I picked up the bedside phone and punched in 734-8818.

"Pastor Tim Rouzerville. How may I assist you?"

"Tim, Paul Stepping. I know it's late. I apologize."

"Hey, Paul! No problem. Hey, my big day is over. I can sleep tomorrow. By the way, I didn't notice you two in the service this morning. Anything wrong? Beyond what we've talked about?"

"Nothing about that—not directly at least. It's Kay. We're not doing well. She's staying with a friend of hers. She won't say who, or even where. She did leave a number. I'm worried." I paused, not quite knowing where to go with this. I hated talking on the phone. When communicating, body language is huge, and in that regard the telephone delivers zero. Cells, with their quavery voices and spotty reception and perpetually degenerating batteries, are the worst. I appreciate the freedom from wires they provide, and how valuable they can be in emergencies, but this technology has a long way to go in my estimation. And what is it with these people who can prattle for hours—*on* one of these miserable cell phones? To me, that's the very *definition* of hell on earth, but obviously not to—

Tim broke into my two-second reverie with, "Listen, Paul—why don't I come out to your place? We could chat for a while—see if we can get a little perspective on things."

"Oh, no Tim—it's almost 10:00."

"Hey, I told you—Sunday's my big day, and it's over. I have nothing scheduled until noon tomorrow. I'll sleep in. And listen—Grace isn't even here. She left after church today to go visit her sister over in Aberdeen. You know where that is? North Chesapeake Bay, near the mouth of the Susquehanna. You've heard of the Aberdeen Proving Ground. Right in that area. She won't be back until Tuesday. So we're *both* bachelors," he yelled. "Look, I can be there in fifteen minutes. What do you say?"

126

"Well thanks Tim—if it's not too much trouble."

"Trouble's my middle name," he cackled. "Hey, put on some coffee."

I hung up, cheered already. Thank God there are people like Tim Rouzerville in this world: people who are undaunted by your problems, who don't blast you for having them, and who see it as their calling to help you through them. Thank God.

I threw my clothes back on, then went to get that fresh pot of brew started. I set out mugs, spoons, milk, sugar. I walked over to Kay's La-Z-Boy. Mr. Coffee was beginning to percolate. I stretched out, staring at the blank TV screen, struggling to assemble my thoughts.

Before long I heard rap, rap-rap, rap, rap—rap, rap. That little clichéd tattoo was one of Tim's signatures. When I opened the door, he was standing there bright-eyed, grinning, swaddled in his hooded parka. "Man, it's *cold* out here," he announced.

I took his coat and we headed straight for the coffee. We fixed our drinks, wrapping our hands around the warm mugs.

"We keep the thermostat on 68 in the winter. I've probably told you that before." He took the pine rocker and I returned to the recliner. "But you see there's a space heater at your feet. Feel free if you're too cool."

There were two negatives I really liked about this place: no basement, and no fireplace.

Mother's house in Virginia, the one I grew up in, the one Daddy built, has a basement, and a history of basement problems. Every time we got a good rain, water got in. It never flooded, but little rivulets snaked across the cement floor, and things stayed damp. We ran a dehumidifier all the time; because of the water issues, Daddy left the area unfinished. After he died, Mother finally had to have the whole thing redone. It involved major excavation, the installation of underground drain tiles, and waterproofing of the walls, inside and out. It cost Mother a pretty penny. I told her at the time she should just fill the damn thing in. I had decided long before that no house of mine would have a basement.

Fireplaces are different—to a degree. There is something special about a cozy blaze on a chill winter's night, especially if the snow is sifting down outside. It brings on feelings of contentment and well-being; it

127

encourages contemplation. Much of that is mitigated however, if you are the one who has to tend it. In our house, that was me. Keeping us in wood took a lot of work, a lot of time. And it was a dirty proposition: lugging the cut limbs and split logs into the house, flaking off bark and chips and wads of lichen—then shoveling out the cold remains, transferring them ever so carefully to a five-gallon bucket so a mushroom cloud wouldn't erupt to cover the furniture and every other square inch of surface in the room with a fine layer of fly-ash. Then there's the safety issue. We had two chimney fires when I was in high school—very scary. The first burned itself out after a brief period of roaring. The second went on much longer. It sounded like a jumbo jet on take-off. The house shook. I ran outside and saw flames shooting skyward. I thought for sure the house was on fire. It finally subsided, but the flue liner was cracked and had to be replaced. Daddy was alive for these episodes. He placed the blame on me, as keeper of the flame. He said I was using unseasoned wood. That caused creosote to build up in the flue, and this deposit eventually caught on fire. I didn't recall him having warned me about the green wood issue, but he swore he had. It took me a while to get over the trauma of that situation. In addition to the work, the time, the dirt, and the danger, I later learned just how inefficient fireplaces are. It feels good if you're backed right up to it, but all the while it's sucking heated air from the rest of your house, sending it right up the chimney to warm the chilled atmosphere above your roof. We have a heat pump: all electric, clean, heating and cooling with one unit, a single thermostat on the wall. Sweet.

Tim took a sip of coffee, and started rocking. "You said you and Kay aren't doing well. Could you tell me a little more about that?"

I tried to summarize the events of the past nine weeks. I provided considerable detail concerning the walk Kay and I had taken on the Catoctin Trail. I confessed the slapping.

"Well," Tim said, looking thoughtful, "things certainly haven't been routine, have they? You've been a busy boy since we last talked."

"More than I'd like. But time is of the essence."

"Right: three months is what you told me back in September."

I explained my calculation of the Death Period. "It's a nine-day window. Today's December 2. The first day of the window, what in shorthand I refer to as DP-1, is December 13."

He nodded. "Things are indeed narrowing down." He drank more coffee, then stopped rocking and leaned toward me. "Would you say any of your recent actions or activities fall into the extreme category?"

I knit my brow at the question, then said, "No—well, the thing with Kay, but . . . ." I shook my head. "That wasn't planned. That was a stupid reflex."

"What about your colleague, Dr. Smalls?"

I had disclosed my two less-than-professional encounters with Joy. "Certainly out of the ordinary—no doubt about that. I went to her with the idea of sharing my feelings, but I never intended for things to go beyond that—believe me."

"I do believe you." A pause, a small squint of the eyes, then, "And you were not intimate with Dr. Smalls—no sex."

"No—no sex. I can't say I didn't think about it—and that embarrasses me—but no." I could have taken offense at Tim's probing. I considered doing so, concluded I had no grounds, and instead asked, "What's this about extreme?"

"One more thing: Does Kay know about Dr. Smalls?"

"No—no she doesn't."

He resumed rocking. "All right Paul, here's a quote for you: 'I don't like extremes—they get you into trouble.' Who said that?"

"Me—that day we talked in the garden at the church. And that moved us to a discussion of comfort, the status quo, how absence of conflict can lead one to conclude that all is well. I believe at one point you said a good dose of heroin was capable of delivering quite a bit of comfort."

"Yeah, well—" he laughed, "—I guess that was a little strong. I'm bringing this up because you were hoping then that you could find a middle path during your three months—some way for the time to be meaningful, without going extreme—without getting you into trouble. You've now explained that the path you chose was authenticity: being more up front with people, more honest, more genuine." His eyebrows moved up. "Yet wouldn't you agree that you're in a bit of hot water? That this approach

129

has produced some unforeseen consequences?"

"That's for damn sure," I breathed.

"Maybe authenticity is more radical than it seems. There's a spectrum of course, but in my experience, few individuals can be considered authentic; even fewer react well to those who are. And in your case, literally leaping out of the closet as it were, I think it was too much for most people, too much at odds with the Paul Stepping they thought they knew."

I considered that for a moment, taking a swallow of my black brew. "Yep—I think you're right. But it hasn't been all bad."

"Oh, I'm not putting a value judgment on it. That's just an observation—actually a shot at an explanation based on *your* observations, your recounting of how others have reacted to your attempt to be more transparent." He shrugged and wagged his head. "Good or bad? I don't know. I'd say the more important question would be: Has this approach served you? Is it producing the results you had hoped? If your time is drawing near, do you want to run this game to the end, or has your experiment revealed the need to change course—or at least to make some adjustments?"

Good questions. Actually, my results thus far were mixed. Amy was good. I had expected the worst reaction from her, but had gotten the best. I would classify Bill's overall response to my honesty as neutral. He didn't like, or buy, everything I said, but he didn't freak. Joy sort of freaked. I think, like Tim said, that I blindsided her, and being worried sick about propriety, she was thrown off balance. Joel was bad. I really need to go see him. Our interaction that day was incomplete. Pauline was absurd. If I had another twenty years, we might reach some accommodation. And then there's Kay. She's dug in her heels; I've dug in mine: two firstborns, locked in combat. Kay believes she has the moral high ground, and has decided to wait me out. What she doesn't know is how short that wait might be.

Tim must have been reading my thoughts. "My conjecture would be that Kay is your most pressing concern. Do you keep on with her as is, or do you—?"

"Cave—or do I cave? See, that's it. That's been my whole history with Kay. And here at the end, I'm trying to break out of that. It's something I need to do, but I'm convinced it will benefit her as well."

"*You've* decided it will benefit *her* to change her ways."

"Well, yes—it's obvious. If she weren't so stubborn, she'd agree."

"Would Kay like to see you change some of *your* ways?"

"I'm sure she would, but that's just tit for tat."

He gave me a long look. "You still love Kay, don't you? You're not falling for this Dr. Smalls?"

"Of course not. I love Kay—more than ever. I just want to get some things straight before I go."

Another long look. "Why not give her a call?"

"Now?" I looked at the wall clock hanging behind the TV. "It's 10:30. She'll be in bed."

"You're not. Maybe she's having trouble sleeping too."

I doubted that. "I'm not apologizing, and I won't beg her to come home."

"No, no—you don't have to do that. In fact, I wouldn't recommend it." He stopped rocking again. "But I'll tell you one thing: if you dial that number, regardless of what you say or don't say, one message will be sent loud and clear."

"And what's that?"

"Kay, I love you, I'm worried about you, I just wanted to make sure you're okay." He watched me as I evaluated his suggestion. "Paul, she left the number. What do you suppose that means?"

I eased out of the La-Z-Boy and walked to the kitchen counter. I saw the scrap of paper on which Kay had jotted the digits. I picked up the cordless and punched.

"Hello? Who's this?"

I hung up. It had been a groggy male voice. I felt the color drain from my face. I started back toward Tim when the phone rang.

Was it Kay, calling back? "Hello?"

"Daddy? It's Amy." It sounded like she was crying. "Daddy, I'm pregnant! It's Frank!"

131

43

I kept Amy on the phone long enough to calm her down. I told her to get some sleep, and that I would be back in touch. I ended with, "Sweetheart, you're not the first person this has happened to. Try to relax. We'll work things out. I love you."

I placed the receiver back in its recharging cradle.

"Amy—" Tim said, "—she's down in Louisiana, right?"

"Yes." I walked back to the recliner. "She's pregnant—and upset."

"I see," he said, leaning forward, looking up at me, his hands wrapped around his mug of coffee. He waited for me to elaborate. When I didn't, he asked, "And no answer when you called Kay?"

I dropped into the La-Z-Boy. "There was an answer. It was a man."

He blinked and frowned. He eased back and began rocking. "Did you dial correctly?"

"I think so."

"There could be explanations other than what you're thinking."

My mind was frozen, numb. I tried to process the input of the last few minutes. "Yeah, well—I suppose," was my response.

After watching my face for a few seconds, Tim said, "You must be feeling like our Old Testament patriarch, Job: the announcement of one difficulty is hardly complete, before news of the next arrives."

"Yep, that's pretty much it." I was bone tired. It had been a long, worthless day. All this seemed so stupid, so hopeless. Despair welled up—a black, empty, barren thing. It crushed me. For the second time since the accident, I broke down.

44

Tim suffered with me, but was not overcome. What a phenomenal line he walked. His empathy was genuine, yet he remained focused on the big picture. I didn't know if it was a natural gift, or if he had worked to develop this skill over time. Whatever, it was what I needed. I sobbed out

132

my misery; I felt no embarrassment.

My pastor offered to stay the night. I declined. I told him I felt much better, and that was true. "I'll sleep now," I said. "Tomorrow's a big day."

As I left for Ft. Detrick the next morning, thoughts of Amy and Kay were heavy on my mind. But I didn't feel overwhelmed as I had last night. Though somber, I was thinking clearly. Tim Rouzerville was a true man of God. He made the face of the Almighty real in this world.

45

It was Monday, December 3. If I could complete the synthesis of the new protectant today, there would be time for animal tests and self-dosing prior to DP-1. If it took longer, I would have to eliminate this option from my arsenal of hope.

Joy reported another hike in the liver enzymes from Friday's blood work. Still outside the danger zone, she said, but the trend was becoming clear, and it was not encouraging. I asked again about medication. She reiterated her reluctance to go that route, given the poor state of our knowledge concerning the cause or causes of this pathology, and the fact that per se the damage to my liver was neither extensive nor life-threatening. I told her that I might put the finishing touches on RPA-73 today. That brought a smile to her face. We kept things cool. We were professional. I said nothing about Kay moving out. It was like old times: low-key, pleasant, inauthentic.

The EKG again revealed heightened disruptions of the electrical activity in my heart. Mellwood clucked his tongue as he scrutinized the printout. "If this drift continues in Wednesday's test, I'm recommending that pacemaker."

I recalled a deacon in our church. He'd had a heart attack while getting a tooth filled. The dentist had administered CPR, which had saved his life, but his heart was seriously damaged. A pacemaker had been installed, and the man still ushers and helps serve the Lord's Supper at First Baptist. That was fifteen years ago.

I went to my lab, hoping I would not be interrupted by Emmerton or

133

Essex. Emmerton would be absorbed in testing varying concentrations of his most vigorous bond-breaker on the RPA-72/heart protein complex. We had talked about this on Friday, so it would surely be a day or two before he had any results to report. And I figured Essex wouldn't call me unless there was movement on the transplant front, which, from his previous information, seemed improbable.

I settled down to work. On the flight back from Daytona I had come up with three possible pathways for completing the synthesis of RPA-73—three potential methods for slicing off that methyl radical, and replacing it with an aldehyde group. The first approach, the one I considered most likely to succeed, did not. It amputated the targeted methyl, but in addition ruptured several other bonds in the modified RPA-72 molecule. This was confirmed by running multiple samples of the reaction mixture through our gas chromatograph, our mass spectrometer, and our infrared spectrophotometer. My techs worked at top speed, but such tests take time. It was noon before I learned these results. I labored through lunch while my colleagues headed to the cafeteria. Soon after they returned, I had samples from Method-2 for them to analyze. I was amazed when our instruments revealed no changes—none whatever. I debated repeating the reaction. Perhaps I had made a mistake. It was getting late. I rejected the re-do, and went on to my third avenue. This was the procedure in which I had the least faith.

It worked! I hollered for Boyd Markham. I told him to prepare four 20-mouse groups. Tomorrow was Tuesday: no morning appointments with Joy or Mellwood. It was almost quitting time. If Boyd got on the mouse prep first thing tomorrow, and if I synthesized and purified sufficient RPA-73 in jig time, we could begin animal testing before the lunch break. I was excited.

46

Tuesday, December 4. Boyd and I worked steadily through the morning. The prime requirements for test mice is genetic purity. They're not clones (though that is the holy grail for test animals), but their genomes

134

are sufficiently similar that they "breed true," like AKC-certified Weimaraners or Chihuahuas. Still there are slight variations that the expert eye of a Boyd Markham can detect: minor differences in snout length, whisker distribution, pelt sheen, claw curvature, etc. Boyd selected the most anatomically similar mice from a given generation of our population, rejecting any that seemed sluggish, or sickly, or behaviorally aberrant in any way. He chose 80 (40 of each gender) for the groups. He cleaned them up, then placed 10 males and 10 females in each of the four test cages. Meanwhile I performed Method-3 on several batches of RPA-72, converting this compound into its successor, RPA-73. The new molecule had to be extracted from the reaction mixture by cooling until it crystallized. The crystals were then dissolved in a polar solvent, and subjected to low-temperature vacuum distillation. The purified product, a liquid at room conditions, would be given to the mice orally.

Making sure each mouse got the proper dosage was a technically demanding task—another reason Boyd Markham was so valuable. One group would be given 73, then the ricin mist; another would be given 73 only—no ricin; the third, again with no ricin exposure, would be given 72, then six days later would be administered 73. The regimen for this third group was designed to mimic my situation, to see if non-ricin mice exposed to 72 could be saved from death by subsequently being given 73. The 72 had killed mice in a week; giving the 73 on Day-6 would be roughly analogous to my predicament. If Group-3 survived Day-7, I would probably dose myself with the new protectant. The last group would be given RPA-72, then turned over to Emmerton. On Day-6 he would treat these mice with his decoupling agent—if his in vitro tests proved successful.

47

On Wednesday Joy reported that the enzyme levels in Monday's blood had once more inched up. She looked concerned. "There is a medication," she told me as she prepared to take today's sample, "that's billed as a general liver-enhancer. It works by stimulating cell division, the idea being

135

to produce more cells than are dying."

"Sounds good," I said, glad she had finally decided to fill me in on this possible treatment.

She cinched the rubber cord just above my left biceps. "There are side effects," she said, slipping the needle into a bulging blue vein. The Red Cross came often to UVa, and during my student years I donated on a regular basis. I remember one occasion when a smiling phlebotomist referred to such a vein as "juicy." Joy released the cord as the vial began to fill. "It raises your risk of liver cancer. By stimulating general cell division, it also increases the mitotic rate of cancerous cells."

I frowned. "That means the person already has cancer."

"Not usually. Most people have a small population of pre-cancerous and cancerous cells in their liver. DNA repair mechanisms, in conjunction with the immune system, are generally successful at keeping this population low. Sometimes the drug can tip the balance in favor of the cancer. That's why it's reserved for near-terminal cases of cirrhosis and hepatitis."

"I'm near-terminal."

"We don't know that. According to your calculations—assumptions, really—your time is growing short. Your liver function *is* deteriorating, but you are not close to the situations I mentioned. I'm holding off for now."

I moved on to Mellwood, expecting more discouraging news. I was wrong.

"Well I'll be damned," he breathed, showing his stained teeth. "What the hell is going on now?"

"Pacemaker time?" I asked, trying to catch a glimpse of the EKG graph he was holding up to the light.

"No—these serrations have evened out. They're not gone, but you're less arrhythmic than you were two days ago."

Though I was still lying prostrate, still hooked to the leads from the instrument, I didn't protest. Instead I asked, "Could this mean I'm getting better? It's not your machine, is it?"

"No. These newer models have an internal diagnostic that's run before every test. If calibration wanders, it resets it. If there's a hardware defect, it identifies the problem, and you can't continue until that's rectified. So no—it's not the instrument."

His eyes began to dart. I knew what that meant, so I hurried to assert, "Then I'm getting better—things are improving."

Fingering the stubble on his chin, he said, "Your heart is more normal than when we took our snapshot on Monday—forty-eight hours ago. Are you *getting* better? We don't have enough data points to conclude that." I watched his hands begin to search. He wasn't even aware he was doing it. "Let's say my ten-step/threshold phenomenon hypothesis is correct. And let's say we're at Step-7 in your heart. Maybe the products of Step-7 don't interfere with the firing of the nodes, and the tissues begin to heal. But as we move to the final steps, maybe we encounter problems again, and Step-10 is still the killer."

"If you're right," I said, trying to act as if the wind had *not* just been knocked out of my sails, "then the blood taken today would show an improvement in the enzyme levels."

"Yeah, Smalls has this distress hormone theory. So sure: less nodal damage, less hormone, less liver damage, lower enzyme levels. We'll see if that plays out." Then Mellwood seemed to lose interest. He crushed the EKG printout into an ill-folded wad and threw it toward my open chart on the counter. He ripped the electrodes off my body. "I gotta go," he said, then vanished like a ghost.

48

Thursday, December 6. *It's been eleven days since Essex told me about that brain-dead kid in Hampton who has my heart.* I winced as that expression of entitlement wafted through my brain. I didn't feel desperate. Correction: I didn't *allow* myself to feel desperate. I had spent a lifetime keeping my emotions in check. So the bubbling up of this crass uncharitable thought, while disappointing, was likely authentic—which made it doubly disheartening.

I showed the guard at the gatehouse my ID. I snaked the Tahoe through two lefts and three rights before easing into my assigned space in the MMDA lot. I had been doing this for a hell of a long time. MMDA had gone through two renovations during my tenure, but had not changed locations within the fort. I killed the motor. I tried to think back. I couldn't remember that even my parking spot had changed over the last twenty-nine years. Unreal. And now, as the old song said, the days were dwindling down to a precious few.

I sat there feeling nostalgic—lonely. Kay had not come back yesterday. She had mentioned something about mid-week, but . . . . I had gone to the internet and done a reverse check on the number she left, hoping to get a name and address. No luck. Either it was unlisted, or maybe one of those cells you buy at Wal-Mart with no contract and the pre-paid minutes. Courage would have dictated that I call the number repeatedly until I got the information I desired. But I was low on courage. To learn that in addition to being angry with me, Kay was so disenchanted she had felt justified in being unfaithful—that was something I'd as soon not know. I was bereft, weak. I was facing the end essentially alone. If Kay was forsaking me in this way, the Death Period was moot. I was already dead. Ignorance in this matter would not produce bliss, but it might help me stay the course in my final days.

I got out of the car having decided to query Essex about the transplant. Face to face would not be necessary. Once in the lab, I greeted the techs, then walked to the wall phone in my alcove.

There was one ring, then, "Essex."

138

"Paul Stepping sir."

"How may I help you Dr. Stepping?"

"Any further word on the transplant possibility?"

"No. Had there been, you'd be the first to know. Anything else?"

I should have shown some modicum of displeasure at this man's continuing disregard for my feelings. Instead, I felt embarrassed, and trying to sound businesslike, said, "No sir—that's it." I did manage, "We're only a week from DP-1."

"I'm well aware of that Dr. Stepping. I'll keep you informed. Is that all?"

I had planned on asking Essex to contact the boy's doctor again, to impress upon the surgeon the urgency of the situation here, to implore him to plead with the grieving family for my life. But I fell short there as well. "Yes sir," I said. "That's it. Thank you."

No sooner had I hung up the phone than it rang—much like Sunday night at my house. I remembered Tim's comment about Job.

It was Emmerton. "Listen, Paul—just wanted to give you a progress report." He sounded excited. Then again, Ward is perpetually upbeat. "I've found the lowest concentration of the harshest agent that works. You were absolutely right—that approach saved a ton of time. So first thing Monday, if you can spare Boyd, I'm going to dose my group. I know it should be Sunday."

The prep of the four groups of mice had been finalized on Tuesday around noon. If Tuesday is Day-1, then Sunday is Day-6—the day Groups -3 and -4 would be given RPA-73 and Emmerton's decouplant respectively. Only we don't work on Sundays. So Monday, early, would have to do. The timing we had established was certainly not precise. To agonize over this constraint would have been silly.

"Sure. He'll do my group, then I'll send him right over."

"Great! I'll have everything set up so there won't be a second lost."

"Any further theoretical thoughts on this?" I asked.

"Oh, why *some* of the 72/protein complex in the heart might be participating in the sequence of reactions, and some not?"

"Right, and why the portion that does not might later get into the

139

pipeline, causing the end-of-sequence products—the presumably lethal ones—to mushroom?"

There was a pause. "I've thought about it of course. There's just so little hard data. If I had to speculate, I'd say it has something to do with the architecture of the cardiac protein. Proteins in general are big, complicated molecules. Sometimes they can fold in different ways. Maybe this one has two forms. Maybe both of them bond to RPA-72, one less strongly so than the other. Could be after the initial capture, the weaker complex allows its 72 to be lured away into the cascade of reactions. If the strong and weak versions are in equilibrium, depleting the concentration of the weaker would cause a shift—a conversion of strong complex to weak—and a new injection of 72 into the pipeline." Another pause. "A lot of ifs. Just guesswork."

Emmerton stopped talking. I was trying to process what he had proposed. Dead air. I hated phones. Finally I said, "Listen, thanks. We're moving forward regardless of the details. I'll get Boyd to you. Thanks for this good work."

49

With 80 mice to monitor, Boyd Markham had his hands full. Since Tuesday much of his time had been spent observing and recording the behavior of these tiny rodents. Several years ago he had devised a numbered adhesive patch which he had applied to the backs of his subjects. This allowed notes to be kept by animal instead of by group. He had trained two other techs to help him with this tedious and time-consuming task, while he retained sole dominion over the aspects of animal testing that required special expertise. Boyd and his assistants spent Thursday afternoon documenting the activities of our experimentees. I worked with my other technicians synthesizing additional RPA-73. If it proved effective in saving the lives of the Group-3 mice previously exposed to 72, I would need a sufficient quantity with which to treat myself.

The next morning Joy reported that Wednesday's blood *had not* shown an increase in enzyme levels over Monday's. She was pleased, but

140

not surprised, since she had been informed of Mellwood's last EKG results. "Let's trust this trend continues," she said with a bright smile and a pat on the arm as I prepared to leave.

"We can always hope," I replied.

I walked down to Mellwood and discovered that the trend had not continued. The level of arrhythmia was back in the almost-time-for-a-pacemaker range. Recalling our last conversation I said, "Looks like we're past Step-7."

"Yeah," he drawled, his face more thoughtful than usual. "I guess Monday will tell the tale."

Monday would indeed be a big day: Group-3 would receive RPA-73; Emmerton's Group-4 would be treated with his low-concentration decoupling agent; I would see if my heart had continued deteriorating, or if it had somehow changed course yet again; we would discover if my liver enzymes were consistent in mirroring the cardiac changes; and there was always the possibility that Essex would have transplant news.

Things were coming to a head.

50

It was December 7: Pearl Harbor Day. It was almost dark as I pulled out of the MMDA parking lot. This would be the last weekend before DP-1. I dreaded these two days. I needed the structure, the intentionality, of work. If Kay were home—if we were on good terms—I'd welcome the change of pace, even as the eleventh hour drew near. We'd walk The Trail, we'd go to church, we'd watch TV together, we'd make love. I left Ft. Detrick realizing how much I had lost, even before, like the over 2400 Americans had on this date in 1941, I lost it all.

51

Kay was home! I was excited as I crunched to a stop beside her Civic. Then my brain replayed the sound of the voice that had answered the phone Sunday night when I'd tried to call her. That sobered me. What did

141

I do about this? Just ignore it? Let it slide? I had maybe a week of life left—two at the most. As was happening with increasing frequency, a wave of fatigue swept over me. It was not the fatigue that comes at the close of a long workday; it was like the plug was being pulled on my emotional strength; whatever reserves I had drained away, leaving a deep weariness of soul.

At such junctures my end-of-days authenticity program seemed just this side of idiocy. As my time drew near, instead of offending and pushing away those I loved, those who could bring me succor and support, shouldn't I be reeling them in, holding them close, cherishing my dwindling moments among them? That had felt dishonest to me. But why? What about the flip side of honesty? Every human being I know is a mixed bag, including myself. Why is it more honest, more authentic (God, I'm getting sick of that word), to harp only on the problematic? "Ac-cen-tuate the positive, e-lim-inate the negative," an old tune advises; "latch on to the affirmative, and don't mess with Mister In-Between." Why isn't that approach just as genuine as mine? Answer: This is what I've done my whole life; I haven't been satisfied with the results, so I'm changing.

Away from the template of work, when my energy flagged, I went back and forth on this. "A double minded man is unstable in all his ways." So wrote James, the brother of Jesus, in his little New Testament epistle. That's precisely how I felt as I exited the Tahoe and moved toward the front door—and Kay.

52

She was in the kitchen. "Oh, hello Dear. Listen, here's a snack. We can have our meal later if we like. To tell you the truth, I could drop a few pounds. I might skip supper, but I'll make you something."

Literal whiplash involving my neck muscles could not have been more real. I was caught off guard, and it was more than a few seconds before I could reply, "Thanks—what have we here?"

"There's tuna fish sandwiches, celery sticks, peanut butter, Triscuits—and I put us on a pot of coffee."

142

Was this a peace offering? Spread out on the counter were the exact menu items from our Catoctin Trail walk of three weeks ago. Should I comment on that—perhaps make a joke? Was Kay ready to reconcile? Maybe this was her way of exemplifying the issue, of saying in symbols, "Hey, Paul—I'm still waiting for my apology." How was I to know her state of mind?

I was spent, confused, without the resources or the will to engage in mind games. So I fell back to my life-long default position: I played it safe. I said, "Well this looks really good. Let me change and I'll be right with you." In five minutes I returned, clad in the gray sweats I wore around the house in winter.

"Nice match to your hair," she observed with a smile. She had said this kind of thing before, always as a compliment. Maybe she *was* ready to move on.

We took our items to the table. If she wanted to pursue our present complication, fine. But first I needed to tell her about Amy. "Here's some unexpected news," I said as we began to eat.

"Ft. Detrick is closing and you get to retire early with full benefits." Another smile and a little laugh.

"That would be nice—but no, this is about Amy. She called the other night."

"Oh, is she coming home?"

"I don't know. She didn't say she was." I dipped a celery stick into the open jar of peanut butter. I watched Kay. She was steady. I considered raising my eyebrows to indicate I remembered this was the spark that had ignited our now smouldering blaze of contention—but I did not. "What she did say was that she is pregnant."

Kay's face lost its hints of playfulness. "That redneck you told me about—what was his name?"

"Frank. Yes, Frank's the one: the one she can talk to; her emotional water wings."

To me, the definitive characteristic of a true redneck is a kind of good-natured surliness. It's their life force; it allows them to survive, and to accomplish things you'd never think possible for ones lacking in so many

143

ways. I knew boys like that in high school. I was fascinated by their inner strength—their twisted drive. While I wanted to go to UVa and become a chemist, their goal was to get MCHS behind them and become woodchucks. Everyone in Madison County knew the term. Woodchucks were guys who made their living cutting, splitting, and selling firewood. Many of them transported their product to the DC suburbs of northern Virginia, and did damn well peddling to affluent lobbyists, diplomats, and high-ranking government officials. I hoped Frank was such a redneck.

"She's keeping the baby, isn't she?"

"I think so. I reiterated our stance. I told her we'd support her through the pregnancy. I urged her to pressure Frank to step up to the plate—to be by her side until the kid comes, and beyond if she decides to raise it. It takes two to tango; he has a responsibility here as well."

"Indeed," Kay said, nodding. She sipped her coffee. "So you talked with Amy about adoption?"

As was true of most big questions, Kay and I were on the same page here. If you had to go with labels, we were pro-life, seeing abortion for the sake of convenience as a demonstration of inferior morals at best. We were sensitive to the complexities surrounding the issue, but abortion as birth control, a surgical morning-after pill? No, we were not on board with that.

"Yes, I did. She seemed open to it."

When Amy had called Sunday night I had tried to reassure her, and had told her I'd be back in touch. I had called the next evening. That's when we had discussed the possibility of her giving the child up.

"Well good. That would probably be best. I mean, Amy's so young. What kind of mother could she be at this point? And the redneck as a father? Of course I don't know anything about him beyond what you told me. But really, does it seem like either of them is ready for parenthood?"

"It doesn't look good."

"Now, as you said, we'd back her up during the pregnancy. I mean, she can stay here if she wants—if she agrees to a few commonsense rules. You'd go along with that, wouldn't you?"

It had been disingenuous for me to extend *our* hand to Amy, when the likelihood was great that this burden would fall on Kay alone. But what

144

real choice did I have?

"Oh, yes—yes I would. But I'd say wait a month, maybe six weeks. If she's having a lot of morning sickness, missing work, if Frank gets spooked and turns out not to be the great counselor and guide she thought he was, then she'll be anxious to come home under any conditions."

"If she doesn't opt to terminate."

"Well, right—but I don't sense her leaning that way."

Kay hunched her shoulders and squinted. "Morning sickness can definitely turn your head around."

"Oh—Joel," I said. The early stages with Bill and Amy had gone smoothly, but Joel had been another story. With him, Kay had lived in a state of perpetual nausea for the first three months. At one point she had begged me to find a way to render her comatose until the onset of labor. She had not been kidding. "Let's hope Amy doesn't have *that* kind of experience." I smiled at my wife, marveling at her great strength in bearing our three children. "Speaking of Joel, I'm thinking of driving down to see him tomorrow. Would you like to come? I was thinking, *My last encounter with Joel ended in his threat to call the sheriff on me*, but I didn't need to stir that pot. Perhaps Kay would.

She likewise refrained, saying instead, "I'd love to."

I blinked at her quick reply, then asked, "Should we call, or just pop in?"

"Let's pop in, like we did that time at Georgetown."

Kay's reference was to an unannounced visit we had made when Joel was a sophomore. There had not been one square foot of that dorm room not ankle-deep in papers, articles of clothing, and food scraps. The look on Joel's face had been priceless. When I asked how he functioned amidst such chaos, he had given me a wide-eyed look and breathed, "Dad, believe me, I know where everything is."

"Should be fun," I said to Kay. "We'll see if six years has made any difference."

We finished our snack—no commentary on the peanut butter from either of us. We settled down to watch the original 1951 black-and-white version of *The Day the Earth Stood Still* on TCM. Kay relaxed in her La-

145

Z-Boy; I eased to-and-fro in the pine rocker. Half way through the movie she offered to make me dinner. I told her no, not necessary—I'd nuke up something from the freezer. "I think I saw a box of Lean Cuisine Swedish Meatballs, 300 calories—unless that's yours." She glanced over and gave me the go-ahead. I was back in three minutes with my steaming entrée. We enjoyed the rest of this classic film, making occasional comments about the plot, the characters, the acting, how movie-making had changed since The Fifties.

This was warm; this was like old times—almost. It was Friday night, our once-regular love night, but when bedtime came, as we had for some weeks now, we retired to separate rooms.

Still, I was happy. Repairing my relationship with Kay might not save my life, but this evening had felt restorative. I had hope. And tomorrow we would surprise Joel. That *would* be like old times.

53

We took I-270 from Frederick down to the DC area. The Saturday morning traffic wasn't bad. After a short drive east on the Beltway, we turned south, wormed our way through the Chevy Chase shop district, and entered the Capital City on Connecticut Avenue. This took us by the entrance to the National Zoo, the site of many happy summer outings with our children.

I was behind the wheel of Kay's Civic. She avoided the frustration of big-city traffic when possible. Allowing me to pilot her vehicle was another good sign. If she had been nursing residual resentment, she would likely have gritted her teeth and borne the exasperation of driving.

We chatted about this and that, surface topics, neither willing to disturb the scab on our half-healed wound. Kay updated me on the sex ed controversy in her school district. I told her I had decided against more life insurance for now, explaining that maybe we needed to see exactly what our post-retirement income would look like before making that move. She was fine with that. What I could not share was that I had been unable to justify lying about my situation, even to a giant corporation, even to secure

146

significant financial benefits for my wife. It simply wasn't right. At least I had moral clarity about that. Another factor in the decision had been the developments with my liver enzymes and heart arrhythmia. When first considering the insurance deal, they had not been on the radar. Now, it was a good bet the health check would reveal these abnormalities, and I might be turned down anyway. So maybe my morality was not so pure. It helped to know that my death would be ruled accidental, in which case double indemnity would apply. Kay would receive twice the face value of my government policy, and that was a decent chunk of change. We were comfortable as we talked, glad for a respite from the contentiousness that had plagued us.

Joel lived on Florida Avenue, near Gallaudet College, the famous school for the deaf. His apartment was a mile or so from the Capitol. Priding himself on his athleticism and fitness, in addition to regular gym workouts and a jogging regimen, he walked to and from work.

It was late morning. After a little cruising, we found a parking spot on a side street two blocks from his place. We turned our collars up against a biting breeze off the Potomac, and struck out. Not calling ahead was a risk of course, and we had decided if Joel was not home we would leave a note, go for a nice long walk on the National Mall (with Capitol Hill on one end, the Lincoln Memorial on the other, and the great spire of the Washington Monument in the middle), then return to check on him again. If we didn't catch him at all, at least we would have had our exercise for the day.

He lived on one side of a brick duplex: one bedroom, small, but nice. We had been there before, not long after he had gotten the job with Representative Brooks. Joel made decent money. I had asked him at the time why he didn't go ahead and buy a place. He had told me he wasn't sure what direction his life would be taking. The duplex was inexpensive, he had said, and he was pouring all his extra cash into some promising investments. "I'm hardly ever home Dad," he had laughed. "I probably should just get a good-quality tent and camp in Rock Creek Park. Then I'd save even more money." He had gone on to say that when he got married he'd think about buying a house.

We walked up the short sidewalk to the plain white door. "Should we

147

knock?" Kay asked.

"*He* never does," I said. That was true, not that we minded, or had ever insisted that he do so. I placed my hand on the knob and turned. "It's open. Looks like we're in luck." I pushed the door open a few inches and called, "Joel, it's your parents. You hiding someplace in here?"

We stepped inside, shutting out the cold air and the street noise. On a small table just inside the door I saw a wool scarf and a pair of designer sunshades. Joel never wears sunglasses. His rationale is that they weaken the eyes—make them less able to properly adjust to natural changes in light intensity. That made some sense, but I suspected his major motivation was not wanting to hide his striking baby blues from the next admiring female. Amy has blue eyes—sky blue—but Joel's are crystalline, like a couple of Hope diamonds glittering beneath his brows. I nudged Kay, then nodded toward the scarf and the glasses.

We heard noises from the bedroom. The door opened a little, and Joel extruded himself through the crack. He was running a hand through his hair and smoothing down the front of his shirt. "Hey, Mom—Dad; listen— good to see you; have a seat; hey, I was just taking a nap; let me go wash up and I'll be right with you."

The light was low, but his face looked flushed. He pulled the door until it clicked, then disappeared into the bathroom. I thought I detected more sounds from the bedroom, but the burble of running water made it impossible to be certain.

54

Joel emerged more together. He walked over to the sofa, gave his mother a hug, and offered me his hand. "So what brings you two out this brisk December morning?" He backed a few feet across the tiny living room and sat on a metal folding chair. He leaned forward, his forearms on his thighs.

"Well," Kay said, "we hadn't seen you since before Thanksgiving. Plus, we haven't been to DC in quite a while. We thought we'd kill two birds with one stone."

"Yeah, well—it's good you caught me. I'm going out in a few minutes to run some errands." He paused, watching us, perhaps thinking we would take that as a cue to make this visit brief. When we didn't respond he said, "You can go with me if you want. We could eat lunch out. There's this great little place on New York—not far from the White House actually; they know me there; they're busy on Saturdays, but I can get us a table—no problem."

Here we went with the ostentation again. I said, "Oh, no Joel—that won't be necessary." I glanced at Kay. She was cool. "We just wanted to visit a while—you know, touch base."

"Okay—whatever." He sat up straight. He propped an ankle on a knee, shook his Sperry boat shoe a few times, then uncrossed his legs. "So, you guys doing okay? I mean, are things going well now?"

He was of course referring to the slapping incident. And that was the question, wasn't it? How *were* we doing? My answer would be, "Better." Then, if I were to properly qualify that response, I would go on to explain that though we were now speaking to each other, we were not back to normal: we still slept in separate rooms, for instance; and since Kay and I were as yet unwilling to discuss our root difficulty head-on, it had for the moment been by-passed, not resolved. I waited to see how Kay would characterize our status.

But she didn't go there. Instead, she asked, "Joel, isn't it a little early in the day for a nap? I didn't know you took naps."

Bill had always been a nap guy, but not Joel or Amy. Maybe things had changed since they'd gotten out of the house, but based on Joel's history, wasn't this a tantalizing question his mother had asked? I had wanted to hear Kay talk about us; I was almost as interested to see how Joel would respond to this.

"Did I say nap? Shows how groggy I was. Actually I was just getting up. I slept in. Last night was very late for me: work—some things at the office that couldn't wait until Monday. Yeah, I was just trying to catch up. You'd be surprised how many sleep-deprived aides prowl the halls of Congress. I don't want to become one of *those* zombies." He chuckled, shaking his head, glancing back and forth, trying to gauge if either of us

149

was buying this particular line of BS.

A creak, then a light thump, came from the bedroom. "You got someone in there?" I said.

"No, I tell you—this cold weather—the window frames—this is an old building, and when you get these rapid changes in temperature—listen, these windows groan and bump something fierce. In fact, that's what roused me just before you came. Otherwise, I doubt I would have heard you. I mean, I was zonked."

Our younger son was one cool customer, and quite creative. But I said, "I'd like to see that window. Ours are starting to show their age. I'm thinking about replacing them. I've been investigating different designs."

Alarm showed in Joel's eyes. He was about to respond when Kay looked toward the door we had entered and inquired, "Have you changed your position on sunglasses? You used to hate them."

I watched Joel's face relax. "I'm a little older now, Mom. I'm hearing more about UV rays and cataracts and such. I figured I'd better hop on the bandwagon."

"Aren't those women's?" I said.

"No, but to tell you the truth, there's not much difference between male and female styles. I noticed that when I was picking them out."

"And a scarf?" Kay said. "You in a scarf?"

"Believe me, I don't like it," Joel answered with a laugh. "But it's been wicked cold around here. I was freezing walking back and forth to work. The scarf has helped a lot. There were a few jokes around the office, but I figured the increased comfort level was worth it."

Kay nodded. "Good for you. It's a nice item. Must have set you back a little—the shades too."

He grinned, waving a hand around his cramped domain. "You see how I live. I figured a couple of nice things wouldn't break the bank." He raised his eyebrows. "Listen, I need to get to those errands. You guys are welcome to come along."

We rose together. He walked over to give his mother a peck on the cheek and another hug. When he turned to me, I said, "I'm going to take a quick look at that window." Before he could object I was at the bedroom

150

door, my hand on the knob.

I turned it and pushed. A woman stood there, looking at me. She was somewhere in her thirties, almost my height, with short black hair and a smooth face. She had on an overcoat. She was ready to leave.

"I'm Paul Stepping," I said, extending my hand, "Joel's father." Her paw was damp. "You're Representative Brooks, Joel's boss. I've seen pictures."

She nodded, her lips pressed tight. She eased past me and moved toward the front door, where Kay and Joel were standing.

Joel looked ill. "Versa," he said to the woman, "this is my mother, Kay Stepping; Mom, Congresswoman Versa Brooks." The two shook hands.

The moment was awkward, riveting. What would happen? What did authenticity demand of me? Perhaps it was enough that Joel's little charade was being disclosed to his parents.

Versa Brooks said, "Good to meet you both." Then to Joel, "Bright and early Monday morning." She reached down for her wool scarf and her designer eyewear. "Bye-bye," she said, and was gone.

55

Joel's face had lost color. He stood there, looking at us, at a loss for words.

Kay broke the silence with, "I guess those errands can wait. Let's talk about this for a while."

When I had broached the issue of the congresswoman with Joel the day of the slapping, he had told me it was none of my damn business, that he was a grown man, and he didn't have to answer to me. Of course the context then had been much different. Let's see how he would respond to his mother.

We returned to our seats. Kay and I waited for Joel to go first. Finally he said, "Mom, I'm seeing Versa—socially. I guess that's obvious." He stared at the floor between his shoes.

151

"Is that what they call sleeping with the boss these days? Joel, this can't be healthy."

The response of my brain to this stimulus was a replay of the sleepy male voice I had heard the night I tried to call Kay. Maybe she was sleeping with *her* boss. I knew she liked her principal. She raved about him all the time.

"Mom," Joel said, "it's okay. We're discreet, and it doesn't interfere with our work."

"Discreet? You didn't even lock the front door."

"Well, that was an oversight."

"A fairly large one," I breathed.

He shot me a look, but said nothing.

Kay said, "Why all that foolishness about the window, and lying about the scarf and sunglasses? We're your parents. Be straight with us. Maybe we'll have something helpful to offer."

I should have held my tongue, instead of saying, "Joel has quite a bit of trouble being straight with anyone. He puts people on—even his parents. And he's good at it; now he does it professionally. Only this time things didn't go so smoothly. He messed up."

"Do we want to re-hash all this, Dad?"

Kay frowned. "Re-hash?" She looked at me. "You two have had this conversation before?"

"Basically, yes."

"That day before Thanksgiving," Joel elaborated, "when I came to Frederick: you and I talked for a while, Dad came in, you went to your room, then the two of us had quite a discussion. He enlightened me about how I snow people—BS them all the time. I informed him that he likewise is a snowman, but a passive one. He keeps his head down, hoards information, allows others to conclude things about him he hopes will be positive, regardless of whether they are true or not. I'm more pro-active, attempting to mold the opinions others have about me."

"Regardless of whether they are true or not," I interjected.

"Well, of course—that's the whole object of putting people on, isn't it?" I was prepared to respond, but Joel continued. "Dad thinks his passive

152

form of BS is morally superior to my aggressive form. I disagree."

Kay was taking all this in. She said, "That's an interesting slant on the masks human beings wear. I've never thought about passive BS." She gave me an appraising stare for a moment, then turned back to Joel. "And I never considered you a con man—exactly. You're clearly more outgoing than Bill—even than Amy. That's the way I've seen you: outgoing and gregarious. But I suppose those characteristics can shade over into putting people on. That's definitely what's happening with your lady friend. You—and she—are hoodwinking every constituent in her congressional district. What do you think would happen if the voters back home knew about this?"

"They're not going to know," Joel said, "unless you or Dad tell them. And it has nothing to do with them. Versa does her work, I do mine, life goes on." When Kay's face indicated that this glib pronouncement was insufficient, he added, "Look Mom, people have jobs, and people have private lives. Some things they do in their private lives affect their jobs, and some things do not. The things that do affect their jobs *should* be known to those the job impacts. The private things that do not affect their jobs are of no concern to those the job impacts. And that's the situation with Versa and me. Our private involvement has zero effect on our jobs, thus zero impact on those our jobs serve, and is therefore of no legitimate concern to them."

I had to give Joel a thumbs up. He sounded like a Georgetown Jesuit theologian, steeped in logic, laying out his argument for papal *ex cathedra* infallibility, or perhaps for the necessity of purgatory. "Your syllogism is impeccable," I said, "but your conclusion is suspect if your premises are debatable. How have you determined that these hush-hush liaisons with your boss have nothing to do with your job performance, or with hers? How could you know that?"

"Easy," Joel said. "I know what we did before we began our relationship, and I know what we do now. There's no difference."

Kay spoke up. "Maybe you and Ms. Brooks are conning *yourselves*—fooling *yourselves* into thinking there's no problem, so you can continue playing around."

The tack Kay was taking with Joel gave me comfort for two reasons: she wasn't using my spat with him as a pretext for renewing *our* hostilities (she could easily have taken his side against me); her seeing Joel's involvement with the congresswoman as objectionable, increased the odds that she herself was not seeing anyone—unless, of course, she was playing the hypocrite.

He looked at his mother and shook his head. "No Mom, we're not. This is no big deal. And to be honest, as I told Dad, it's none of your business. No disrespect, and I appreciate that you're worried, but you need to forget about this. It's not a problem." A pause, not long enough for Kay to reply. "What *is* a problem—well, maybe not a problem, but something that screams for an explanation—is Dad's recent conversion from BS-passive to BS-aggressive." Joel laughed, but I didn't, and neither did Kay. "I'm guessing it has to do with getting close to retirement at Ft. Detrick. Dad's probably thinking, *Less than a year; time to take off the happy face; they won't like it, but what the hell; as long as I pull my weight—do my job to the last day—there's nothing they can do.* Am I right Dad?"

Joel was turning the tables. But that was okay. We now knew his secret. He knew that we knew. And Versa Brooks knew that we knew. That should throw a fair amount of ambiguity into their little set-up. So if Joel wanted to shift the focus to his father for a while, fine.

"Somewhat," I replied. "It does have to do with work. Something happened there that made me re-think my position."

"Your BS position."

"That's your terminology. But yes, I began wondering about transparency—about the value of that, versus the value of being more opaque. As you observed, I tend toward the opaque. But I began questioning that stance, questioning if it has served me adequately, and to what extent it has benefitted those I interact with. I disagree that being more open about what I think and how I feel, equates to the kind of spinning and manipulation I've seen in you. It certainly hasn't resulted in my improved reputation among others." I chanced a look at Kay.

"Maybe you're not that good at it, Dad. You need to hone your skills. I can help you with that."

154

Joel said this with a straight face. I didn't know if he failed to get it, or if he was pulling my leg. I said, "It's an experiment of sorts. It's my own deal. I don't need help."

He gave a shrug, and Kay said to me, "So that's what the peanut butter was about?" She squinted. "What in the world could have happened, at *work* of all places, to provoke this 'experiment' of yours? And why the abruptness? If you'd given me a heads up—some context, like you're doing now—we might have avoided what happened on The Trail."

I was saying too much. If I died within the next two weeks, and if Essex got wind that Kay or anyone else outside Ft. Detrick had any inkling that my demise was work-related, he would go right by the book in denying her the financial benefits that would normally convey. He wasn't about to put his promotion on the line just because Paul Stepping talked out of school. I needed to backtrack.

"I say it has to do with work. That's really not accurate. Years ago Tim Rouzerville gave a sermon entitled 'Blunt Is Not Bad.' His point was that even Jesus had not always been a nice guy—that he confronted people, from the Pharisees to Simon Peter to his own parents, when the occasion demanded—and that we today might profit if we stopped dancing around certain issues in our lives. That stuck with me, probably because it's so different from the way I've historically operated." This much was true. Now I began to obfuscate. "A couple of months ago I overheard two of my techs having a conversation. These guys are friends, and it had to do with something they had done together the previous weekend. One of them complained that the other had been late picking him up. He went on to state that this was a chronic problem, that it inconvenienced others, and that the friend should be thoughtful enough to correct it. That reminded me of Tim's sermon, and I thought maybe I should give this approach a try." There had been no such conversation. "So this triggering event, if you will, *happened* at work, but it had nothing to do with my *scientific* work. It could have happened anywhere."

Had I repaired the damage? My attempt to do so had led me to out-and-out lying. Ah yes—very genuine, very frank, thoroughly authentic.

"So just like that," Kay said, frowning, "this new approach. Why not

155

clue me—us—" she indicated Joel, "—in?"

I tried to wrap up my song-and-dance with, "You're right—I should have. I just didn't want to introduce another variable. If you knew what I was up to, it might have mitigated the effect." That was weak, lame, but it was all I could come up with at the time. "Sorry," I said.

So here I was again, ducking my head, apologizing, dissembling, reverting to type. Yet it was not *sheer* weakness. Of course I wanted to deflect criticism. But this instance of backsliding was for Kay, to preserve her shot at a decent life after I was gone.

She looked at me with somber eyes. Then she reached over and pressed my arm. I hadn't felt her touch in weeks. A mild shudder rippled through my shoulder blades. I placed my hand on hers, and offered a smile that came from the most authentic place I could find.

Joel widened his eyes and said, "Maybe I should go—leave you two alone. I really do need to swing by the bank and post office."

I watched for Kay's reaction, thinking she might accept that offer. But she said to Joel, "I know our walking in on you was awkward. And you're right—it's your life, your business. Just give the whole situation some serious thought." She stood and I followed. "We love you son. We only want what's best for you."

Joel's relief was evident as we said our good-byes.

Kay and I decided to walk the Mall, stopping to eat in the subterranean cafeteria of the Natural History Museum. It was a long hike. Including the lunch break, it was three hours before we made it back to the car. The skies had been clear when we left Frederick this morning. Now they were turning gray and lowering.

The weather held until we reached home. The first flakes began to drift down as we pulled up beside the Tahoe. We hurried inside, glad to be under our own roof this snowy winter night.

Kay shrugged out of her jacket, placed her purse on the kitchen counter, then said, "Guess who I saw in town a few days ago?"

"I'll go with my ultra-religious cousin, Fake Blake." Blake lived in Virginia. He never came up our way, but I thought it might be a good joke.

She laughed. Still smiling she said, "No, it was your colleague, Joy

156

Smalls."

56

My heart thumped. The thud was so powerful, I heard it as much as felt the impact. I wondered if the sound waves had propagated to Kay, because she cocked her head. Then I wondered if my unsound pump could take such an abrupt change.

"Are you all right Paul? You're frowning. You look pale."

I guess she hadn't actually heard the hammer blow, but was reacting to a change in my expression. "Oh, sure—I'm good. It's just surprising you would see her." I took a breath and formed a smile.

Kay had met Joy once, at a Christmas get-together for MMDA personnel. This was BE (Before Essex). When he came on board five years ago, he put a stop to such foolishness.

Kay watched me with alert eyes. "Like you," she chided, "the good doctor *does* have a life outside Ft. Detrick."

Now why would she put it like that? Joy has a life outside work, *like me*. And why the reproof in her voice? "Well, of course," I said. "Boy, don't *you* have a good memory?"

"She's hard to forget." Kay headed to the refrigerator. "Want a Diet Coke?"

"Sure. Let me change."

I went to my room, returning minutes later in my house sweats. Kay was in her recliner. She handed me a cold can as I dropped into the rocker. She had already popped the top.

I realized I was tired. The Mall walk had been a good seven-to-eight miles. We'd burned a lot of energy; we'd depleted our fluids. I also realized I was chilly, so I leaned forward and dialed on the electric heater at my feet. Why cold drinks instead of hot chocolate or coffee, I didn't know. Too much trouble for either of us at this point I figured. We just wanted to relax. But Joy Smalls was not a relaxing topic of conversation—not for me at least. Still, I wanted to know more about this encounter.

I took a swallow of the soda, enjoying the frosty tickle of the

157

carbonation as it slid down my dry throat. Then I asked, "So what did you two talk about? Or maybe you just caught sight of her from a distance."

"No, it was at the Walgreens on West Patrick."

"Did she recognize you?"

"It didn't seem so. She was in the card aisle. I was headed to the pharmacy to refill my Premarin prescription. I said, 'Hello, Dr. Smalls.' She turned to me with this blank stare. 'Kay Stepping,' I said. 'We met at a Christmas party seven years ago.' Her mouth flew open and her face transitioned from white to sunburn-red in a matter of seconds. It was remarkable. She was still silent, so I added, 'You work with my husband, Paul.' The color began to drain, she apologized for her exaggerated response, and we began to chat—about you: the only thing we have in common."

Kay was watching me again with those vigilant eyes. I chuckled, "No doubt good things were said," hoping my little laugh didn't sound nervous.

"Oh, for sure. She's deeply impressed with you: considers you a top-notch chemist, and a—how did she put it?—'a sensitive and understanding friend.'" Kay scrunched up her face and blinked. "I didn't think you actually worked with her."

I knew the elaborated version of this question was: If you don't really see her all day every day at work, and if you don't have contact with her outside of work (you don't, right Paul?), then how have you become this sensitive and understanding friend? I took a deep pull on my Diet Coke before saying, "Joy compliments everyone—often to excess. It's just the way she is. We've known each other the biggest part of a decade. I like her. She's a good doctor, and a nice person. On some level I guess it's accurate to say we're friends." I was over-explaining here, as I had at Joel's. I stopped talking and drank more beverage.

"Nice-looking too," Kay stated.

I tried to seem thoughtful, clinical. I shrugged and said, "I suppose—but not in your league."

"Come on Paul: that skin, those eyes, that hair—don't tell me you haven't noticed. I was struck, and I'm a woman."

"She does stand out," I acknowledged, "but so do you. Listen, I'm

158

glad you saw her."

I wanted this to end. I was uneasy. I was playing a double game, and I couldn't find the strength to come clean."

Kay said, "Look, on Monday tell Joy I'd like to get together with her sometime. Try to get me her number. I'm thinking maybe we could strike up a friendship." Then she asked, "Hey, you want to watch a movie?"

Darkness had fallen—always a surprise on these short winter days. We didn't actually have a porch: just a small shingled overhang protecting the cement slab in front of the door. There was a light for this area, and it was on. Through the small window in the top half of the door I could see that the snow had picked up. It was wet, falling in clumps straight down. If this kept up all night we'd be snowed in.

"Sure. What's on?"

"Are you picky?"

"Not at all. You choose."

"*Doctor Zhivago* on TCM. That is one gorgeous production—a real classic too."

As the film began I found myself thinking, *Kay and Joy, friends—now there's a disaster waiting to happen*. But that was based on the belief that at some point these women would clash over me. The arrogance of that assumption soon struck, along with the absurdity of it. Two weeks from today I'd likely be gone. I doubted they would clash much over a dead man.

And speaking of friends, what about Kay's woozy-sounding chum? Maybe that guy had not been sleepy. Maybe he'd been drunk. So when I had called, Kay was either sleeping with the man (likely her principal), or at some party with him, and they would hop into the sack later. At least *Kay* didn't drink. Or did she, on certain occasions? We were teetotaling Baptists, right? Not that you heard much about total abstinence from alcohol from the pulpit or in the denominational literature anymore. There were good reasons not to drink. You didn't need a religious doctrine to persuade *me*. (I took a swallow of my soda.) The night of the phone call, Tim Rouzerville had told me this did not necessarily mean Kay was being unfaithful. Sure, Tim. God, I wish I'd never heard that groggy voice! (I drew in a deep breath, then let the air escape slowly through my nostrils.) This was stupid. Stewing over this, as I had since that night, was stupid. What I needed was *facts*—hard data. I should just come out and ask Kay. She'd tell me the truth, wouldn't she? But had I told her the truth about Joy Smalls? Then it hit me, and I almost said, "Oh my God!" out loud. The last time we had sex, the last time we shared a bed, the night before our disastrous November walk on the Catoctin Trail, *had I talked in my sleep*? Kay has told me I do that from time to time.

I tried to focus on the long movie, tried to banish these thoughts from my mind. The 1965 production, starring Omar Sharif in the title role, was based on Boris Pasternak's novel. It was, as Kay had said, gorgeous. Set against the backdrop of the 1917 Bolshevik Revolution, the ensuing Russian Civil War, and World War I, the scenery was indeed stunning. But the violence, the political turmoil, was discomfiting. Yuri Zhivago's tangled relationships with his spouse and two lovers troubled me. And near the end, the scene of Sharif shambling after a streetcar transporting his wife, calling her name while clutching his chest in the throes of a fatal heart attack—that seemed prophetic.

We had decided against supper, instead munching popcorn and pretzels as the film ran. Though we'd had a longer than normal walk, our lunch at the Natural History Museum had been high-calorie; we could easily forego the evening meal.

I was wrung out. Kay and I had spent a good day together. She let me give her a kiss on the mouth before we retired to our rooms. I closed my door wondering what she knew about Joy Smalls.

57

Sunday morning dawned clear. It had not snowed all night. I estimated four inches of wet near-slush on the ground. Travel would not be impeded. Church would not be called off.

It was egg day. I remembered the spat Kay and I had had shortly after my accident. We had run out of eggs. I had gone to Virginia that Saturday to visit my mother. Kay had stayed home. When I returned that evening,

160

she told me she had noticed we were out, but then had forgotten, and had not gone to town to replenish our supply. I was in the early stages of my get real crusade, so I made some comments about her shortcoming. She had been hurt. I had gotten back in the car and headed for Wal-Mart, where I had an altercation with an obese woman, and had attracted the attention of store security. I fled, and on my way home had picked up a dozen very expensive hen-fruit from a convenience store. The next morning we'd had our eggs in silence, then had gone to church where Tim Rouzerville had preached a sermon on The Golden Rule. The upshot was repentance on my part for general un-Christlikeness, and a verbal apology to Kay.

All that seemed eons ago. I scanned the hard drive document in my brain entitled "Since September 19." So much had happened. Though I had not opted to "go big time" (as Tim had put it during our first talk), I was definitely getting my money's worth of living.

It had been weeks since Kay and I had enjoyed our traditional Sunday morning breakfast. But today we did. I scrambled the eggs to perfection while she prepared the toast, coffee, and juice. We ate and chatted, deciding to skip Sunday School, but to attend the worship service. I was getting little from Clay Winslow's class. Kay joked she'd rather have the 613 Old Testament laws, plus the genealogies from the book of Numbers, read to her for three hours straight, rather than sit through another of Clay's arid forty-five minute monologues.

That afternoon we walked The Trail—north this time—agreeing with a look not to re-visit the scene of our crimes. It was so domestic, so normal, so much a part of our lives together for all these years. We smiled, talked, held hands, laughed. It simply was not possible that this joyful journey, this great blessing, was coming to an end.

58

When I arrived Monday morning, Boyd Markham was already there, preparing to deal with the four groups of mice. This was the day. What the

161

animal tests revealed, together with my EKG results later in the morning, would provide data to guide some important decisions. This was December 10. Thursday would be DP-1, the first of my calculated nine-day Death Period. I draped my jacket on a wall-peg in the alcove, then slipped into my lab coat. I walked to the center of the laboratory where three stainless steel cages, clearly labeled, were lined up on a cart. It had been rolled from the animal room directly under one of the banks of bright fluorescents. Emmerton had the fourth cage.

Boyd was bent at the waist, his face close to the top of Cage-1, peering through the wire at his subjects. As I approached he glanced my way and said, "So far so good. They're still alive. They look fine."

Last Tuesday Group-1 had received RPA-73, then had been exposed to ricin mist. So the 73 was protecting the mice against the ricin (as had 72), but it had not killed them (as had 72)—yet. The 73 could prove fatal; it might just take a little longer. Still, it was encouraging news for the project. If this band of rodents outlived me, MMDA personnel stood a chance of witnessing a first: Essex smiling.

I nodded, said, "Great," then looked into Cage-2.

"This is the 73-only group," Boyd said, running the back of a fingernail across the closely-spaced wires. The mice rustled amongst their bedding of cedar shavings. "These guys are good too."

Welcome information—but again, who could tell about the timing with this new molecule?

"Now for your group," Boyd said. All the techs knew my situation. He stood straight and turned to face me. "We're all pulling for you Dr. Stepping."

"I know you are Boyd." I reached out and touched his shoulder. "Thanks so much for all your good work."

More could have been said, but time was of the essence.

"Group-3 here was given 72 last Tuesday," he said. "They're fine now, but we know from previous testing that these animals will die later today, tonight, or early tomorrow. So I'm about to dose them with the new compound. We'll soon know if RPA-73 will function as an antidote."

I took a deep breath, then let the air balloon my cheeks as I puffed it

162

out. "Very good. I'll let you get to it. And as soon as you're done, hustle over to Emmerton's lab for Group-4."

This last bunch was also "my" group. Having likewise been administered RPA-72 almost a week ago, Boyd Markham would now give them Emmerton's decouplant, the hope being that *it* might prove a counteragent.

My talented technician gave me a smile and a thumbs up. "I'm on it Boss. I think we've got this thing licked."

59

Until the results on RPA-73 were in, my work was on hold. If the Group-1 mice survived, the next step would be to tinker with the dosage— to find the upper and lower limits of 73's protective ability. Generally speaking, when any foreign substance is introduced into the body, less is better. Calculations would then be done to translate this optimum dose into a per pound value, making it useful for human application. The test animals were being given the pure liquid product, the tiny amounts delivered orally with micro-pipettes. I had discovered RPA-73 to be soluble in a polar organic solvent. Water is polar, but it did not work. Dissolving the protectant would allow a dose to be delivered in a larger volume of liquid, making it easier to work with. But testing was needed to find a diluting agent less harsh than the one I used in the purification process. Then there was the question of stability. Perhaps to extend its shelf life, a preservative would have to be developed. If the Group-1 animals survived, I would address all these issues—or someone would.

I returned to the alcove, busying myself with realigning the several dozen chemicals I used most often. They were arranged alphabetically. I decided to rank them in order of frequency used. Wouldn't that be more efficient? Whatever. I was just trying to stay occupied until it was time to go see Joy Smalls.

60

When I walked into her office, Joy was studying a single-page document—my lab report from Friday, I presumed.

"Enzymes are back up," she said, her face serious.

"The last EKG showed the arrhythmia had returned. The enzyme levels continue to track the heart situation, which lends credence to your distress hormone theory."

"I guess," she said. "But that's cold comfort, because it doesn't suggest a treatment. What about your mice?"

As Joy drew my blood I filled her in on the status of the animal tests, ending with, "It'll be later today—maybe tomorrow morning—before we know anything definitive. The next big thing will be Mellwood. He said if this EKG showed further intensification of the electrical problem, he was going to recommend a pacemaker."

She taped a pad of sterile gauze over the puncture site. "Not a bad idea. Any word from Essex on the transplant?"

"No. He won't pressure the people in Virginia. I've about given up on that option." I moved to the examination table.

"Have you considered going yourself?"

"Where?"

"To Virginia. Essex told you the hospital. You go down, make some inquiries, appeal to the family yourself."

"That wouldn't fly," I said, reclining, waiting for Joy to begin palpating my upper abdomen. "It would surely get back to the Major—soon to be colonel—and since that would constitute a clear violation of my security obligation, Kay would get nothing upon my death. Should I survive, my employment would be terminated, and my retirement benefits would be down the tubes. So, no—I have not considered going to Virginia."

"You don't think Essex would cut you some slack, given the uniqueness of this situation?"

"I don't think he'll let much of anything stand in the way of his promotion."

She considered that for a moment, then nodded. "Paul," she said, pushing harder up under my ribs, "I'm feeling some enlargement here—not

164

much, but it wasn't there Friday."

"I'm assuming that's not good."

"Enlargement is generally a sign of a liver that's struggling. It's minor, but it's something new." She removed her hands. "You can button up."

"What about that medication you mentioned? Should I go on that?"

"Let's see what Mellwood finds today, and what this new blood shows. I'm reluctant to prescribe it, but I haven't ruled it out."

I slipped off the table. While Joy made notes in my chart, I tucked in my shirttail and got back into my lab coat. "Don't wait too long," I cracked. "DP-1 is Thursday. I'm practically dead man walking."

She turned to me, her green eyes somber. "We don't need that kind of talk Paul. I told you before, these calculations of yours about the Death Period—they're based on debatable assumptions. That means you could certainly be off on the time frame. Then there's the mouse/human liver comparison. True, my vet friend over at MRIID confirmed the differences in physiology are few. But who knows? Maybe they're significant. What about your own specific genome? Could be there's something unique in your genetics that will enable you to weather this storm." She moved a step closer. "I know you were joking, but . . . ."

We watched each other for a moment. I said, "You're right—there's always hope." Then I tacked on, "Kay says she saw you in town last week."

Joy broke eye contact. "Yes, I think it was Tuesday." Color seeped into her cheeks.

"She said your response was exaggerated."

"Well, she surprised me."

"You might have mentioned it."

"Was it important that I do so?"

I thought about that. "I guess not—not really. It's just that to my knowledge you've only seen her one other time, and given what I've shared about the difficulties she and I have been having, I figured actually bumping into her—well, it seemed that would have made quite an impression, and that you would have told me about it. But important?" I

165

gave a shrug. "No."

"If she brought it up, you two must be doing better." The look on her face was bland, almost blank. She spoke without inflection.

"Somewhat," I said, then wondered why I had chosen that response. But I knew. I didn't want to close the door on the possibility of Joy and me. That was it. I wanted to believe I was a half-way decent man. Reactions like this made me wonder. I hurried on to add, "By the way, she asked if I would get your number. She wants to get together with you. She thinks you two could be friends."

Now Joy's face showed some expression. "I'm not sure that would be wise," she breathed.

I couldn't pursue this. It was time to go see Mellwood.

61

Mellwood met me with the words, "I've made the preparations." Then before I could ask what that meant, he said, "I told you not to hold your breath."

I remembered him saying something along those lines in the initial meeting with Essex. "The transplant," I said. "Yeah, that's a no-go."

"The Man wouldn't step up to the plate for you, would he?"

"He could have done more—in my view."

Mellwood snorted. "In *anybody's* view. Hey, you don't have to be nice. This place isn't bugged—I hope. If I were in your shoes, I'd go ahead and tell Essex what an ass he is."

I looked around the office. "If you're wrong about the bugging, you just did."

"Yeah, well—I'm not your warm fuzzy type, but that bastard is cold."

Mellwood was a strange one: blunt, brusk, sarcastic—but with a soft spot in there somewhere. Physician-wise, with little-to-no bedside manner, Ft. Detrick was a good fit. His patients, rule-oriented businesslike types, needed little coddling. "Are you married?" I asked.

Malcolm had come on board when our previous cardiologist, an Army

166

doctor, had been transferred to Walter Reed. That had been a couple of years before Joy. I still didn't know his marital status, this basic fact about him. I realized my question was a forward one, but I was no longer that concerned about propriety.

"Divorced," he said.

"Children?"

"Yeah, two—with their mother. I see them pretty often. They're in high school, over in Bowie."

I smiled and said, "Well good. Listen, you planning to quit smoking?" Anther nosy question: this one I wanted to ask Mellwood every time I saw him. He seemed stumped, so I elaborated. "You know, your kids and all." Anger flashed in his eyes. I retreated. "None of my business Malcolm. Sorry."

He looked away. "No problem. You're right. It's stupid, but I'm hooked. The illustrious C. Everett Koop said tobacco is more addictive than heroin. I don't know about that, but it's got me. I'd rather smoke than eat."

"That's powerful," I said. "But there are plans, medications, patches, gum—even hypnosis; you know all this." I reached out and tapped his arm. "Hey, I might be checking out soon. You don't want to beat me to it. They won't admit it, but kids need their dads at least through college." I gave a little laugh, trying to take the edge off this serious talk.

Mellwood said, "Yep. Maybe I can work this into some kind of New Year's resolution." I started to offer that my one and only hope for the new year was to actually make it *to* the new year, but he was already moving toward the EKG area.

"You mentioned you've made preparations," I said to his back.

"Yeah—in case we need to go the pacemaker route. Go ahead and lie back." He began fiddling with the leads to the EKG unit. "I've lined up an anesthesiologist and a surgical nurse from MC4. If what we find in the next few minutes warrants it, they'll come tomorrow morning. I can do the procedure here, but I need help." (MC4 is the Medical Communications for Combat Casualty Care unit.)

Mellwood hooked me up, and while the details of my heart's electrical

167

activity were being traced out on graph paper, he gave me a briefing on pacemaker/implantable cardioverter defibrillator (ICD) insertion. I would be on my back, and would be sedated via IV, though not to the point of unconsciousness (unless I became agitated or otherwise unruly). A local anesthetic would deaden the area under my left collarbone. A blood vessel there would be opened, and a plastic tube inserted into it. Through this sheath, the lead wires for the pacemaker and/or ICD would be introduced and advanced to my heart. Mellwood would follow the progress of the leads by means of a fluoroscope. Once in the chambers, they would be tested to verify proper functioning and placement. More topical anesthesia would be injected beneath the collarbone, and another incision made near where the lead wires protruded from the sheath. The wires would be attached to the heart-regulating device; it would then be slipped under the skin through the new opening, and the wires pressed into a slit made between the sheath and device incisions. More tests would be done to insure all systems were go. Everything would then be closed tight with surgical glue, and a sterile dressing applied. In preparation, I would have to fast overnight—no food or drink after 10:00 PM. Some recovery time was required, but assuming the procedure was done before noon, I could likely drive myself home at quitting time.

Mellwood's explanation was clear and concise. And he was into it. He bent over so I could see his face, maintained eye contact, and didn't seem dogged by the need for a smoke. "If you get this thing," he concluded, "forget about MRIs. The magnetic field plays havoc with the programming. Same with airport security. Walking through the screening portal might be okay, but the hand-held detectors—no. They bring them too close. If it were me, I'd tell the guy, 'Hey, I've got a pacemaker—frisk me,' and steer clear of *all* that." He glanced over at his instrument. "Anyway, we're getting ahead of ourselves. You're done." This time he promptly removed the electrodes from my chest, wrists, and ankles. "Let's check your readout." He walked over to the machine and tore off the tape.

I sat up, waiting for the verdict. It was not long in coming.

"We have an escalation," he announced. "Look." He stepped over and smoothed two feet of the narrow graph out on the cushioned surface

168

beside me. "The serrations have deepened significantly."

It was true. The notches in Friday's graph had looked like those in the blades of Kay's steak knives. These reminded me of Grandpa Stepping's crosscut saw. "How bad are we?" I asked.

Mellwood continued studying the printout. "The good news," he said, "is that your heart is strong, the rate is steady and mid-range, and there's no evidence of disease or any valve issues. I've been saying pacemaker because it's the familiar term. You don't need a pacemaker; you *do* need an ICD. You're headed for a fibrillatory event. That's likely what happened to your mice. If your heart begins that uncoordinated flutter, this device will deliver a corrective shock. A fibrillating heart can't pump blood. You'd be dead in minutes." He folded the graph. "So, first thing tomorrow morning. I'm assuming you're willing."

"Yes, I am. Given the new data, it makes sense to go this route. It sounds like the ICD is a tested technology that's minimally invasive. The transplant option I'd classify as dead. The two chemical possibilities have yet to play out. So sure—tomorrow morning, me, here, with an empty stomach."

"Good. I'll notify Essex."

Now Mellwood's eyes were beginning to dart.

"But look," I said, "one request."

"Yeah, what's that?"

"Before I place my life in your hands, please, have a cigarette."

It was a joke—sort of.

62

I had had enough social interaction for one morning. After notifying Boyd Markham, I took my lunch and left the building. I would eat in the Tahoe.

It was cold. I cranked the big engine; soon warm air was issuing from the vents. Wasteful, but what the hell? I flicked on the radio to AM 790, where I knew I would find "America's Rude Awakening," Neal Boortz. Today, "The High Priest of the Church of the Painful Truth" was railing against our "hideous government schools," by which he meant, public schools. I listened while I ate my chopped ham and mayo sandwich, crunched my little bag of barbecue corn chips, and sipped black coffee from my thermos. Public schools, striving to educate everything from the next Einstein to the village idiot, had challenges. No one debated that, or that there were improvements to be made. And while Boortz often hit the nail on the head, in this case he was absurd. If his analysis of public education coincided with reality even fractionally, this country would have long since been reduced to a smoking ruin. Visualizing him frothing at the mouth, I extinguished Neal in mid-sentence, and turned my thoughts to this afternoon and tomorrow.

When I returned from lunch, Boyd and I would check on the mice. That might reveal something significant—or not.

Then Tuesday morning, the procedure. Joy had vouched for Mellwood's competence. I trusted her, so I guess I trusted him. I spent a few moments wondering if Joy's assessment was up to date: maybe things had changed with Mellwood since she formed her elevated opinion of him. What did she base that on anyway? Did she know enough about cardiology to give him such a glowing report? Maybe doctors *always* watched each other's backs. I gave a mental shrug. I was getting the ICD. I had agreed. Why worry? Malcolm Mellwood was a little twisted, but decent. He wouldn't put me in danger by attempting this if he suspected he was incapable or unqualified.

I moved on. What about tomorrow night? Assuming everything went okay and I drove home safely, what would I tell Kay—another accident in the lab? We still had our own rooms, so I could dress and undress behind closed doors. It was winter; concealing clothing was the norm. Maybe I could actually keep this from her—if the IV needle in the back of my hand didn't leave a bruise, that is. The narrow-bore needles Joy used never left a mark. Even if this one did, something like that could be plausibly explained away. My goal was to drop dead, or reach retirement, whichever came first, with Kay entirely ignorant of this whole unbelievable mess. But what I needed, was to tell her everything.

Lunch time was over. I killed the engine and downed a last swallow

170

of coffee. Time to see if Boyd's rodents had anything to say.

When I re-entered the lab, he was there to greet me. "Well, Dr. Stepping," he said, rubbing his hands together, "shall we?" I had encouraged him to call me Paul, but Boyd was in his thirties, I was old enough to be his father, plus I was his boss, so he had never acted on that authorization.

We walked to the animal room, a cramped antechamber off the main lab. There was a sturdy table whose legs were cement columns built into the floor, a refrigerator/freezer, a double sink made of porcelain, and shelves of wire enclosures up each wall. Boyd placed the three cages of interest on the table. The news was mixed.

Group-1, the 73 + ricin group, was alive and kicking. The same was true for Group-2, which had been dosed with 73 only. All the members of Group-3, "my" group, were dead. RPA-73 had not protected the animals against the lethal effects of the 72 administered a week ago.

Boyd Markham appeared stunned. He bent down for a closer look. He tapped on the stainless steel. The small white bodies remained still among the cedar shavings. He turned to me. "I checked them not an hour ago, Dr. Stepping. They were fine."

I grabbed the wall phone and punched Emmerton's extension.

"Yeah, Paul—I was just about to buzz you. It's weird: of the twenty mice, seven are dead, ten seem sick, but the other three are bright-eyed and bushy-tailed. I looked in on them mid-morning. No problems with any of them at that point, so this is recent. And get this: the three live ones, they're all male."

63

I relayed the Group-4 information to Boyd, and told him to continue monitoring the remaining groups. He watched me with worried eyes, so I added, "Listen, the main thing is the ricin project. That's for the troops, and right now that looks promising. And who knows? Maybe Emmerton's decouplant will work out." Then I retreated to my alcove to think about the animal results—to try and put them into perspective.

171

The first two groups did indeed look good for the ricin initiative. But they were far from conclusive. It was too early to celebrate. Several more days of survival were needed before our cautious hope could become more robust. Even then, the issue of side effects, both short- and long-term, would loom. Perhaps RPA-73 would protect soldiers against a ricin attack. But what if it also caused blindness or hearing loss or kidney damage? I thought of all those pharmaceutical advertisements on TV. By law the drug companies were required to reveal the unintended consequences unearthed during the clinical trials of their products. Sometimes the list was quite scary. The announcer would hurry through them of course, but that information often left you wondering if the risk associated with the purported cure was worse than the condition. If these forty mice lived on, additional groups would first be tested to see if the results were reproducible; if they were, the question of side effects would then be confronted. It would be a lengthy and thorough endeavor. If specific problems surfaced, they would be addressed either symptom-by-symptom, or, if the numbers and types of symptoms proved overwhelming, via an entirely new protectant: an RPA-74 might be required.

The test animals related to my personal situation had not fared so well. I had been exposed to RPA-72. Group-3 had suggested that subsequent dosing with RPA-73 could not save me. If time permitted, this experiment could be re-done, and other tests could tinker with the quantities of 73 used. But time did *not* permit. Which brought me to Group-4. Emmerton's compound, which *in vitro* had succeeded in forcing a mouse cardiac protein to release bound RPA-72 molecules, *in vivo* had produced a mere 15% survival rate. Looking only at the male mice, the rate was 30%. Still not stellar. If that number had been 70%, I might feel encouraged—I might take the risk and treat myself with Emmerton's decouplant. But again, time: whether three healthy survivors or seven, these lucky ones might succumb later today, or tonight, or tomorrow. I'd just have to wait, at least until Wednesday—the last day before DP-1.

The only thing really settled thus far was that tomorrow morning Malcolm Mellwood would be threading wires into my heart, and inserting an ICD under the skin of my chest.

64

By quitting time, Emmerton's ten sickly mice had died, but the three healthy males were still good. The forty subjects of Groups -1 and -2 likewise were alive.

Kay had an inservice class after school. She had told me she wouldn't be home until 6:30 or so. When she had provided that information I found myself wondering if it were true, or if instead it was a pretext for a tryst with her principal friend. That had been a fleeting thought however. I hadn't dwelt upon it. Since our encounter with Joel on Saturday, I had felt more confident about Kay's fidelity.

She arrived home closer to 7:00, gave me a nice kiss, and proceeded to fix supper. After we ate she said she wanted to call the children—all of them. I told her I had some internet work to do. She settled down in her La-Z-Boy; I retired to my room where I had the computer, leaving the door open. I Googled "implantable cardioverter defibrillator," and read as much as I could about ICDs before hearing her say good-bye to the third child. At that point I went offline.

Kay gave me a quick update on the kids: Bill and Pauline were debating taking Eva to a child psychologist for help with her impulse control; Joel was apologetic about what had happened Saturday, but insisted his relationship with Versa Brooks was serious; Amy and Frank were contemplating marriage.

After this briefing I announced that I was bushed, that tomorrow was "a big day" a work, and that I was turning in.

"No *CSI: Miami*?" Kay asked. She knew I was a fan. I often watched re-runs on the weekends. "It's a new episode—more about Horatio and his wayward son."

I liked the original series set in Las Vegas. Gil Grissom was truly my kind of guy. The New York and Miami variants were likewise compelling. I was drawn by the science. And though I would rate the Miami show my narrow favorite because of the water, the vivid colors, and the semi-tropical backdrop, when producer Jerry Bruckheimer strayed into these personal melodramas, my interest flagged. "Not tonight," I said to Kay. "You enjoy."

65

The forty-three mice made it through the night. Boyd Markham was excited about that. Then, before I headed down to Mellwood's, he gathered all the technicians in a white-coated semicircle around me. "Dr. Stepping," he said, "you're the best boss ever. We're behind you one hundred percent." There were nods, smiles, mutterings of agreement.

I felt an ache behind my eyes; looking from face to face I said, "That means a lot—thank you. And I can tell you this: I seriously doubt there's a more competent and hard-working group in all of Ft. Detrick. You guys make me look good." We watched each other for a few seconds. "Guess I'd better go. I'll be fine."

Mellwood was waiting with the anesthesiologist and surgical nurse from MC4. As I walked in he said, "I just had one. While these people prep you, I'll have another." He was referring to cigarettes. He was assuring me that his addiction would be appeased while he performed the procedure.

I was led to the EKG room. An IV pole and a metal cart had been positioned near the head of the couch where I reclined for my regular heart tests. It had been draped with operating room green sheets. The cart bore an array of shiny surgical instruments, as well as a small black box which I assumed contained the device.

I was told to remove my lab coat and shirt. As I lay back the nurse confirmed that I had fasted as instructed. She began to shave and sterilize a fairly wide area beneath my left collarbone. Meanwhile the anesthesiologist found a vein on the back of my right hand. He began a drip. Mellwood entered the room wearing a mask the same color as the sheets. He presented his hands, fingers spread, to the nurse, who snapped a pair of latex gloves on them. I supposed he had just scrubbed. The other two then tied on masks.

"How are we doing?" the anesthesiologist asked.

174

"A little woozy," I managed.

"That's the idea," he replied.

I was kept on the edge of consciousness, fading in and out. There were distant voices, faces bunched above me, blurred images on a monitor. It was dream-like, not unpleasant, time-free.

"We're done Paul. It went well." Things were coming back into focus. That was Mellwood. He was seated at the counter, jotting notes in my chart. "The nurse will stay a while—an hour or so. Before I release you, we'll have a chat."

The hour went fast. The nurse was friendly, but thank God, not overly talkative. She allowed me to doze off and on. Before I knew it, Mellwood had scooted a swivel chair up beside the couch.

"How do you feel?" he said, looking directly into my eyes. "You alert?"

"Yeah—I'm good."

"Starting to feel a little discomfort in your chest? The local's wearing off."

"Yeah, a little."

"I'll prescribe something for that. Can you sit?"

The nurse assisted me. There were shooting pains, replaced by a dull ache.

"I'd suggest you eat and drink something soon," Mellwood went on. "Do you use the cafeteria?"

"I brought something from home."

"Go ahead and consume that as soon as you get back to your lab." He reached out and touched the gauze and tape poultice covering the incisions. "This stays in place until Friday. Keep it dry—so no showers. Come to me for removal. At that point I'll determine if a fresh dressing is required."

I nodded.

"Now, about the device itself. It comes with default parameters telling it under what conditions to fire. These parameters are appropriate for eighty, ninety percent of patients. Your case is different. Number one, because of all the recent EKGs, I have unusually complete information on the condition of your heart; and two, again atypical, except for the

175

intensifying arrhythmia, your heart is quite healthy and strong. Most people who need an ICD have a host of corollary problems. What I'm getting at is this: the device is programmable, and with the wealth of data I have, I've been able to customize those parameters to fit your particular situation."

"Sounds good," I said.

"It should be. Now, here's another feature." He handed me a dark green object about the size and shape of, well, a pack of cigarettes. It had a sturdy clip. "This is a wireless modem," he said. "Have it with you at all times. If the ICD fires, a signal is sent to the modem. It beeps, then relays certain information to me. You may or may not feel the firing. It depends on the voltage, which can vary. Regardless, it's not painful. But what you do if you hear the beep, is get to me as soon as possible. I'll hook you up to the EKG and see if we need to do anything further. Chances are, the device will have straightened out the problem."

"What if it happens at night or on a weekend?"

"Come here. We have access 24/7. I've cleared it with Essex. The last thing he wants is for you to show up at some off-base emergency room."

I took a breath and said, "Well, I'm glad we did this. I think it's going to help."

"Unless there's something massive," Mellwood said, "this should do the trick." He began to move his chair away, then stopped. "One more thing—no sexual activity for one week. No intercourse, no masturbation, no orgasms from any source. That's only prudent."

I glanced at the nurse. She had looked away, her cheeks pink.

"Any questions?"

"No—listen, thanks Malcolm. The level of care you're giving me is—outstanding."

He ignored that tribute, saying instead, "Henrietta here is going to wheel you down to your lab. Who's your main tech? Markham?"

"Yes."

"She's going to tell Markham to keep an eye on you throughout the day, and to call me if you keel over or whatnot. She'll leave the wheelchair with you. Bring it back at 4:45. I'll tell you then if you can drive home. If

176

not, I'll take you, and pick you up tomorrow morning. And I'll have the prescription for your pain meds. Until then, take acetaminophen as needed." He handed me a bottle of Extra-Strength Tylenol. "You get dressed and I'll see you this afternoon."

The anesthesia cobwebs continued to clear, and by noon I felt almost normal. I popped a few of the Tylenols as I worked in my alcove, doing some preliminary tests on the thermal stability of RPA-73.

Shortly before returning to Mellwood I checked on the status of the mice. All, including Emmerton's three, were still enjoying life.

I walked the wheelchair back to Mellwood's office. He asked what I had done since leaving him that morning, had I been able to concentrate, had I felt dizzy or lightheaded at any point? He spent two very attentive minutes listening to my heart via his stethoscope. Then he handed me the promised prescription and told me I was good to go.

On the way home I stopped by Walgreens to get it filled. I walked down the card aisle where Kay had encountered Joy Smalls.

It was dark when I pulled in beside the Civic. I removed the Band-Aid covering the IV puncture on the back of my hand. The anesthesiologist had done a good job: no bruising. I rubbed with my thumb to remove telltale traces of adhesive. I found myself wondering, *What do I tell Kay if this modem goes off?* I needed a cover story.

We passed a typical Tuesday evening: supper, some conversation, a check of the day's news on CNN, MSNBC, and Fox, then an old movie on TCM. I was nervous, though I tried to hide that fact. Kay was sweet, smiling a lot, giving me soft looks.

We watched *The Agony and the Ecstacy*, the 1965 film based on Irving Stone's novel. The battle of wills between Michelangelo and Pope Julius II while the great master painted the Sistine Chapel, was compelling.

As the credits rolled, Kay turned to me and said, "Paul, it's been a long time. I know it's not Friday, but . . . ?"

66

Kay didn't finish her sentence. She didn't need to. Twenty-nine years

177

of marriage allows time to develop the non-verbal. I was lonely for Kay. We were talking, relating comfortably now. But I hungered for her touch, to lay beside her through the night, to reach out in the morning and find her there, sleepy and murmuring and warm. I longed for that once-common consolation. And she was inviting me back to our bed. But tonight, of all nights!

She watched me, waiting for an answer. My mind raced, searching for a plausible way to reject what I so desired. I felt confused. Perhaps it was the residual effects of the anesthetic. My chest ached. I needed my pain medicine, the oxycodone Mellwood had prescribed.

Then, the brain-scramble went quiet. I wondered if something had happened with my heart, if the blood flow to my head had decreased. The wireless modem was clipped to the waistband of my sweat pants, in the small of my back. If the ICD fired, it would beep. I waited—no beep.

"Paul, are you okay?"

I was looking right at Kay, yet her voice startled me. "I'm okay," I said. Then it seemed as if somewhere in my cerebrum, three identical slot machine icons clacked into place. I was a winner! The mechanism of my speech center unlocked, and these word-coins poured from my mouth: "Kay, I am dying. Something happened in the lab—an accident. Back in September: my hand—you remember. It's affecting my heart. This morning, at work, I had a device implanted in my chest." I raised my shirt.

Kay's hand went to her mouth. "Oh Paul!" she breathed.

"If my heart malfunctions, the device will try to compensate, but it's uncertain if it is capable of doing that under all circumstances. If it fires, this thing will beep." I leaned forward in the rocker, then reached behind me and showed her the modem. "If that happens I'm supposed to rush to Ft. Detrick, day or night, to see Malcolm Mellwood, the cardiologist assigned to MMDA. He's the one who implanted the ICD."

Kay was mute. She just stared with wide eyes.

"Other treatments have been considered, even a transplant. We've done all we can, but the chances are high I'll be dead within two weeks. I'm sorry Kay. I should have told you before. Just—" I took a ragged breath, "—just stupid." My chin began to tremble.

178

67

Her eyes filled with tears. "Paul, no—isn't there some mistake?"

"I'm afraid not. In September I was exposed to a chemical that had killed test animals. The mice didn't die immediately, and they didn't appear to have suffered. We determined that the substance had affected their hearts."

As I began revealing these details, my emotions settled down. But Kay was shaking her head, starting to sob. I rose from my rocker and moved to the La-Z-Boy. I pulled her to her feet. I wrapped my arms around her, held her while she cried, stroked her honey-colored hair.

After a while, once she began to calm, I whispered in her ear, "Let's go to bed." I led her down the hall to her room—our room for all these years. Before we went in I took her face in my hands. "But here's the thing:" I said, "I can't have sex for a week—and by then I might have croaked."

"Paul!" she yelled, the tears still standing in her eyes. "Stop that!" Then she gave a chopped laugh and added, "You fool!"

I raised a forefinger. "Mellwood said *I* can't have sex; he said nothing about you."

Kay knew what I meant, but she wailed, "Nooo! I just want to be *with* you. You need to rest. Come on."

We went in, undressed, and turned down the covers. We slipped in. With the blankets snugged around us we kissed and fondled and toyed. We wore nothing to bed. We never had. God, this felt good! This felt right! I was aroused, but also relaxed. The tensions that had developed since the accident drained away. I told my wife, "I love you Kay. I've missed you *so* much. I'm sorry I was mean to you—about the peanut butter. That was wrong. Forgive me."

"No," she said, nuzzling my neck, "you were right. You *were* mean, but you were right. I need to change. The problem is, I depend on you to compensate for my deficiencies. You're so smart and organized—I feel I don't have to worry. Paul will take care of things. That's been my mind-set forever. But it's not fair to you." She kissed me while laying a gentle hand on my chest dressing. "Oh Paul," she said, "what are we going to do?"

"Let's just be cool-headed and honest. We'll examine the situation— what we know, what we don't know—and we'll make some decisions." The modem lay on the bedside table. I hoped it wouldn't interrupt this bittersweet reunion. "We'll keep our feelings in the background—just try to be sensible. How does that sound?"

"This is your life we're talking about," Kay said in the semi-darkness, "our lives together. I feel strongly about that."

"Well of course—me too. All the more reason to be hard-eyed. It's more than easy to be carried away by sentiment. But that likely wouldn't serve us very well."

Kay agreed this approach was best, and said she would try to avoid any undue drama.

The first thing I impressed upon her was the supreme importance of secrecy in this matter. "By talking even to you, my wife, I'm breaking my non-disclosure agreement with the Army; I'm breaking the law. Should this become known, there will be consequences." I explained the legal and financial impact. "As long as you're absolutely silent, there's no problem."

"You don't suppose your implant is really a bug, do you?"

Now there was an idea that had not occurred to me. "Well I hope to God not. If so, it's already over. No, I doubt it. If it is, somebody went to a world of trouble to keep tabs on me."

"I was joking," Kay said. "You know, yanking your chain a little." There was just enough light from the LED clock for me to see her smile. "Sorry." She touched my nose with hers and gave it a few light rubs.

"That's all right." I thought of Essex. "Suspicion *is* our middle name at Ft. Detrick, so it's not out of the realm of possibility. But hopefully, no."

I told her about the ricin project, and the results of the animal tests with RPA-72. I gave a few details on how I had calculated my nine-day Death Period. "Day after tomorrow is DP-1," I said.

Kay listened to all this, watching my face in the dim light. Right away she zeroed in on the assumptions underlying my computations. "This is not certain," she stated, encouragement sounding in her voice. "This might not happen."

"You're a quick study," I said. "Here's a suggestion: come to work for me at MMDA. Then we'd both have security clearance, and we could talk about this legally and at will."

"Paul, I'm six months from retirement." She must have made out my slick expression; after a moment she pulled back and rapped me on the chest, saying, "Very funny."

"Ouch!" She had struck my poultice.

"Oh no—Paul! I'm sorry!" She ran her fingers over the bandage, pressing lightly, as if to repair any damage she had caused.

I thought to fake a seizure or some such, but why carry things too far? The moment was perfect as it stood. I took her hands and kissed the palms. "You cannot harm the Bionic Man. It's not possible."

"Paul, stop. Are you all right?"

"I'm good. But listen, I *could* use that brain of yours in the lab. You picked up on the fuzziness in my Death Period projection. Your average 3rd-Grade teacher wouldn't do that. You're not average. You're way above average—here," I touched her forehead, "and here." I found one of those nice breasts.

She pushed against my hand. "So how much confidence do you really have in these calculations?"

"I'm estimating the likelihood of my death from this exposure is 70%. The likelihood that I will die within the nine days, I put at 50%.

"I don't get that."

"Well, a 70% chance that the RPA-72 will kill me; only one out of two that it will happen within this particular nine-day period."

"So if you expanded the number of days, maybe adding two on either end, making it thirteen, the 50% would go up."

"That's the idea."

"And the 70%—that's before the implant. The implant's supposed to improve your odds, right?"

"Yes." She snuggled up to me, seeming to have taken comfort in that affirmation. "Kay," I said, "we don't know if the ICD will be effective."

181

She pressed closer. "And you realize not even the children can be told—no one."

"Yes."

"I mean, you've integrated this, correct? You clearly understand that if it is revealed that I've talked to you, there will be no retirement benefits, no life insurance, no Cadillac health-care—nothing, nada, zero."

"Paul, I understand—and I can keep a secret. I'm just glad something's been done, and that your predictions aren't pinpoint accurate."

Joy Smalls had emphasized the statistical nature of my calculations, that there was clearly a margin of error, and that a ray of hope lurked therein. Kay was doing the same. Both these women now knew of my dire situation. Both were rooting for me.

As long as I was coming clean, I needed to tell Kay about Joy. I said, "And we agreed to keep emotion out of our discussion."

"Yes. I think we're doing pretty well on that score, don't you?"

"We are, we are. But I have something else—something that might put our agreement to the test."

"You mean put it to the test more than telling me you're going to die within two weeks?"

"Well, no—not more than that. It's a different kind of thing. In a way, it's nothing. But in the spirit of transparency—of authenticity, if you will—I just need to lay this out."

"Okay. What is it?"

Kay was beautiful. In the pale blue light, those crow's feet she worried about were invisible. I moved my hand over her shoulder, down the middle of her back, and around her waist. No, this was not the twenty-something Kay Bishop of our college days. But she remained trim, fit, and at fifty-one, remarkably firm. I felt myself responding even as I said, "I kissed Joy Smalls—twice."

She stiffened. I heard her draw in air. "Why?" she breathed, inching away.

"It's more accurate to say I kissed her once, then on another occasion she kissed me."

"Why? Why did you do it?" Kay was trying to keep our bargain—

trying to stay calm.

"It was after our big blowup on The Trail. I was upset with you. I was scared about my accident—that I would soon die. It seemed I couldn't even be honest with you about the peanut butter without a fist fight, and I certainly couldn't tell you what had happened at work. But Joy knew. She was sympathetic. We'd been friends for quite a while—well, friendly. And in my shaky condition, one day in her office, I kissed her. I'm just explaining. It's not excuse; I'm not defending what I did."

"She's gorgeous," Kay said.

"That played a part."

"And later you say she kissed you."

"Yes."

"Why?"

"I don't know for sure."

"Did she find you attractive?"

"Well, I guess—in some sense. She probably felt sorry for me."

"Do you kiss someone you feel sorry for? Is that the normal response?"

"Kay, I don't know why she did it. You'd have to ask her."

"If I'd known all this before seeing her at Walgreens that day, I would have." I heard Kay chuff. "No wonder she almost fainted."

This was out, thank God. Kay had done well. I was ready to move on. "She was embarrassed. I was embarrassed. That was it."

"So no more kissing, or hugging—no sex in some back room at work?"

"Kay, that's not necessary."

"What's the answer?"

"The answer is no. Listen, I didn't have to tell you this at all."

That was defensive, but she drew closer. She kissed me in a way she knew I liked. "So it's over between you and Dr. Smalls?"

"Kay, there was nothing to be over. This was no relationship—no affair. It was a couple of mistakes, and yes, it's over."

"Good," she said, delivering another of those kisses.

There was one more thing to be revealed. Could Kay continue

183

keeping her cool? Could I? Should I even ask? Yes, I had to know. "That number," I said, "the one you left when you were away."

"Yes."

"I called it."

"You did? No one told me."

"It was late at night. A man answered."

"What did he say?"

"Nothing. I hung up."

"Hung up? Why?"

Was Kay playing dumb? Surely she could connect the dots. "It surprised me. I expected you to answer."

"Maybe you dialed the wrong number."

Tim Rouzerville had raised that possibility.

"Maybe—but I don't think so."

"Did you call back?"

"No."

"Why not?"

"It was late, I was tired, and I—well, I knew you were angry—with me. I didn't know if I had the strength to deal with whatever was—happening." I stopped, giving Kay time to respond, to explain. But she just watched, her face six inches from mine. She was waiting for my question. "That man," I said, "was he your principal?"

Her eyes slid to the side. I saw her lips compress. She shifted under my hand. "Yes," she said.

I knew the blood was draining from my head. I felt woozy, just as I had when the anesthesia began to bite before the ICD procedure. I thought there was a buzzing in my chest—the device firing—but the modem didn't go off. Just my imagination, or something to do with the freshly-glued incisions. Was Kay going to leave it at this? Was she going to make me go further?

She said, "I was in another room. His wife was with him."

Thank God! sounded in my brain. Then, striving to keep my voice emotion-free, I asked, "Was she okay with you staying over? I mean, did she have any questions?"

184

"If she did, she didn't raise them with me."

"So no sex with—what's his name?"

"Dave Holcolm."

"In some broom closet at school?"

"Paul," she warned, "no. And no kisses either."

"What about hugs?"

"One," she said, "when I told him you and I were having problems. I got a little misty, and . . . ."

"Did you like it?"

Now she was looking into my eyes. "Paul, if you want me to beat you in your chest again, just keep it up."

All the cards were on the table. It felt good—a weight lifted. I pulled Kay closer. I kissed her. I loved this woman. I loved her energy, her spark, her good heart. Though I had certainly felt otherwise, at this moment even her instances of unmindfulness seemed endearing. I cherished the fact that she had chosen me—that she had stayed with me; I found it almost unbelievable. Her body here in the dark, her familiar inviting body, was a metaphor for what I found even more soul-stirring about my wife.

I said, "I love you Kay. I'm so sorry about all this. Three months ago the world was our oyster. Now . . . looks like I've messed up everything. You're the purest person I know. You deserve the best, but you're getting the worst. And I'm helpless. I apologize, but it doesn't rectify the situation. Kay, I don't want to leave you."

She enfolded me. She held me. Yes, again I cried; she cried too. It was awful, but it was authentic. Afterward, I felt limp—so weak—yet clean, calm.

"We need to sleep," Kay said. "Now we can face this together."

68

Wednesday morning was our first normal good-bye in some time. I was almost fooled into thinking that our *lives* were normal, that our careers were winding down according to rule, that retirement beckoned just over

185

the horizon. None of this was true of course, but there was little to do except go to work and carry on as if it were.

All mice had survived the night. That was good. Boyd and Emmerton were happy.

Joy informed me that the enzymes from Monday's blood had spiked. That was not good, but was expected, as it was the Monday EKG that had prompted Mellwood to recommend the ICD. I told Joy that Kay and I had made up. She seemed relieved and said, "Good. Every external stress factor needs to be minimized these next two weeks." I thought it unwise to tell her all I had shared with Kay. We discussed again the possibility of a medication for my worsening liver. She reiterated its dangers, said the trend of my blood chemistry was pushing her toward prescribing it, but that she wanted to see if the mere installation of the device, the leads embedded in the heart tissue, might change the equation. "And," she added, "if that thing has occasion to fire, we might be looking at an entirely new ball game. I wouldn't want to jump the gun."

Mellwood did a wireless diagnostic on the ICD. All was well. He asked about discomfort, or if anything unusual had happened. I told him I had experienced one instance of lightheadedness, accompanied by an odd buzzing in my chest. "You weren't having sex, were you? I warned you against that." I told him no, but admitted there had been a "sexual context" to the symptoms. He suggested I avoid such contexts until the full week from the procedure was up. The EKG revealed further problems. "Look," he said, showing me the printout. "Not only do we have deepened serrations, but things are getting erratic." He pointed out that not all the dips were of the same depth, and that some were considerably broader than others. "This kind of electrical chaos generally precedes a fibrillatory event. Don't be surprised if your ICD fires within the next twenty-four hours. And I'm assuming you remember what to do if that happens."

I left Mellwood not encouraged, but convinced he was on top of my situation. I returned to the lab, working most of the afternoon on the thermal stability tests I had begun yesterday. I spent some of my time contemplating a 3-dimensional model I had made of the RPA-73 molecule. Compared to flat, pen-and-paper representations, this effigy was more helpful as I considered possible solvents for the new protectant.

I left Ft. Detrick with two thoughts peppering my brain: Mellwood's portent concerning the firing of my ICD; and the fact that tomorrow would be the first day of my calculated Death Period.

69

Emmerton met me Thursday morning with bad news. Standing in my alcove, he disclosed that his three surviving male mice were ailing. They were alive, but they were listless and would not eat. "I'm sorry Paul," he said, regarding me with sad eyes. "I know I've let you down."

"Nonsense," I told him. "You've done everything you could—amazing work, actually. Our problem is time."

"Should I pursue a different decouplant? You might recall, I've zeroed in on two other classes of compounds that might serve. They're harsher than the one that failed, so that's counterintuitive. Still, you never know."

"Essex would have to approve," I observed in what I thought was a neutral voice.

Emmerton frowned. "Are you saying he wouldn't?" I guess my voice hadn't been neutral enough.

"He might. But our meeting back in September—right after the accident?"

"Uh-huh."

"I told the group I had done some computations."

"Right. You had calculated a span of days when you would be in jeopardy."

"Yes."

Still looking sour, Emmerton said, "Hey, I remember Essex being callous to your situation." Then he brightened. "But Joy stood up for you. She's something, isn't she?"

"That she is. But see, this is the first day of what I've dubbed the Death Period. This—today—is DP-1."

Emmerton blinked. "Exactly. This is it: DP-1."

187

"So Essex will say it's over—there's no time to pursue anything else."

"But your predictions might be off. Maybe there *is* time."

"I'm just saying—I mean, you can ask—but this has taken you away from your assigned work for over two months. Essex is probably thinking: *Forget this lost cause; Emmerton needs to get back to his own project.*"

He shrugged and shook his head. "What can be more important than saving your life?"

"Well thanks—thanks Ward. I appreciate that. You've done so much."

He left saying he needed to inform Essex about his mice, and promising to seek the Major's approval to continue his decouplant research.

Boyd Markham informed me that all the Groups -1 and -2 mice had again made it through the night and appeared normal. Every day these forty little rodents lived, improved the likelihood that I had indeed synthesized a substance that would protect our military personnel in the event of a ricin attack, while being well-tolerated by the human body. Encouraging, but again, too early for unbridled jubilation.

I continued my thermal stability tests. These consisted of subjecting samples of RPA-73 to different temperatures for varying periods of time, then running them through the infrared spectrophotometer to check for any degradation of the molecule. Preliminary results were suggesting the protectant was stable over a fairly wide range of temperatures: good, of course; you didn't want battlefield medical materiel that was too delicate.

Based on scrutinizing the model I had constructed, and after consulting several handbooks of physical constants, I had identified six polar organic liquids I thought might serve as suitable solvents for RPA-73. A satisfactory substance would naturally have to dissolve the compound. It also could not chemically alter it, or be unduly harsh to human physiology. As I worked into the afternoon, I began checking the eligibility of these liquids for their potential job.

Around 4:00 PM I was startled by a piercing beep. It was the wireless modem clipped to my belt.

Boyd came sprinting into my alcove. "You all right Dr. Stepping?"

I had felt nothing. "I'm fine. Listen, when this happens I'm supposed to go see Mellwood right away."

"Shall I go with you?"

"No, just carry on. Hopefully I'll be back before we knock off."

I walked down the corridor to Mellwood's suite. As I crossed the threshold the modem sounded again—this time a double beep.

He ushered me directly to the EKG couch. While I unbuttoned my shirt he said, "Looks like your calculations were right on target."

70

Mellwood hooked me up, saying, "The first firing didn't successfully defibrillate. The ICD waits a programmed period of time to see if things even out. If they don't, it delivers a second shock, this one at a higher voltage. That's what just happened. How do you feel?"

"Fine."

He walked over and switched on the EKG unit. "We'll soon get a picture of your electrical status." While the test proceeded he explained that the device had five voltage levels. He hadn't gone into that before. "You reach a certain degree of disorganization, you're zapped with a low voltage; the modem chirps, the device waits; defib achieved, fine—defib *not* achieved, Punch-2, with more zing; modem squawks again (this time twice), the device waits; that's where we are now; and so on with increasingly powerful jolts until Level-5 with five beeps is reached."

I asked the obvious question. "What if this highest voltage doesn't work?"

Nothing if not blunt, Mellwood replied, "You're probably a goner. Now if you get to me in time, I'd use my defibrillator with the paddles." He pointed to a corner where a machine under a plastic dust cover rested on a cart. "It's capable of more robust shocks than your ICD, *and* it can deliver more current—volts and amps being two different things, as of course you know. The implantable can rev up a respectable electromotive force—which is the key thing in correcting a fibrillation—but that little battery can only cough up so many electrons per firing. If you're plugged into the wall," he waved again toward the corner, "you're not faced with

189

that limitation."

"Yeah, well—I'd get here as fast as I could."

He ignored that stating of the obvious. "There *is* a risk with high-amp defib," he went on, "and that would be what we call heart-fry, where the flow of current is great enough to damage some of the heart tissue. It's like electrocution. But if you're going under . . . ." He shrugged. "Now, if you come to me at Level-5, before I went high-amp, I'd inject epinephrine directly into your heart—take the chemical approach. Sometimes that's just what the doctor ordered." He chuffed air through his nose and threatened a smile. "If that didn't work I'd grab my paddles. If *that* failed, I'd crack open your chest and do something manual—which actually would not be advisable in this office, by myself. But again, last ditch effort."

There was something reassuring here. It wasn't the content of what Mellwood had said. That was rather grim. It had to do with the fact that he had a plan—he knew what he would do given certain eventualities. It had to do with his careless use of terms like "heart-fry" and "high-amp defib," which conveyed a familiarity that spoke competence. And it had to do with my growing confidence that whatever developed regarding my case, this man would not panic.

As I tried to muster a decent response to Mellwood's narrative, he moved toward the EKG unit saying, "Let's see what we've got here." He tore off the six-foot printout and took it to the counter. He secured one end with a glass container of wooden tongue depressors. He ran the edge of his hand along the tape, smoothing it, then placed a dispenser-box of latex gloves on the other end. He returned to the start, bent his face down close, and began a slow left-to-right scan of the graph. I heard grunts and mumbles. Several times he backtracked to linger over a certain segment.

After a long five minutes he stepped over to me. "We caught this right after the second jolt. Everything is smooth, normal. The ICD did its job. You want to see?" he asked, then seemed surprised that I was unable to comply. "Oh—yank those things off."

I disengaged from the adhesive-tipped leads and joined him at the counter. "So the device is working as planned."

"Yes. Check this." He moved a forefinger along the first eighteen

190

inches of the printout. "Remember how these peaks were jagged? Now they're not—a nice continuous flow of electrical energy."

"But how long will this last?" I said. "I don't suppose I'm cured."

"Unlikely," Mellwood replied. "Now, look further along." I followed his finger the next couple of feet, at which juncture he straightened up, turned to me, and said, "We got no third jolt during the test. That's good of course, but it would have been interesting to see the details leading up to a firing. I've read about it in the literature—seen photos of the EKGs—but then your case is unique, isn't it?" Not waiting for my response, he harkened back to the graph. "During the final third of the test period—it's hard to see, but there are the beginnings of fresh aberrations." Switching to his middle finger he traced an invisible circle around the last three peaks on the tape.

At first they looked no different than the others. But as I drew closer, the ever-so-slight irregularities became clear. "Damn," I breathed.

"What we don't know is how long it will take for the disorganization to build and trigger another Level-1 burst. It's clear though, that the RPA-72 is still needling your nodes." He flicked his eyes over the long graph several times, then looked at me and said, "This thing is not over."

71

That night I told Kay what had happened. Echoing Mellwood, I said, "Looks like the time frame I calculated is pretty accurate."

She responded with a very good question: "If you make it past the Death Period, are you in the clear?"

What I had done was compute *the date* of my death—Monday, December 17. That had been extrapolated from time, weight, and dosage data on the mice who had died from exposure to RPA-72. I had then assumed that this was not *the* date, but only the most probable one. Moving away from it, both forward and backward, the probability diminished. Earlier than DP-1, I put the chance at zero; likewise for later than DP-9. Yesterday was earlier than DP-1, and no problem; today *was* DP-1, and I had a fibrillatory event. Not much data, true—but thus far the

191

bell curve distribution of probabilities for the time of my death had been predictive.

"That's what my numbers say," I answered. "Trouble is, our mice all died on a given day (their equivalent of DP-5), and we didn't have a separate group of test animals outfitted with tiny ICDs to see if the devices would get them past that day, and if their heart problems would diminish *after* that critical point. So I'm really just shooting in the dark from DP-5 on. It could be that the risk actually continues to *rise*."

"But maybe not," Kay said.

"Right—maybe not."

When I went to see Joy the next morning she told me she had arranged for same-day results on my blood samples. "I thought that might be helpful until you're in the clear."

In the clear. Kay had used that exact phrase last night. "When would they be ready?"

"By noon."

I arched my eyebrows. "You *do* have the power."

"Oh, I have my ways." Then she said, "Actually, it was Emmerton. He dropped by to tell me Essex nixed any further decouplant work. We talked a while, and he offered to have one of his people do the enzyme tests, rather than me send the samples over to JVAPO. This fellow's a new hire. He was the main blood tech for a hospital lab down in Rockville, so he's familiar." She gave a little laugh. "Funny guy, Ward."

Emmerton had already called to inform me about Essex. I was not surprised, as I had predicted the Major's response.

Joy took my blood, palpated my liver, then sent me on to Mellwood. The EKG was encouraging. The re-serrating of the peaks that had begun near the end of yesterday's test persisted, but had not intensified. Mellwood told me a fair number of people live with this level of irregularity and never have a problem. I left his office thinking, *Maybe I am cured.* Before breaking for lunch, Joy called to say that my enzyme levels were significantly down.

On Saturday Kay and I walked The Trail south, replicating our ill-fated trek from a month ago. She packed the same lunch, remembering the peanut butter this time. It was cold, the trees were bare, but it was crystal clear with no wind. We talked about the events of that day, and their aftermath. We were serious, but we were able to laugh as well. I found myself looking up into the icy blue sky and breathing, "Thank you," to the Great Spirit that is all and in all. I was alive, I was functional, I felt no pain, and I had my treasure, my Pearl of Great Price, Kay.

Sunday morning we ate eggs, then went to church. We even risked Clay Winslow's Sunday School class. It was as dry and uninviting of participation as always, but I basked in the normalcy of it. Even Kay didn't squirm too much. I hardly heard Tim Rouzerville's sermon. I focused on the music and the rich sunbeams filtering through the stained glass windows of the sanctuary. I held Kay's hand. I wondered if this was worship, or close to it? I thought about what I'd heard of the Quakers— how they gathered, then sat quietly, each one attending the "inner light" of God's presence. Maybe I was doing that. Whatever was happening, I felt nourished, refreshed.

The weekend had been gorgeous, but Monday dawned overcast, though a tad warmer. This was DP-5, the apex of my statistical curve.

Kay held me close as we stood at the door, ready to leave for work. "I love you, my darling," she whispered in my ear. "My prayers are with you. I love you—always."

72

The test mice continued to prosper. I gave Essex a ring to report that fact, and to inform him of my progress on the thermal stability and solubility studies. We conversed a good five minutes on all this; I expected him to comment on my emergency visit to Mellwood last Thursday, perhaps to explain his rejection of Emmerton's request to continue his decouplant research, and certainly to acknowledge that this was DP-5. He raised none of these items.

Before hanging up I said, "RPA-73 is looking more like a winner every day."

"In this business," Essex replied, "we never count our chickens before

193

they hatch." Then, without pause or segue, he said, "You and your technicians are fully documenting your work, as I've instructed."

His voice gave no rise in pitch as he spoke the last three words. That would have indicated a question, which would have suggested the possibility that his underlings might dare disobey. Major Leonard Essex always projected power and authority to his subordinates: no hint of weakness, ever.

Still it was clear he wanted assurance, so I said, "Yes sir—absolutely." And that was it. I heard a click and a dial tone.

My EKG showed an increase in electrical irregularity from Friday, but not to the level preceding the firing of the ICD on DP-1. The concentrations of hepatic enzymes in my blood showed an uptick: the hypothesized distress hormones from my heart were once more killing off some liver cells; again, not serious.

I was encouraged. I ate lunch with Emmerton and Joy Smalls in the cafeteria that served MMDA and two other Ft. Detrick agencies. It was comfortable, enjoyable. Ward threw out a few observations about some of his family members located in Minneapolis; the cracks were lame, but Joy found them hilarious. We didn't discuss my situation. There was a sense that things were looking up. We returned to work smiling.

At 2:15 the modem sounded. I stoppered the flask I was working with, then removed my lab coat and hung it on a wall peg.

Boyd Markham appeared at the door to my alcove.

"Yep," I said to him, "gotta go."

Before I reached the entrance there were two beeps.

I brushed by him with my hand on the modem, looking down at it and joking, "All right—you don't have to yell."

I walked across the lab. At the door to the corridor the modem gave a triple chirp. I felt a tingling in my chest.

I pushed out into the brightly-lit passageway, hurrying toward Mellwood's suite. There were footsteps behind me.

Halfway down the hall the modem sang out again. My legs felt weak. I began to crumple. Things were going dark. As I went down I blinked and squinted. I saw Mellwood rushing toward me.

194

73

"Paul—Dr. Stepping. This is Malcolm Mellwood. How are we doing?"

The first thing my eyes focused on was a wall clock. It showed 2:45. "Thirty minutes," I mumbled.

"Yeah, you were out for a while."

My tunnel vision widened. I was in Mellwood's EKG nook. I was on the couch. The defib machine was at my head. Near it, on a separate cart, was a beeping oscilloscope. My heartbeat was being traced out with a bright green line on the dark screen of the monitor. I looked at Mellwood who had pulled a chair up to the couch. "You were coming toward me," I said.

"Probably the last thing you remember. Yeah, you went down hard, but your tech made a dive and kept your head from banging on those ceramic tiles. Kind of like a dig in volleyball." He chuckled, seeming to enjoy that image.

"So I'm okay?"

"I don't know about that. You're stable—for the moment. I'm going to watch you another half hour or so. If you don't go sour, I'll replace your battery at that point. It's not a big deal: a local, then ten, fifteen minutes." I guess he saw me frown, because he went on to explain, "I know, it's a brand new battery. But these two episodes have drained about two-thirds of its power—especially this thing today."

"What exactly happened?" I was feeling more alert and I wanted some details.

"Big event—much bigger than Thursday. Your ICD was at Level-4 by the time I got to you. Before your man and I could get you here, you reached Level-5. While I was putting you on the oscilloscope and cranking up the high-amp defib, you Level-5ed twice more. When your device tops out, if the fibrillation is not corrected, it delivers the maximum voltage repeatedly until its juice is gone."

"So the ICD didn't work this time."

195

"It worked—it did not malfunction—but it was unable to cope with the degree of disorganization your heart was experiencing." He watched me a moment, then said, "Paul, you flatlined."

That sank in, and I breathed, "Oh my God. For how long?"

"Less than a minute—probably not dangerous."

"What do you mean?"

"Heart stoppages under a minute generally do not result in measurable damage to the brain, or to other organs or tissues."

"That's good."

"Well, yes. But your resurrection required three shocks with the paddles. That's a lot of high-speed electrons blasting through. You remember our discussion about heart-fry."

"You tried the epinephrine first?"

"I did—no effect. So I went high-amp. I think we're okay." He turned the oscilloscope cart to more easily see the screen. "Your heart beat is regular, and I don't see the kinds of anomalies normally associated with electrical damage to the heart. But the plot is low-resolution and fleeting. I'm going to do a quick EKG to satisfy myself that your pump came through the defib okay." Mellwood set me up for the test then said, "Listen, I'm going to go grab a smoke. Dr. Smalls will watch over you while I'm gone."

Unbeknownst, Joy had been standing behind me, quiet as a mouse. "Hi Paul," she said. "Good to have you back."

Mellwood started the EKG unit then walked out.

As I raised my head and turned to see her, Joy moved into my field of vision. She was smiling, but her eyes were full of concern. I said, "Were you here the whole time?"

"Pretty much. Malcolm sent Boyd to get me. When I arrived, you were unconscious, and he was about to inject the epinephrine."

"How do you think this has affected my liver?"

"That's a good question. My guess is, adversely. The blood tests will tell. I'm taking a sample in a few minutes—as soon as Malcolm gives the okay. But if you're over the hump, if the RPA-72 has finally cleared your system and the arrhythmia fades, the damage will heal."

196

I asked questions about what had happened while Mellwood had worked on me. Her answers were complete and disturbing. I said, "Looks like I was lucky to be here at work when this happened."

She put a hand on my arm. "I'd say very lucky."

Mellwood returned looking relaxed. He examined the EKG printout. Everything was good. Joy assisted him in giving me a new ICD battery. Pressing a fresh bandage into place over the incision, he said, "Sit up and tell me how you feel."

I felt drained, weak; I told him that.

"But not woozy or lightheaded, like you might faint?"

"No, not really."

"Good. Then I'm going to ask Dr. Smalls here to walk you back to your lab, and like the other day, just before we knock off, come check with me."

The rest of the afternoon went well. Mellwood praised my quick bounce back, called it "atypical," and pronounced me okay to drive home. I left Ft. Detrick one grateful man.

74

I told Kay what had happened. She welled up, and holding my face whispered, "Oh Paul!" Then the tears began to flow. She cried a while, then snuffled a while longer. We talked for some time, and when we went to bed I slept like a baby in her arms.

The next morning I felt wrung out, but not ill or incapacitated. Kay and I were subdued as we said good-bye. We were sad, worried, but not desperate. To the extent possible we had made our peace with this situation.

Mellwood had reported to Essex, and had requested daily EKGs at least through Friday, the last day of the Death Period. Joy had done the same regarding blood tests. The Major had approved, without argument I was told, telling the doctors only, "I want feedback immediately. Don't wait until the end of the day. And I want details." I was gratified by the boss's concern. Maybe he was on my side after all.

197

The blood Joy had taken revealed a huge spike in enzyme levels. The assault on my heart had delivered a punishing blow to my liver. But today's concentrations, while still above normal, showed a marked improvement.

The EKG disclosed the return of some arrhythmia from yesterday's post-defib perfectly smooth readout. That caused Mellwood's brow to furrow. "Not encouraging," he said. "I had hoped . . . . But a snapshot is not a trend. Tomorrow we'll get some sense of direction." Before I left his office he added, "Today is the end of your one week sex ban. Considering what happened yesterday, it's wise to extend that at least through Friday— and that includes sexual contexts, as you put it, that arouse, but do not terminate in orgasm. Until we see what shakes out in the aftermath of your Level-5, that's my advice. Can you hold out?"

I was disappointed, but not surprised. I told him yes, I could hold out.

Wednesday's test results for both liver and heart eclipsed Tuesday's; Thursday's were better yet.

When Mellwood finished his examination of my EKG graph Friday morning, he turned to me with a rare smile and said, "Ban lifted! Go have some fun. This thing is perfectly normal."

I let out a whoop, and gave the cardiologist a bear hug.

Around noon Joy Smalls appeared in my alcove to deliver the news that for the first time since we began testing for them, the levels of the two liver damage enzymes had fallen to within acceptable limits. "Congratulations Paul," she said, her eyes bright, her chin trembling. "I can't tell you how happy I am."

I hugged Joy too—a soft, brief, respectable embrace. I wouldn't forget those kisses, but we were beyond that now.

Two hours later Essex called. "I've heard the good news, Dr. Stepping. No one knows for sure of course, but it looks like you're out of the woods. Tell your people to knock off at 4:30—a little gift from me in honor of this positive development. But if you would come to my office at, say, 4:40, I'd like to chat with you about the future."

The request seemed odd—I mean, why not wait until Monday morning when we would know if my normal status had survived the weekend?—but my spirits were high, and the man *was* making a gesture of sensitivity, so I replied, "Yes sir, I'll be there. Thank you."

I informed my techs of their early dismissal. They were thrilled, but one of them commented that it took a near-death experience of the head of an MMDA lab to pry thirty damn minutes out of "Major Hard-Ass." There were laughs all around, and I worried for a moment if I had properly hung up the phone. What if Essex had heard? Then I figured, hell, what if he had? Surely he knew his reputation. As long as his servants were obedient, he probably didn't care what they thought, or even said.

I labored the rest of the afternoon in my alcove. I called a good-bye as the workers left for their extended weekend. I cleaned up and headed down the corridor toward the Major's office.

When I arrived the door was open and the lights were on, but Essex was not there. One of the chrome chairs had been pulled from its normal place against the wall and positioned in front of his desk. I assumed that was for me, so I sat down. Perhaps he had stepped out for a bathroom break. I waited five, ten, fifteen minutes. No Essex. Could be an emergency had called him away. I saw a pad on the edge of his desk. I jotted a note, tore it off the pad, secured it with his quartz paperweight, then left. Whatever the boss had to say could wait.

Christmas was next Tuesday. Washington County Schools had dismissed at noon today for the winter vacation. Kay would be waiting for me when I got home. We had planned to eat out (Red Lobster), take in a movie (a new Clint Eastwood flick), then come home to resume our Friday night trysts, put on hold for so long. We were excited. It was beginning to look like we had a future again, and we wanted to celebrate.

The lab was empty and dimly-lit. A few low-wattage perimeter lights stayed on all the time. I walked past the tables laden with high-tech instruments, glassware, and amber-colored bottles of chemicals. I entered my alcove where only a few rays penetrated. I shrugged out of my lab coat and hung it on the wall, feeling as much as seeing. I lifted my jacket from an adjacent peg and slipped into it. I was out of here.

A click sounded behind my left ear. A familiar voice said, "Dr. Stepping, your Death Period is not quite over."

199

75

"Major, it's you." I had frozen at the click, then had relaxed when I realized it was Essex. "I was just at your office, but—"

"Sit down, Dr. Stepping." He moved to the alcove door and pulled it to. He flicked on the light. Leonard Essex had a pistol leveled at my face. "Sit down," he repeated.

I backed to my wooden desk chair and lowered myself into it. He remained standing, but took two steps toward me. "What's going on?" I said. "Has there been an intruder?" It was the only thing I could think of that made any sense.

"Not to my knowledge." His blue eyes blinked rapidly, almost fluttering, then stared straight at me.

"So what's with the gun?"

A hand went to his strawberry blond crewcut. He ran it over the short hairs twice, then examined the palm. He was wearing latex gloves. Returning his gaze to me, he said, "This is for your suicide."

"My suicide," I echoed. "Major, are you—is everything okay?"

"Fine, Dr. Stepping. In a few moments you will commit suicide. All that's happened over the past three months has taken its toll. You've cracked under the pressure. It's tragic."

I watched him for several seconds, trying to make this compute. "Why would I do that? Today I got the best news of this whole ordeal. You yourself told me I was probably out of the woods. Why would I kill myself now?"

He advanced another few feet. The pistol did not waver. "The mind is a mysterious thing, Dr. Stepping. We all have our demons. It's not unusual to read in the paper about some individual blowing his brains out, and nobody, not even his closest associates and family members, saw it coming. With you, with the stress you've been under, I doubt it will be deemed outside the realm of possibility—nor even outside the realm of expectation."

I was not afraid. And that surprised me, because something was very wrong here. Perhaps these months of living with the prospect, the likelihood, of death, had immunized me against that emotion. I told Essex, "I'm not shooting myself."

"Of course not, Dr. Stepping. I'll do that."

"You'll murder me."

He frowned and shook his head. "No, no—that is improper terminology. This is all about the greater good."

"Then you *won't* murder me."

More fluttering of the eyes. "I thought you understood." He sounded exasperated. "Isn't it clear that leadership in the upper echelons here at Ft. Detrick has been slipping over the last two, three years?"

"I know nothing about that."

"Well I do, and it's pathetic. Because of high-level misfeasance, our national security is being compromised."

"What do you mean? Give me an example."

"Now Dr. Stepping, you know I can't do that. But trust me, there's a problem."

"And what does that have to do with me—with you holding me at gunpoint?"

Essex ignored the question. "I can put a stop to this slackness—this abomination!" He was grinding his teeth. "I can bring order and efficiency to this entire installation, as I have to MMDA. You see what I've done here." He inched toward me. "Protecting the United States of America: that is our mission, is it not, Dr. Stepping?" His voice was louder. "We're in a war here—a battle for our way of life, our civilization. And I'll be *damned* if I'll sit idly by and let this great nation go down the drain because the top brass at Ft. Detrick is asleep at the wheel!"

Now I felt the fear rising. Essex was agitated. I thought of Kay—of our possible new life together. I had everything to lose. In what I hoped was a calming monotone I said, "Major, the gun—they'll know it's yours."

"No, Dr. Stepping, they won't. Some time ago—shortly after your accident, in fact—I made a trip to Baltimore. There I procured this weapon on the black market. Likely it had been stolen from some law-abiding citizen. It's probably registered, but not to me. When the investigators find

201

it in your hand and check it out, they will conclude that *you* stole it, or perhaps purchased it illegally. So no, I can't be connected to this firearm in any way."

My fear was being replaced by anger. The bastard had planned this all along. I took a different tack. "You know Major, I don't think you're going to get that promotion."

I saw him stiffen. His eyes narrowed. "And why is that?"

"Because of my accident and all the uproar it's caused. You talk about order and efficiency under your command at MMDA. The last three months has been chaos. I doubt your superiors are looking kindly on all that."

Essex laughed (I had never witnessed that behavior), then turned hard. "Dr. Stepping," he said, "my superiors are ignorant of your accident."

My jaw dropped. "That's not possible."

"It *is* possible. I am the sole conduit of data from our agency to the next level of organization. I have told no one at that level." He watched me digesting this news—realizing its implications. "As you noted, your carelessness has proved quite an interruption to our projects here. That is no fault of mine, yet as you likewise noted, it has the potential to place in jeopardy my vision of a revitalized Ft. Detrick. What then would be my motivation for informing the higher-ups?"

"It is your duty," I said.

His cold eyes grew colder. "My duty, Dr. Stepping, is protecting America from her enemies. As I ascend the ranks, my impact will increase. At some point I will have the ear of the president. If, however, my record is blemished, not by any failure on *my* part, but by *your* violation of laboratory protocol, then the possibility exists that I would be denied my destiny. That, for the sake of our country, I cannot allow."

"There will be an investigation," I said. "Someone will find my body and the military police will be called in."

"Of course."

"They'll ask questions. My techs, Dr. Smalls, Dr. Mellwood, Emmerton—they'll tell the MPs everything."

"Well, possibly. Before the investigators start nosing around, I'll call

202

the group together and remind them of the highly classified nature of our work, of the secrecy rules under which they operate, and of the penalties for transgressing those rules. After that, I doubt they'll tell the police *everything*. But regardless—whatever is divulged, the investigators will conclude suicide; they will write their report, then submit it to me, and to me alone."

"They'll keep a copy."

"I'm sure they will. But the only version that goes up the chain will be *my* version."

God in heaven, I thought. *Is the man crazy, or just ambitious beyond belief?* I said, "You're taking a huge risk."

"Some, true—but not huge. The military police have their own code of silence. Once they close a case and file their report, it's over for them. No one will talk. It will soon be forgotten. The huge risk, Dr. Stepping, is for the nation. It is looking the other way while Ft. Detrick slides deeper into irrelevance. I won't do that."

I'd played all my cards. Essex had thought of everything. He had an answer for everything. He even believed he inhabited the high moral ground. I knew one thing: I would not beg for my life.

"Dr. Stepping, I've observed that you are right handed."

"That's correct."

"Then would you please turn to the left, presenting your right temple to me?" He inched forward. "The muzzle must be pressed against your head, and the angle must be appropriate. It will be instantaneous, Dr. Stepping—no suffering. Rest assured, your country will be eternally grateful for your sacrifice."

I stared at the barrel of the pistol as it moved toward me. I thought of Tim Rouzerville and my flirtation with authenticity. I thought of my children. I thought of Kay, wondering if my suicide or murder (whichever was determined) would result in double indemnity benefits for her. Remembering the morning's forecast, I turned my head as Essex had instructed, thinking, *December 21—the shortest day of the year. It's cold, snow is predicted: it's the perfect day for a death.*

203

76

One more step, Major Essex. I would not let this maniac gun me down without a fight. He had to get closer, but I had to act before he pulled the trigger. My eyes slid far right. I felt myself tense. One more step, Major.

"Good-bye, Dr. Step—"

Two sharp raps cut him off. His head jerked toward the sounds. The revolver, inches from my temple, moved a cigarette-length to the side.

From beyond the door I heard, "Dr. Stepping, you in there?"

I began to rise from the chair; my right arm struck like a coiled cobra. I caught Essex hard on the left side of his chin. I felt my knuckles break as the gun exploded. Essex staggered back and went down, still gripping the revolver.

Boyd Markham burst into the alcove. "Dr. Stepping? Oh my God!"

Essex tried to get up. "No!" he screamed. "Get back in your seat! The plan!" On his knees he aimed at my chest.

I was standing beside my chair, six feet from him. There wasn't time; I was too far away. I closed my eyes.

The pistol roared. I flinched, waiting for the burn of the bullet.

I felt nothing. My ears were ringing, but I thought I heard a voice wail, "Noooo!"

I was confused. I was not dead. I was not wounded. What had happened? I chanced a look. Essex had no weapon. His wrist hung limp and there was an odd angle to his forearm. Boyd was standing over him, daring him to move. The gun was on the floor near the fume hood.

My lead tech looked at me and said, "I guess I never told you, Dr. Stepping—I was a place kicker in high school."

And all I could think was, *Thank God Essex didn't lock that door.*

77

I collected the revolver and secured it in the bottom right drawer of my desk. I pulled ten feet of quarter-inch Tygon tubing from its dispenser on the side of the hood. I sliced it off with a scalpel Joy Smalls had given me for that purpose. Boyd and I hog-tied Essex with the tubing, ignoring his protests concerning pain and loss of circulation. Then I stepped to the wall phone and called the Ft. Detrick military police.

The MPs arrived ten minutes later. After a few questions they led Essex away, muttering about "the plan," and calling out to me, "Dr. Stepping, I already had your replacement picked out!"

Boyd insisted that we wrap my hand with an Ace bandage until I could see a doctor. While he worked on me I said, "The lab was dark. I thought everyone was gone."

"I was in the animal room, working with the mice."

"You caught the announcement, didn't you?" I tried to remember if he had been in the group when I'd brought the news.

"Oh, sure. But the last thirty minutes every Friday there's a different sequence to prepare the guys for the weekend."

"You could have done that half an hour earlier."

"Right, but the little fellows are temperamental. You don't want to introduce an extra variable into their situation." He had wrapped the bandage tight, causing me to wince; now he fastened it with a metal clip. "There we go. Beside, thirty minutes: whoop-dee-do; big deal; Essex is a regular Mother Teresa. So I decided to stay with the routine. And by the way, the mice are still fine—active, eating well, sleeping well, having sex. RPA-73 is looking good. I think you've hit the jackpot."

I had made a similar comment to Essex earlier in the week. He had replied, "In this business we never count our chickens before they hatch." He was being his usual non-encouraging bastard self, of course; he was also right. Still, I smiled at Boyd and said, "Great—let's hope it continues." Then I asked, "How did you know we were in the alcove? Did you hear us talking?"

"Not really. I'm all the way across the lab, and both our doors were shut, so the sound didn't carry. What happened was, as I started to leave, I glimpsed light under your door."

I frowned. "When I walked through, I glanced over toward the animal room. I didn't see any light."

205

Boyd stroked his chin. "Yeah, I noticed that a while back. My door fits very tight, but yours doesn't." He gave a little laugh. "Funny how things can depend on small details."

78

It was almost 6:00 when I finally got away from the lab. It was dark and snowing. I put the Tahoe's headlights on low-beam and headed for home.

"Small details," Boyd Markham had said, suggesting that I had been very lucky today. On the other hand, some of the New Age gurus preach that there are *no* coincidences. Though I couldn't recall him having addressed the issue as such, Tim Rouzerville would probably agree with that pronouncement. I remembered a quote from Einstein, something to the effect that, "Either there are no miracles, or everything's a miracle." I guess that's the big question—or one of the big ones. Either a person believes there's more going on than meets the eye, or he doesn't.

Snow was already accumulating on the roads. I had to go slow. These storms usually moved in from the west, so they hit Washington County before reaching Frederick. With her mid-day release from school, hopefully Kay hadn't had to deal with this.

Crawling along Hamburg Road toward Yellow Springs, it hit me that in all the excitement my ICD had not gone off. My heart rate no doubt had escalated, yet there had been insufficient arrhythmia to provoke a discharge from the device. I considered that a very good sign.

Not counting the slapping incident with Kay, or the fight I'd had in 3rd-Grade with Sonny Blankenbaker over a girl, *or* the few times I'd had to spank the kids when they were young, I'd never struck another human being in anger. So it surprised me how effectively I had dropped Essex. I was like a pro. Maybe I just caught him off guard. I did pay a price though. My knuckles were aching. I'd have Joy take a look Monday.

Yes, we had to work Monday. Then we'd be off Tuesday for Christmas, but back to work Wednesday. As head of the lab I could have taken some time off around the holiday. I often did, to be with Kay, who

206

always had a long break spanning Christmas and New Year's Day. This time I figured I'd best stay close to Mellwood.

The western Maryland snow machine was cranking up. I flicked on the Frederick AM station (the one where I occasionally caught Neal Boortz) to get the weather. They were now predicting eight-to-twelve inches in our area. About a mile to go. The edges of the roadway were blurring, and the center line had already been obliterated. Careful, Paul. You've dodged three bullets here lately—two of them literal. Don't be snuffed by a few slippery little ice crystals a stone's throw from your damn house.

I made it in one piece. Kay met me at the door with shining eyes and a hungry kiss. She looked through the falling snow illuminated by the circle of porch-light, out into the darkness of the gathering storm. "Scratch Red Lobster and Eastwood," she said. "I'm making prime rib—medium rare." That was how we liked our beef. "And on the way home, considering the forecast, I picked up a dozen large. We might be stuck here all day tomorrow." She watched me, doubtless wondering if I remembered our egg problem from shortly after the accident.

I did, and I said, "Thank you Sweetheart—good thinking. We'll be all set for Sunday morning, come what may." Kay beamed. After all these years, after these three trying months, she still coveted my approval. I marveled at that; it humbled me and brought a lump to my throat. Before this got mushy I said, "Have I got a story for you. Can you take more drama?" I asked, stepping inside, shutting the door on the cold and snow.

She watched my eyes. "I hope so. It's nothing bad, is it?"

Shedding my coat and holding up the bandaged hand, I said, "It has to do with this."

I told Kay my tale over supper. Other than fingers to her mouth when I detailed the gunplay, she took it well until I mentioned seeing Joy Smalls Monday about the knuckles. That provoked a cool stare, but only for a moment.

After watching a little TV, I looked over at Kay in her easy chair and said, "Mellwood gave me the green light."

She turned my way, squinting a question mark.

207

"It's Friday," I stated from the rocker. "It's our night. Mellwood gave the okay."

"Oh," she said, "yes. Friday night." She pointed at me. "I hope that mummy hand of yours won't cramp our style." She quit her recliner and stood before me. "Come on Big Boy," she invited, "give this schoolteacher a lesson.

79

It's Tuesday, January 1: a new year with new hope—and a day off. Nearly a month since exposure, the RPA-73 test mice continue to thrive. My hand is much better. Joy said the knuckles were not broken, only bruised. Over the last ten days my arrhythmia and liver enzyme levels have fluctuated, but have not exceeded acceptable limits. So am I cured? Can I put this nightmare behind me?

Though Bill and Amy bowed out, Joel had come up from DC for Christmas dinner. He brought Versa Brooks with him. He had arranged that with Kay. I was wary, thinking it would be awkward at best, with a potential for some serious unpleasantness. I was wrong. Representative Brooks had been genial, hadn't tried to dominate the conversation (a real danger with any politician), and had displayed a keen sense of humor. Joel made a good-faith effort to go light on the self-aggrandizement and the BS. I set aside my authenticity foolishness. It had really been quite enjoyable.

When we returned to work on December 26, several of us had been summoned to the office of General Wick. He had identified himself as the immediate superior of Major Essex. When the General looked at you, here was the message: "Tell me the truth, or by God you'll wish you had." And *this* was the guy Essex withheld information from?

The purpose of the meeting was to determine what actually had transpired at MMDA since September 19, the date of the accident. Mellwood, Emmerton, Joy Smalls, Boyd Markham, and I all testified. We were told that Essex, as well as the military police who had been involved in his arrest, had been interviewed in separate sessions. I asked to whom did the MPs routinely forward their reports? Essex had said after

208

investigating my supposed suicide, the account would come only to him. The General, watching me for long seconds as if I were a source irritation, finally shared that in addition to delivering a statement to the head of the unit in question, copies were given to the commanding officers of the next two higher levels. "That's standard procedure," Wick growled, "and the point is to defeat just this kind of crap." So Essex had been wrong—or perhaps delusional. We were also informed that one of the General's aides, a Colonel Blasingame, would be temporary head of MMDA. Joy inquired as to what would become of the Major? Wick turned a lascivious eye on her, and showing his chipped, yellow teeth, cooed, "Dr. Smalls, your former boss will get his due process. Then I hope his sick ass will be drop-kicked out of this man's Army."

The rest of the work week had been fairly normal. Kay and I had another outstanding Friday night. The weekend had been typical, nice. Yesterday, Monday, had been productive: I had zeroed in on what I think will be a suitable solvent for RPA-73. Also I had eaten lunch with Mellwood in the cafeteria. At one point, referring to Essex, he had snarled, "What was the crazy bastard going to do? Kill everyone who knew the truth?"

This New Year's morning I got up around daybreak, careful not to disturb Kay. She told me last night she'd like to sleep in. "Wednesday it's back to the little would-be hell-raisers," she had said. "I need to build up my sleep credits."

I started some coffee and flicked on the TV. I caught the weather— cold, windless, clear—then aimed the remote again and killed the program. Kay and I would likely walk The Trail this afternoon. I took my coffee to her La-Z-Boy, the plan being to continue some reading.

Peter Noll's *In the Face of Death* had rested on my shelf a good twenty years. I had bought it at a used book store in Charlottesville one summer, then had forgotten it. A few days after I flatlined, I pulled it down.

Noll was a Swiss jurist who had been diagnosed with bladder cancer in his fifties. Accepting only palliative care, he had opted for no surgery and no treatment, not wanting to sacrifice his freedom by being caught up in what he called "the medical machinery" of doctors appointments, harsh regimens, and hospital stays. Confronting a sure and early demise, instead of disengaging from life, Noll found that his interest in religion, philosophy, even politics, intensified. Given my situation, this man's dramatic choice intrigued me. So far his account had been thoughtful and forthright. I was half-way through. I wanted to see how it ended.

In the last month or so I had run across two other somewhat related items in our local paper.

One was a piece on Edwin Shneidman, retired professor of thanatology (death studies—I had never heard of such) at UCLA. Referring to Shneidman, Thomas Curwen had written, "He never asked to live to be 90, to see the breadth of his life diminished, the allure of the world fallen further out of reach." Quite a different tone from the Noll book; but then again, the circumstances were dissimilar. "Today will be the same as yesterday," Curwen had continued, "the same as tomorrow, every day a waiting and a hoping for a good death, a death without suffering." The article had appeared originally in the *Los Angeles Times*.

The other was a book review for the *New York Times* by Garrison Keillor, the Lake Wobegon guy. Knowing little about him, I had gathered that Keillor is basically a humorist. I had therefore been surprised to find him commenting on *Nothing To Be Afraid Of* by Julian Barnes—a book about death. Barnes is 62, a novelist, an agnostic, not sick, his death not imminent; yet fear of dying is a fact of his life. This book is his attempt to address that fear. According to Keillor, Barnes dismisses not only the traditional comforts of religion, but also those of the modern secular dogma of self-fulfillment. He turns instead to science, whose conclusions are more certain, but quite restricted in scope. There is scant metaphysical solace there. Keillor's final thought: "I don't know how this book will do in our hopeful country, with the author's bleak face on the cover, but I will say a prayer for retail success." Maybe Garrison *is* a humorist.

Sitting in the La-Z-Boy, with all this murmuring in my head, with the rising sun beginning to stream through the eastern windows, I too breathed a prayer. "Almighty," I said, looking toward the light, "I know so little; I understand even less—about You, about life, about what lies beyond. It's a mystery, very deep. Yet we humans, in our anxiety and pride, claim to know. In our frailty, with clouded vision, we bluster certainties. But not me—it's not honest. My beliefs are fuzzy and few. Still, despite the exaggerated insecurity in which I continue to live, I feel gratitude and confidence. My great overarching sentiment is hope. And that is good. Thank You—thank You for that possibility."

I was whispering, muttering really, trying to be authentic. My eyes were a little wet. I took a sip of coffee. It was a new day, a new year, and Kay would soon awake.

EPILOGUE

If you have read my story, it's because the statute of limitations on telling it has expired. Even so, there are certain strictures, and those I have endeavored to follow. The purpose of these final words is to tie up loose ends—tell you how things have turned out.

Kay and I retired. We sold the place in Frederick, our home for so many years, and moved south. We settled in the little town of Big Pine, two-thirds the way from the Florida mainland toward Key West. We live a semi-anonymous life on this island, which is fine with me. And though the aesthetics can be stunning, if I never see another flake of snow, I won't feel deprived.

In my last months at Ft. Detrick, I continued the work on RPA-73. When I turned the lab over to my successor (*not* the one Essex had picked), no major problems had yet surfaced.

Essex was court-martialed. He was found not guilty by reason of mental defect, and confined to a government facility for the criminally insane. It came out during the trial that there had been harbingers of his psychosis during his graduate years at Rensselaer, but that an agreement with his thesis advisor, who was also Chairman of the Biophysics Department, prevented the Army from learning that. The advisor had since died; his replacement had had no occasion to delve into his predecessor's files, where memos concerning all this were kept. Leonard Essex, therefore, had passed all his background checks, and was eventually granted the high-level security clearance he enjoyed at Ft. Detrick. Another tidbit surfaced during the proceedings: not only had Essex kept knowledge of my accident within the confines of MMDA, he had also lied about exploring the transplant option for me. There had been no brain-dead boy down in Virginia who was a tissue match and potential donor. It had been a fabrication—a part of the master plan.

A word about Boyd Markham. When I left, he was offered the position as head of the lab. That's unusual, as he doesn't have a doctorate. His master's is in animal behavior. He loves his mice, and as I've noted, is highly-skilled at working with them. As lab chief he would have had to

213

give that up, and would have been saddled with administrative duties and paperwork. He (wisely, in my view) said no. I keep in touch with Boyd— nothing technical of course, but he keeps me apprised of the general goings-on.

Colonel Blasingame's temporary stint as top man at MMDA turned out to be permanent. Boyd says he's a good guy, and since he had been an aide to General Wick, there was no way *he* would ever try to keep anything from his scary boss.

Joy Smalls married Ward Emmerton. They eloped. I thought Boyd was pulling my leg when he e-mailed me that. But it's true, and I couldn't be happier. Thinking back, there actually were a few signs pointing to this. Two decent people finding each other and tying the knot—sort of renews one's faith. Plus, they can talk about their work over dinner.

One sad note: Malcolm Mellwood died. He did make that New Year's resolution to stop smoking. In the months leading up to my retirement I watched him struggle with his addiction. He tried, but he lost. Soon after I left Ft. Detrick he was diagnosed with lung cancer. Within a year he was gone. I went back to Maryland for the funeral. Malcolm had become my friend.

Bill and Pauline have another kid. Winthrop Paul Stepping was born a month after Malcolm died. Winthrop is *Pauline's* father's given name. So once again . . . . But Bill seems happy, and if it works for them, who am I to judge?

Something I never thought would happen, did. Joel and his politician boss got hitched. They moved out of their respective apartments, and are buying a nice place in McLean. She was a divorcée, a life-long Catholic; Joel had turned Catholic; I've wondered how Church doctrine deals with such a situation, but to this point I've not asked. Versa Brooks has retained her House seat, *and* her last name. Joel continues as her top staffer. Working for your wife in a clearly subordinate position would seem awkward at best, nepotistic at worst. But to hear Joel tell it, things are hunky-dory. The boy's a spin doctor, and a good one. Yet I've come to see that beneath the slick veneer, there's something solid.

Amy dragged her redneck to a Rapides Parish justice of the peace and made it legal. They decided to keep the baby. Kay and I flew down to welcome little Wilma Jean Broussard into our family. After Amy got Frank promoted from dishwasher to server at the Paradise Catfish Kitchen, she enrolled at Louisiana College, and is majoring in (of all things) chemistry. Says she wants to teach high school. Cousin Eileen remains at LC, and keeps informal tabs on our youngest. And oh, Frank stopped smoking because of his new daughter. Good man.

Clemmie Finks has passed on, as has Kay's father—a stroke. Mother is really doing quite well; Lucy, my youngest sister, moved back from Colorado to stay with her. I feel good about that. Kay's mom is in an assisted living facility in Newport News.

Tim Rouzerville is *still* at First Baptist, Frederick. I wonder if that's some kind of record. He and Grace have been down twice to visit us.

The National Key Deer Refuge is on Big Pine Key. Kay and I walk there sometimes. Almost always we run across a few of the tiny fellows. They see so many people, they're not that shy. Our main walking place is the shoreline at Bahia Honda State Park, just a few miles east on US 1. Occasionally we'll drive a little further to Marathon. There's a great public beach there. All this is quite a departure from the Catoctin Trail.

Kay does some subbing at the local elementary school. She's met a small cadre of retired teachers, and has made friends with several of them.

I've spent a fair portion of my time authoring this memoir. It doesn't come easy to me, but I'm reasonably satisfied with the result. Maybe I'll do some more writing—maybe try my hand at fiction.

In closing, a comment on my authenticity initiative. After much thought, I have concluded that it was not ill-conceived, but it *was* ill-implemented. Like patience, being genuine is a virtue. Like honesty, it's the best policy. But being kind is also a virtue. Finding the proper balance between the two is paramount, and that is where I fell short. I haven't dropped the idea; I'm working on it.

Life here in the Florida Keys is warm, slow, and as close to carefree as I'm likely to find. I've made the acquaintance of a few people—nothing beyond that. But no problem. I have Kay, my soul mate, my inspiration. I'm a happy man.

There is, as the great Greek dramatist Euripides wrote, "a debt we all must pay." One day I will receive that final summons. When I do, because of the tribulation I survived, because of the edifying turn my life then took, it will be a good death.

About the Author

David E. Lawrence, a Louisiana native, lives in Mechanicsville, Virginia with his wife, Wilma. The retired public school teachers have three children, four grandchildren, three dogs, three turtles, and a hen. David spent most of his thirty-two classroom years at rural Madison County (Virginia) High School, teaching chemistry and physics. He is a graduate of Louisiana College, and his American literature professor there encouraged his early attempts at writing. He has published four other books: three novels, and a collection of poetry. David has been jogging regularly for close to forty years.